# JACKSON'S Jewel

Awakening Desires

# N.J. WALTERS

ELLORA'S CAVE
ROMANTICA PUBLISHING

An Ellora's Cave Romantica Publication

www.ellorascave.com

Jackson's Jewel

ISBN 9781419963452
ALL RIGHTS RESERVED.
Jackson's Jewel Copyright © 2008 N.J. Walters
Edited by Shannon Combs.
Cover art by Syneca.

Electronic book publication July 2008
Trade paperback publication 2011

# JACKSON'S JEWEL

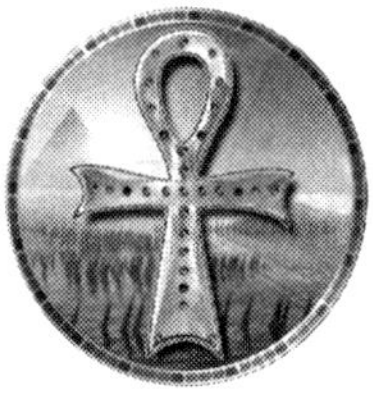

# Dedication

❧

*Thank you to all the readers who haven't forgotten Jackson but continued to ask for his story.*

# Trademarks Acknowledgement

❧

# Chapter One

**ഇ**

Emerald Jewel glanced nervously in her rearview mirror, her hands tightening around the steering wheel as a black pickup pulled out to pass her. *He can't find you here.* She repeated the mantra over and over but it did no good. She didn't believe it. The truck pulled alongside her and she risked a look. The young man driving the other vehicle gave her a wink and a nod before pulling ahead of her.

Her heart pounding, her breathing shallow, Emerald eased her foot off the gas and pulled her car onto the shoulder of the road. When she'd come to a complete stop, she leaned her head against the steering wheel and took a deep breath. Slowly her breathing returned to normal and her heartbeat calmed. Her hands were trembling as she peeled them away from the wheel. Sweat rolled down her back, making her shiver even though it was a hot summer day.

She dragged a nervous hand across her forehead. Her life had gone from wonderful to terrifying in the past two months and she still couldn't quite figure out how it had happened. When the first flower, a beautiful white orchid, had arrived at the offices of Sisters' Jewels, the company she owned with her two sisters, she'd been charmed. There had been no card to indicate who had sent it and her sisters, Topaz and Sapphire, had teased her endlessly about her secret admirer.

Emerald had been flattered at first and had placed the orchid on the corner of her desk, enjoying its fragrance and beauty as she worked on her designs. Sisters' Jewels sold accessories, scarves, journals, stationery, cards and jewelry out of their small New York boutique. Her older sister, Topaz, was the brains behind the business operations while her younger sister, Sapphire, was the creative force behind their unique jewelry creations. Emerald used her artistic background to create designs for cards, stationery, covers for journals and gift bags, and she'd recently branched out into designing fabric for the new scarves and purse line they wanted to carry.

A rose had arrived the following week, a lily the week after. Then had come the chocolates and the slim volume of very graphic erotic poetry. At that point, she and her sisters had started to worry. Topaz had wanted to contact the police, but Emerald hadn't seen the point. No crime had been committed. She'd tried to laugh it off, but she'd started looking at all the males she knew, wondering if it could be any of them.

Opening her eyes, she leaned her head back against the seat and sighed. She'd racked her brains trying to figure out who could be sending her these things, but she'd drawn a blank. Who knew how many men she came in contact within the run of a day? There was the grocery store, the coffee shop, the subway... The list went on and on.

There was no way she could imagine her ex-boyfriend, Beau Vater, sending them. After all, she'd broken it off with him six months ago when she'd caught him cheating on her. Yes, he'd made a few overtures about getting back together, but she'd been adamant in her refusal. She hadn't dated since they'd split, so there were no new boyfriends to worry about.

Now that her nerves were calm, she put the car in gear and eased back onto the pavement. Ignoring the scenery around her, she continued to think as she drove. The only other men in her life on a regular basis were Fred Kirby, who delivered the mail to Sisters' Jewels every day, and Derek Locke, longtime friend and son of their parents' former manager.

"It can't be either one of them." Her voice sounded desperate even to herself. She licked her dry lips, no longer believing her own words.

The letters had been the next thing to arrive. Computer-generated and printed on plain white paper, they contained graphic suggestions about what the sender wanted to do to her. She swallowed hard, glad she hadn't eaten yet today or she might have lost whatever food had been in her belly. As it was, her stomach churned. The possessiveness in the tone had been frightening and she'd finally given in to her sisters' pleas and gone to the police.

She'd come away from that experience feeling more alone than ever. Although they were sympathetic, there wasn't much they could do. They took the letters and dusted them for prints. There were none. The postmark was local, but there was no way to trace it to whoever sent it. The paper and envelopes could be bought just about anywhere. Unless she could give them some ideas, the most they could suggest was being careful about going anywhere alone.

The police had suggested that it could be a crazed fan of their parents. Moon and Aloysius Jewel had been well-known folk singers in the late Sixties and early Seventies. They toured worldwide and had been very successful. The onset of disco and her mother's first pregnancy had led them to retire.

Her father might have been a hippie, but he'd also found he had a talent for business. He'd parlayed their money into quite a bit more and now her parents lived in upstate New York on a large, private estate. That is, when they weren't traveling around the world. The births of all three of the girls had been a huge media event, but over the years, they'd been mostly forgotten about, except by diehard fans. Emerald supposed it could be a fan of her parents, but she really didn't think so.

They were in Europe at the moment and knew nothing about the stalker. Both Topaz and Sapphire had wanted to tell their parents, but Emerald didn't want to worry them. If her father knew, he'd have them all locked behind the gates of the family estate with a battalion of security guards positioned around the perimeter. At the moment, that didn't sound like such a bad idea.

The ribbon of road in front of her blurred and she blinked. All of a sudden, she realized that the interior of the car was extremely hot. Flicking the air-conditioning up higher, she let the cool air wash over her heated flesh. She shivered, but at least the blast of air made her more alert.

The final straw had come over the past two weeks. Someone had hacked into her e-mail account and started writing nasty letters to all her friends and business contacts. By the time she'd discovered what was going on and had taken steps to stop it, Sisters' Jewels had almost lost a very lucrative deal with a large, upscale clothing chain who wanted to carry a line of their products. Emerald had spent days on the phone contacting everyone she knew and explaining that she'd been the victim of a hacker. At first, she'd believed it was just a random attack, but she'd gotten another note from her stalker. He didn't like her working. According to his letter, she should be singing like her parents had, not slaving in a tacky little shop.

Crazed fan suddenly went to the top of her list of possibilities.

At least that had ruled out Derek. She loved him like a brother, but he barely managed to keep his e-mail and appointments straight. The man was a genius at promotion and wheeling and dealing, but his computer skills were just average. In typical Derek fashion, he'd learned what he needed to get by—no more, no less.

When she'd started receiving packages at the apartment she shared with her two sisters, Emerald had moved beyond fear and into terror. This person knew where she lived, had likely been watching her. The final package had arrived just yesterday morning. Large and flat, it had seemed harmless enough, but they weren't taking any chances. They'd called the police.

Her phone rang. Emerald jumped, her heart starting to pound again. "Get a grip," she admonished herself as she pulled over onto the shoulder of the road and fished her phone out of her handbag. She'd told her sisters she'd keep in touch, but she hadn't talked to them since breakfast this morning and it was now after two in the afternoon.

They had protested her leaving and going off by herself, but she'd been adamant. She hoped by leaving that she'd draw the threat away from her sisters. A spark of hope flickered inside her. Maybe they'd heard something from the private investigator they'd hired. "Hello."

"Wasn't my last present to your liking?" The voice was distorted but distinctly male. Emerald froze.

"Who is this?" Her voice was little more than a whisper.

He laughed and the sound sent chills racing over her flesh. "You belong to me, Emerald. Once you admit that, then things will get easier for everyone."

She closed her eyes and swallowed heavily. She was dealing with a lunatic. The last package had contained a long, white wedding gown as well as a pair of heavy black handcuffs. This guy was sick! "I don't belong to anyone, you jerk."

"Temper, temper." He chuckled. "I know you think you can run." He paused for a moment. "I hope you enjoyed your overnight stay in Jaffrey."

Emerald's hand flew to her throat. She'd stayed at an inn in that town last night and gassed up her car there this morning. She'd purposely been taking a winding path on this trip so no one would be able to find her. "How could you know?" She hadn't meant to whisper the words aloud, but he heard them.

"I know everything about you, my black-haired beauty." The good humor fled his voice and it became as hard as ice. "You belong to me."

"No!" she screamed. "You leave me alone."

"I'm coming for you, Emerald," he taunted. "Watch for me."

The line went dead and she sat there shaking for the longest time. The occasional car passed her and when one of them started to slow down, she flung her phone in her purse, put her foot on the gas and spun back onto the road.

How could he have found her? The answer when it hit her was obvious—credit cards. She'd used her credit card this morning when she'd paid for her hotel room and her gas. This guy was even smarter than she'd imagined. After all, if he could hack into her e-mail account it was possible he had skill enough to track her credit cards.

Emerald gripped the wheel tightly and marshaled her thoughts. Okay, she couldn't use her credit cards or her bank card. Any kind of electronic transaction would leave a trail for him to follow. She'd been traveling all day and thankfully hadn't used her cards, so he had no way of knowing exactly where she was.

The sign loomed in the distance. "Welcome to Meadows," she said aloud. This was as good a place as any to get some supplies and check out her cash situation. She pulled into the parking lot of a local convenience store and shut off the car. Her skin was clammy, her hands shaky as she fumbled with her wallet. She counted out a hundred and eighty-five dollars and twenty-three cents. Not enough to elude a stalker. She needed money and a place to hide out while she figured out what to do.

Her stomach growled loudly, reminding her that she hadn't eaten anything all day. Opening the car door, she climbed out. The blast of heat hit her hard, but it felt good against her clammy skin. It was so hot she could see the heat shimmering just above the pavement. Wiping her sweaty hands over the legs of her jeans, she grabbed her purse, shut the car door and strolled over to the store.

Her legs were wobbly, but they held. She needed food and she needed an inexpensive place to stay for the night while she figured out what to do. The bell over the door jingled when she walked inside. The woman behind the counter smiled at her and went back to ringing up her customer.

Emerald strolled down the aisle, trying to find something that might sit well in her stomach. She went down the first row and back up the next without finding anything that tempted her. As she reached the front of the store again, she noticed a large bulletin board filled with notices. Curiosity pulled her toward it.

Trucks for sale, property for sale, a few for rent signs and a smattering of community notices peppered the board. Not much to help her. Emerald figured it was best to ask the woman on the front cash if there was an inexpensive place to stay. The locals always knew the best spots. She made up her mind that she'd also ask about a good, but cheap, restaurant. She needed to get some real food in her stomach before she collapsed in a heap.

She started to turn away, but a notice in the top right-hand corner caught her eye. *Help wanted! Need temporary housekeeper/cook for local farm. Room and board included.* Emerald stared at the note, reading it again and again. This could be the answer to her prayers. Room and board meant that there would be no record for anyone to trace. The fact that it was on a farm was a bonus. Farms tended to be fairly isolated. This could be perfect. She didn't worry about the work aspect. Her mother hadn't spoiled any of her daughters and they all knew how to cook and clean.

Ripping the notice off the board, Emerald turned and marched toward the front counter. This was the break she'd been looking for.

# Chapter Two

ഗ

"You did what?" Jackson Connors glared at his sister. She smiled at him, blithely ignoring his growing anger.

"I hired you a housekeeper." Erin shook her head and threw her hands in the air. "Honestly, Jackson, this place is a disaster zone."

He scrubbed his hand through his reddish-brown hair as he glanced around the kitchen. So there were dishes piled on the counter and in the sink. Yeah, the mail was strewn across the table, the beautiful hardwood floor that he'd stripped and refinished last winter was grungy and the garbage can definitely needed to be emptied. He winced at the mess. He didn't even want to consider the state of the bathroom or his bedroom. He was just thankful that he'd put away his camera and his latest photos last night before he'd turned in for the evening. "I've been busy."

That was certainly an understatement. He was running the family apple farm by himself now that both Erin and Nathan had married and moved out. Yes, he'd hire help when it came time to pick the apples, but for now he was doing almost all the work himself. It was August and that meant that the hay and alfalfa that he'd planted on the land he leased from Erin's husband, Abel, had to be harvested and baled. He sold that to surrounding farms for extra cash.

Added to that, he also had another job that no one else knew about. Several years back he'd started taking pictures over the winter months to help pass some of the time when he wasn't working. That hobby had grown into a passion. On a whim, he'd submitted a few of his photos to contests, and to his surprise, had won several. A gallery owner who'd wanted to feature some of his shots in his shop had approached him. At first Jackson had been skeptical, but he'd ultimately agreed to give it a try. His skepticism had turned to shock when he'd gotten his first check.

His hobby was now providing him with a savings account that was going to allow him to buy out his sister and brother's share of the farm. Now that they had lives of their own, they didn't need the farm. But he did. It was as much a part of him as the color of his hair or the sound of his voice. His goal was to secure it as his very own.

Erin's features softened as she strolled over to him, wrapped her arms around his waist and hugged him tight. "I know." She tilted her head up, her face serious. "That's why you need some extra help around the house." She stepped back and held up her hand before he could protest further. "It's only temporary. Just until the end of the apple season. Think how nice it would be to come home to a clean house, a cooked meal and fresh sheets on the bed."

It would be nice, but Jackson didn't want some stranger in his home. "I don't think so."

"I already told her to come this morning."

"Then you can wait here and tell her to leave." He loved his sister, but there was no way he was having some stranger poking around his home while he wasn't here.

"No." She pursed her lips and got a stubborn expression on her face that he recognized all too well. He ignored it. He was more stubborn than she could ever hope to be. "You wait and tell her. I hired her in good faith."

"I don't have time for this foolishness." Dumping the last of his coffee in the kitchen sink, he piled his mug alongside the rest of the dirty dishes. He'd get to them later today he promised himself. Ignoring his sister's dark glare, he headed for the back door.

"I can't help out here any longer, Jackson."

He whirled, a sarcastic comment on his lips, but he swallowed it back. Now that she had her own home with her husband, he didn't see her enough for his liking. Yes, he saw her practically every day, but it just wasn't the same. Nothing was the same anymore.

Just a year ago all three of them had been living here and working the farm together. Nathan had worked it part-time as he was a deputy sheriff with the town, but Erin had spent many hours working alongside him in the orchards while running her own blueberry farm. He missed the way things used to be.

"Look. I know you mean well." He softened his tone. "But I really don't want or need the help. I know you're busy with your own farm and with Abel. Don't worry about me. I'll be fine."

Tears shimmered in her eyes and he swore inwardly. Erin rarely cried, so this meant that she was really upset about this. *Shit!* He could feel his resolve weakening. She shook her head and started toward him. Her face suddenly paled and she swayed where she stood. Jackson leapt forward, wrapped his arm around her and guided her into a chair.

"I'm fine." She waved him away.

Worry began to burn in his gut. Erin didn't look real well this morning, now that he really took the time to look at her. There were dark circles under her eyes. She looked tired and slightly haggard.

When he was certain she wouldn't topple over, he left her long enough to grab a clean dishtowel out of the kitchen drawer and dampen it with cold water. Returning swiftly to her side, he laid the damp cloth on her forehead. "Just hold this while I get you some water." It had been really hot the past few days, even for August. Perhaps she'd gotten a bit dehydrated. When he'd filled a tall glass with water, he made her take small sips until half of it was gone.

"You need to go home and rest. Or maybe you should stay here and lie down. Obviously, Abel isn't taking good care of you. What the hell were you thinking to let yourself get dehydrated in this heat? You know the dangers of that." Erin's eyes widened as his tirade continued. He knew he should shut his mouth, but he couldn't seem to stop. He'd practically reared Erin, as their father hadn't been much of a parent.

She placed her hand over his mouth, stopping his rant. A tiny smile played at the corners of her lips. She looked for all the world like she used to when she was just a kid and she'd had a secret. "I'm not dehydrated, Jackson."

"No? Then what's wrong with you? You're pale and you've got dark circles under your eyes." He crouched down beside his sister. "Honey, you look a mess."

She laughed. "Thanks a lot. You know how to make a girl feel good."

The back door opened and a large man stepped inside. Jackson slowly stood and glared at his best friend and brother-in-law. "Where the hell have you been?"

Abel cocked his eyebrow as he sauntered into the kitchen. "Good morning to you too. Did Erin tell you the news?"

"Yeah, she did."

"You don't look very happy about it." Abel scowled, his pale green eyes narrowing in anger.

"I'm not."

Abel's hands fisted at his sides. "We'd hoped you would be," he all but growled.

"Umm, Abel." Erin tried to get her husband's attention, but he ignored her for the moment, all his attention focused on Jackson.

"How the hell would you feel if it were some strange woman coming into your home?" Jackson's patience was at an end. He was already behind in his work and every minute he wasted with this foolishness was putting him further behind.

Abel stared at him like he had two heads. "What are you talking about?"

"The damn housekeeper that your wife hired for me. Without asking me, I might add. What the heck did you think we were talking about?"

Abel glanced over at Erin who just shrugged. "I haven't had the chance to tell him yet."

"Tell me what?" He propped his hands on his waist and glared at his younger sister. "I don't have all day. If you have something to say to me, then just say it."

"I'm pregnant," she blurted out.

Jackson felt as if he'd taken a hit to his solar plexus. Staggering back, he hit the counter and knocked into a stack of dishes. They crashed to the floor, shattering into dozens of tiny pieces. He ignored them. "What did you say?"

A huge smile broke out on Erin's face, making her appear absolutely radiant. As she stood, her husband went to her side and wrapped his arm around her waist. There was no mistaking the pride and love in his face as he stared down at her. "I'm pregnant." She laughed as she leaned against her husband's chest. "We're pregnant."

Jackson swallowed hard. His baby sister was going to have a baby. Jeez, he needed to sit down. He looked at her and could see the happiness in her eyes. This was what he'd always wanted for her, but it was still hard to take in. "When?"

"I'm three months along so it should be late January or early February." He knew he had to say something, do something, but he was at a loss. Her smile slowly faded as she stared at him. "Jackson?" She left her husband's arms and came toward him. "I'm going to be a mother. You're going to be an uncle."

He felt the corners of his mouth tipping upward. An uncle. He liked the sound of that. Giving a whoop, he lifted her off the floor and swung her around. When he realized what he was doing, he stopped immediately. "I'm sorry. I shouldn't have done that. Are you all right? Is the baby okay?"

Erin laughed. "I'm fine. I'm just tired is all and mornings aren't the greatest these days."

He scowled at Abel. "She'd been working too hard. She almost fainted this morning."

Abel's indulgent smile disappeared and was replaced by a scowl. "What happened?"

Erin pushed away from Jackson and went to her husband. "I'm fine. I just got up too quickly is all."

"You need to rest more."

"You're damn right she does." Jackson was still trying to wrap his brain around the fact that Erin was going to be a momma. "Does Nathan know yet?"

She shook her head. "I wanted to tell you first."

He swallowed back the lump of emotion that welled within him. It meant the world to him that she'd told him first. "Thank you."

"You're welcome. But if you really want to make me happy, you'll give the housekeeper I hired a chance."

Oh, his sister was slick. She'd maneuvered him right into that one. There was no way he could refuse her now. She stared at him expectantly, a smug look on her face. "All right." He raked his fingers through his hair. "A one-week trial run."

"Two," she countered.

"Ten days," he fired back.

"Done." They all heard the sound of a vehicle pulling up beside the house. "That should be her now. Her name is Emerald Jones."

"What the hell kind of name is Emerald?" He envisioned a skinny, pampered blonde with cool green eyes and a ton of jewelry.

"A very pretty one," his sister snapped. "Now be nice."

"I'm always nice," he muttered as he followed his sister and Abel out of the house. It was time to meet the stranger who would be sharing his home for the next ten days.

Emerald pulled the car to a stop and turned off the ignition. Since there was no one around, she took a deep breath. She could do this. Her stomach was doing flip-flops and had been all morning. She'd stayed at a quaint B&B last night and had shelled out sixty dollars to pay for it this morning. Her cash was quickly dwindling.

She hated the fact that she'd lied to the woman she'd talked to on the phone about her name. She'd started to give her real name, but at the last second had given the false surname, Jones. They probably wouldn't recognize her name, but she hadn't wanted to take any chances. Still, it left her feeling like a complete fraud.

"What's done is done," she muttered as she clicked off her seat belt, opened the door and slid out of her compact car, smoothing down her skirt. It was early morning, not yet seven o'clock, but it was already heating up outside. It was going to be another scorcher of a day. She looked around at the place that was to be her home for the foreseeable future. She'd been honest with Erin Garrett about not wanting a long-term job. But the other woman had assured her that the position of housekeeper and cook was only a temporary one, eight weeks tops.

The back door popped open and a tall redheaded woman stepped out onto the porch. "You must be Emerald." She held out her hand as she strode forward. Emerald liked her on sight.

"I am. And you must be Mrs. Garrett."

"Please call me Erin." She turned to the massive man who was close on her heels. "And this is my husband, Abel."

The guy was huge and very intimidating with his dark hair and piercing green eyes. Still, Emerald met his gaze squarely. "Pleasure to meet you."

Abel nodded and said hello, but before he could say any more than that, the back door slammed open, drawing all their attention. Emerald froze on the spot. The world around her receded, narrowing to the man striding determinedly toward her. And what a man he was.

He looked to be at least a half a foot taller than her, if not a bit more, and she was five foot eight. It was hard to tell exactly how tall he was because he had a very muscular build. His gait was fluid as his long legs ate up the distance between them. The denim of his jeans outlined his thick thighs and she watched, fascinated by the play of muscles as he moved. The tight, faded material also cupped his male attributes. Emerald's mouth went dry as her body began to tingle.

His wide shoulders were encased in a faded blue T-shirt that brought out the color of his incredible blue eyes. They were almost the same color as the summer sky and right now they were focused on her. She tried to swallow, but it was impossible. Her breasts felt heavy and, the closer he got to her, the more she could feel her nipples tightening. A low ache began between her thighs and she had to force herself not to fidget.

His face was too rugged to be called good-looking, but it had something even more important—character. His brown hair had reddish highlights that glinted under the morning sun. It was cut short in the back and brushed away from his forehead in the front, framing his face. His eyebrows were severe slashes that were the same color as his hair. Thin lines radiated from the corners of his eyes. Emerald imagined that they were a result of working outside in all weather his entire life. His skin was burnished a light gold from the sun and it emphasized the blue of his eyes. His eyelashes looked almost too long and thick for a man's, but it was the only softness on his face. His cheekbones were high, his chin firm and stubborn and his nose hawkish.

At the moment, his full lips were pursed in a severe line. They looked soft though. Emerald wondered what they would feel like against her mouth. Or maybe lower as he nibbled on her breasts, teasing the tips. She barely swallowed back a groan. She had to get a grip on her wayward libido. Ignoring the fact that her panties were now damp, she plastered a smile on her face.

Uh-oh, Mr. Hottie wasn't pleased about her being here. Emerald wondered who he was even as she turned back to Erin. The other woman was smiling at the man. Emerald got a sinking feeling in her stomach.

"Emerald, I'd like you to meet my brother, Jackson Connors. It's him you'll be working for."

She'd just known that this wouldn't be easy. Still, she needed this job worse than she'd ever needed anything in her life. She could bury her burgeoning desire for her new boss. Besides which, she wouldn't be here long enough to really get involved with the man. His life was here and hers was back in New York. She was just tired, and like any woman, she could appreciate a fine male specimen. It didn't mean anything.

"Pleased to meet you, Mr. Connors." She held out her hand and his large, tanned one quickly swallowed it up.

"Might as well call me Jackson since you're going to be living with me." His voice was low and raspy, sending shivers running down all her nerve endings. His hand was strong, but he held hers gently. This was a man who knew his own strength and controlled it. Would he show that same control when he took a woman to bed? She suspected so. And she had to get her mind back on the business at hand. She had no time to indulge in sexual fantasies, no matter how much fun they might be.

"Jackson, then," she agreed and tugged her hand away from his, needing to break the contact which felt very intimate in spite of the two other people standing next to them. She turned back to Erin. It was easier to talk to the other woman. "I assumed I would be working for you."

Erin shot Jackson a mischievous grin. "I don't need a keeper."

"Erin," he growled.

She laughed, totally unconcerned. "Come on, Emerald. I'll show you around and get you settled." She gave her brother's arm a squeeze as she planted a kiss on his cheek. "Go to work. I'll take care of this for you."

Jackson looked as if he might say something, but he gave a curt nod and headed toward a large barn about fifty yards from the house. Emerald couldn't take her eyes off him. The man had buns of steel and, boy, did they fill out a pair of jeans. She felt a trickle of sweat roll down her back and knew that not all the heat she felt came from the sun.

He turned before he'd taken more than a few steps and glared at his sister. "You take it easy today."

"I will."

He smiled then and Emerald's breath caught in a gasp. She'd thought his features too rough for him to be good-looking and she was right. He was devastating. His smile changed his face totally. She could stand there and stare at him all morning. He glanced her way and the scowl returned. It was just as well. She didn't need this attraction that was obviously one-sided.

Emerald forced herself to turn her back on Jackson and face Erin and her husband. Abel was leaning down to kiss his wife. Emerald could see the love in his eyes and it made him seem not so intimidating. "I've got to run," he murmured. "You take it easy, okay?"

"I'm pregnant, not sick." Still he waited until she sighed and nodded. "I promise I'll take it easy."

"Nice to meet you, Emerald. I'm sure we'll see more of one another if you last here." Then he was gone, striding across the yard and into a stand of trees.

"Don't mind either one of them," Erin told her as she linked her arm in Emerald's. "Leave your stuff for now. We can get that later after I've shown you the house."

"I don't think your brother wants a housekeeper." Her words were blunt, but Emerald knew that there was no polite way to phrase it.

Erin laughed. "He does, but he's just too stubborn to admit it."

They walked up three steps that led to the wraparound porch. Emerald took the time to have a better look at the house. It was a snug, two-story farmhouse that looked to be in good repair.

Erin opened the back door and ushered her inside. "I got married last year and moved out. I live just next door, by the way, so I'm close if you run into any problems."

"Good to know." Emerald took in the state of the kitchen. She had her work cut out for her.

"I know it's a mess," Erin cut into her thoughts. "Jackson's working the place by himself now, and this time of the year he's busy from dawn to dusk. Now that I've got my own home, and I run my own blueberry farm as well, I just don't have time to help out."

"Not to mention you've got a husband," Emerald added dryly. She'd seen the way the big man had stared at his wife.

Erin chuckled. "There is that. Abel does keep me busy. And now that there's a baby on the way, I just can't manage it all."

"Congratulations."

"Thanks." Erin rubbed her stomach with her hand. Emerald tried to find some evidence of pregnancy but couldn't see any. "I'm almost three months along and I'm not doing so well in the mornings. Anyway," she continued briskly, "my brother needs a housekeeper."

"I have to agree with you there." The kitchen was lovely with its hardwood floor and large wood trestle table. The cabinets were a crisp white and the walls were the same color as a café au lait. It felt welcoming, homey. Except for the pile of broken glass on the floor and counter.

Erin noticed her staring at the broken dishes. "Jackson had a slight accident just before you drove up."

Emerald nodded, not asking what had happened even though she was dying to know.

Erin grabbed a broom out of the utility closet and began to sweep the glass into a neat pile. "The place had gone downhill this past month. I've been busy with my own business and Jackson's been flat out in the fields. He also grows alfalfa to sell to local farmers, along with running the apple orchards. It's a lot of work and he does the bulk of it himself. Our brother, Nathan, helps out when he can, but he's married now and living in town. He also works as a deputy sheriff, so his time is limited. You'll probably meet him and his wife, Carly, in a day or two."

Emerald tried to commit all the names to memory. "So what am I responsible for beside the house and meals?"

Erin leaned the broom against the counter. The glass was in a neat pile ready to be removed. "That's pretty much it. Once you get the house back in order, it will be more maintenance than anything else. Jackson's not a real messy soul, he's just been too busy to cope. He's also a guy, so he doesn't always notice that the laundry is piling up or that the living room is dusty."

Emerald nodded as she followed Erin into the living room. The room was neat but dusty. Again, it was a comfortable room, but a decidedly masculine one. A floor-to-ceiling wall unit dominated one wall. It was filled with books, stereo equipment, a flat-screen television and a DVD player. A stone fireplace stood in the center of another wall, the dark wood mantle filled with family photos. The furniture was a comfortable mix of old and new. The leather sofa was obviously new, but the faded brown easy chair was not. A book was facedown on the coffee table as if waiting for its owner to come back. She was surprised to see it was a true-crime book by well-known author A. B. Garrett.

"That's your husband," she blurted out.

Erin smiled and wrinkled her nose. "Yes, it is. That's his latest true-crime book."

"Wow. You must be really proud of him."

"I am. But I'm also glad that he's switching to writing mysteries."

"That's a big change." Emerald knew how hard it was to switch, even within a profession where you were already well-known. Especially then. Her parents hadn't been able to make the switch when music changed in the Seventies and had retired instead.

"It is, but Abel can do it. Now, as for meals," Erin continued as she showed Emerald the office and laundry room before leading her upstairs. "Breakfast needs to be on the table by six—Jackson usually leaves the house before seven and comes back for lunch at twelve. Soup and sandwiches are fine for then. Supper is at six in the evening. That gives him time to get home and grab a shower. He'll want something substantial then. I'll leave you a list of meals that he likes."

"Thanks, I'd appreciate that." Emerald ran her hand over the smooth wood banister as she climbed the stairs.

"No problem. This is Jackson's room." They stopped in front of a large bedroom. The bed was unmade and there was a small pile of clothes in one corner.

Emerald could just imagine Jackson coming in after a long, hard day's work, stripping off his sweaty clothing and tossing it aside.

*Naked, he moved about the room and then stretched out across his bed. His cock swelled and his muscles rippled as he gripped his length and pumped his hand slowly up and down.*

*He smiled at her and beckoned her forward. "Like what you see?"*

*She smiled back at him as she licked her lips. "I certainly do." Seductively, she stripped off her jeans and shirt, all the while watching him as he continued to work his hand up and down his erection. Naked, she climbed up onto the bed and crawled forward until she was sitting between his spread legs. Cream slipped down her inner thighs as she cupped his testicles in her hand. His skin felt hot. He moaned as she scraped her nails gently over him.*

*Bending forward, she licked the tip of his cock, tasting the salt of his flesh. She made a small sound in the back of her throat.*

"Are you all right?"

Emerald jerked when a hand clasped her arm. What in the world was she doing? This was no time for a sexual fantasy featuring a man she just met. "I'm fine. Just tired. It's been a hard few weeks."

"Are you sure you're up to this?"

Emerald could see the concern in Erin's face and felt her new job slipping away. "Absolutely." She forced herself back to the task at hand. She needed this job. Her libido could darn well take a backseat. She'd never had any trouble concentrating on work before. It had to be the stress she'd been under. Nothing more.

She could see that Erin still looked concerned, so she summoned up a smile. "Why don't you show me where I'll be staying and I'll get my things brought inside. Then I can start on the kitchen."

Relief passed over Erin's face. "Your room is downstairs off the kitchen. It's a large bedroom with its own bathroom. It was the original housekeeper's room. There hasn't been a housekeeper here for about twenty years though, so it hasn't been used." Before Emerald could groan over the probable state of that room, Erin grinned. "But don't worry, we've always used it as a guestroom, so it's been kept up. It just needs a good dusting. The sheets and towels are upstairs in the hall closet."

"Got it."

"You should have several free hours every day once the place is back in order. And, as I said on the phone, Sunday is your day off. Saturday, you just need to make something and leave it for Jackson's lunch and the rest of the day is yours as well. The job only pays two hundred a week because room and board is included."

"That's fine." In fact, it was perfect. She didn't foresee needing to spend much money over the next few weeks. She wasn't planning on leaving the farm unless she absolutely had to. She could use the phone here to call her sisters, rather than use her cell phone. It would all work out. It had to.

# Chapter Three

ॐ

Jackson walked to the barn, although it was difficult with his cock at full attention. He reached down and adjusted himself but it didn't help. His balls were heavy and tight, his erection throbbing. He hadn't had this kind of a reaction to a woman since he was in his early teens.

Emerald was far from the thin, cool blonde he'd imagined. Her hair was a profusion of black curls, which hung below her shoulders and emphasized her slender neck. Her dark, chocolate-brown eyes dominated her heart-shaped face and her full rosy lips begged a man to lick and kiss them. Her skin was creamy and her body lush with curves in all the right places. Her thighs and hips were gently rounded and her breasts full and firm.

He groaned as his erection twitched. She was a walking wet dream. Dressed in a flowing skirt and matching blouse, she looked more like a gypsy enchantress than a housekeeper. He shook his head at the irony of the situation. It had been years since a woman had done more than catch his casual attention. Now he was finally attracted to a female and she was hands-off.

And she was attracted to him too. He was too old and too experienced not to notice the way her eyes glazed over as she stared at him. Her breathing had hitched slightly and she'd unconsciously smoothed her hands over her stomach and hips, pulling the fabric tight on her blouse. The movement had emphasized the shape and size of her breasts. Jackson wondered what color her nipples were. Would they be rosy like her lips?

He licked his lips and then swore under his breath. He had to get his mind off his new housekeeper. She was only here for ten days. He was getting rid of her as soon as his agreement with Erin was up. He wasn't about to get involved with a woman who was just passing through town.

*Why not?* a voice in the back of his brain taunted him. Maybe Emerald would be agreeable to a no-strings affair. Every muscle in his body tightened and he forced himself to take a deep breath and relax. He'd have to think on this some more. The thought of her naked and spread across his bed was almost enough to make him turn around and head back to the house.

He swore again as sweat trickled down his temple. It was hot enough outside without him making himself even hotter. Swiping it away with the back of his hand, he climbed aboard his tractor and started it. It was going to be one heck of a long day.

Heading out of the barn, he focused on the workday ahead. On a farm like his, there was always something to be done, especially this time of year. And if he was lucky, he might get a few minutes to take some pictures.

Since he'd started making money with his photography, he kept his camera close and watched for particularly interesting shots. He enjoyed it and it added another dimension to his day, breaking up the monotony of the daily chores. He glanced back at the house as he drove away. Cursing, he pushed all thoughts of his new housekeeper from his mind, distracting his wayward thoughts by running through his mental to-do list for the day.

Emerald put her hands on her hips and surveyed the kitchen with pride. The place practically sparkled. It was a far cry from what she started with more than three hours ago. It hadn't taken her long to cart her belongings in from her car with Erin's help. She hadn't bothered to unpack, but had gone straight to work. Thankfully, the utility closet in the kitchen was filled with everything she needed to put the kitchen back to rights.

However, her first task had been to start a load of laundry. She figured she had about six or seven loads to do including sheets and towels. While she was waiting for the first load to wash, she'd finished cleaning up the broken glass on the kitchen floor and then had gone to work on the mounds of dishes. It had taken a fair amount of elbow grease to scrape the dried food from them, but she'd done it.

Draining the dirty water, she'd then refilled the sink and started washing down the counter and cupboards. She'd opened every cabinet door as she stacked the clean dishes away and figured out where all the pots and pans were kept. It was a fairly organized kitchen. Emerald reckoned that she had Erin to thank for that.

She'd sorted the mail that was strewn across the table, placing the bills in one stack, flyers and papers in another and what looked to be personal stuff in yet another pile. She'd have Jackson go through them after supper. Then she'd scrubbed down the table. It was a beautiful trestle table made of maple and her hands had lovingly traced the warm wood.

The refrigerator and the stove had come next. The refrigerator wasn't in too bad a shape, but it was getting close to empty. It hadn't taken her long to dump everything after its "best before" date. She'd washed down the shelves with baking soda and water and then had put everything back inside. Somebody would have to go shopping and she was afraid it was going to be her. Her stomach clenched at the thought of leaving the farm. She'd make a list tonight, get Jackson to approve it and go first thing tomorrow. Unless she could convince him to go.

The stove came next, but that wasn't too dirty. She suspected that Jackson used the top of the stove to do most of his cooking and the oven to reheat food that his sister brought over. According to Erin, she'd been bringing him casseroles to keep him from starving. There were still some in the freezer.

Emerald had washed and dusted every surface in the kitchen in between running back and forth to the laundry room and loading clothing into the dryer before starting another load to washing. The curtains had looked dingy, so she'd dragged them down and shoved them in the washing machine while she cleaned the windows. She'd even taken down the light fixture and washed it.

When every surface of the kitchen was clean, she tackled the floor. The hardwood floor was a thing of beauty and looked fairly new. By the time she was finished, it gleamed. Satisfied, she packed away her cleaning supplies for the moment, folded the next load of clothing that came out of the dryer and started another one washing. The kitchen drapes were dry, so she shook them out and hung them back on the windows.

She was more than satisfied with her morning's work and Jackson should be too. Her plan was to make herself indispensable so he wouldn't even think about firing her. Emerald knew that Jackson didn't want her here, so it was up to her to change his mind. She needed to be able to stay.

Nibbling on her bottom lip, she fretted as she slipped off her blouse. It was soaked in sweat after all her hard work. The tank top she was wearing beneath it was much cooler. She realized now that she should have taken the time to change before she'd started work, but she'd been in more of a hurry to make a good impression. What she needed now was a long, cool shower to revive herself.

A glance at the clock told her that Jackson would be home and expecting his lunch in about fifteen minutes. Sighing, she knew her shower would have to wait. There was just enough time for her to slap some ham and cheese sandwiches together. She'd serve them with some chips. It was simple and fast. She'd make something more substantial for supper.

She just finished cutting the last sandwich and piling it onto a platter when the back door opened. "Lunch will be on the table in just a second." When there was no answer, she glanced toward the door. Jackson stood there staring, not at the nice, clean kitchen, but at her. She knew she looked a fright, but she hadn't thought she looked that bad. Blowing a lock of hair out of her eyes, she grabbed the platter and hurried to the table. "Why don't you sit down and dig in?"

He shook his head like a man coming out of a daze. Still not saying anything, he sauntered over to the sink and began to wash his hands. Even though she told herself not to look, she couldn't resist watching him as he lathered his big, work-roughened hands. The bubbles covered his fingers and wrists as he rubbed them together.

A picture of them in the shower together, he rubbing those slippery, soapy hands over her body popped into her head. A restlessness filled her as her womb clenched. She felt empty and achy. The crotch of her panties dampened as Jackson rinsed his hands and dried them in the towel. Her nipples puckered and pressed against her bra. Glancing down, she could see them outlined against the thin fabric of her red tank top. Jackson chose that moment to turn around. It was like waving a flag in front of a bull.

His nostrils flared. His body tensed. She could see the steady rise and fall of his chest as his breathing deepened. Her lips parted as she tried to get enough air into her lungs. She felt lightheaded and totally unlike herself. Her skin felt as if it was on fire as desire pulsed through her veins. It was exhilarating. It was frightening. She'd never had this kind of a physical reaction to any man in her entire life.

She licked her lips and his eyes darkened as he watched. There was no mistaking the bulge in the front of his jeans. The man was seriously aroused. His hands clenched at his sides as he struggled for control.

Emerald took a step toward him as if pulled forward by an invisible thread. Her mind was screaming at her to be careful. Her body was demanding that she go to him. One step became two.

She stopped when she was right in front of him. Their bodies almost, but not quite touching. She could feel the heat rolling off him in waves. The urge to snuggle up close and lay her head against his chest was almost overwhelming. What was it about this man that drew her to him?

His hands wrapped around her shoulders. She could feel the tension in his fingers as he held her. She wasn't sure if he was going to push her away or pull her closer. She didn't think he quite knew what to do. The heat of his hands permeated her skin. She could smell sunshine, sweat and the sweet smell of fresh-cut hay.

"This isn't a good idea." His voice was low and gritty.

"I know." If she were sensible, she'd run to her room and wait for him to leave. But her common sense had deserted her at the moment.

"You work for me." Jackson's fingers tightened.

"I do. But I'm an adult." She licked her lips again and tried to swallow, but her mouth was too dry. "I don't usually do things like this." It was important for him to know that she didn't make a habit of coming on to men she'd just met.

He frowned and his eyes narrowed. "I didn't think you did. This thing…" He trailed off, unable to find the words he wanted.

She nodded in complete understanding. "I know. I feel it too."

"There's still time for you to go." She knew that he meant more than just leave the room. He was telling her that there was time for her to get in her car and just drive away.

The only problem was that she really needed a safe place to stay and, besides that, she didn't want to leave. She wanted to explore this burgeoning attraction flaring between them. She shook her head. "I'm not going anywhere."

She could feel the tension rolling off him as he stared at her, his blue eyes intense. He swooped down suddenly and captured her lips with his. This was no tentative first kiss, but a declaration, a claiming.

Jackson's lips were firm and warm as they melded against hers. His hands slid up the slope of her shoulders and neck until he was cupping the sides of her head. He tilted it to one side to give him better access as he traced the seam of her lips with his tongue.

The moment she parted her lips, his tongue snaked inside, stroking hers. She swallowed a cry of pleasure and snuggled closer. The hard ridge in the front of his jeans pressed against her stomach. Her nipples almost hurt, they were so tight. She rubbed them against the hard planes of his chest. Even through her clothing and his, she could feel his rock-solid muscles. Jackson groaned and thrust himself tighter against her.

She longed to see him naked, to touch him, to rub herself all over him. She creamed her panties as his tongue rasped over the inside of her mouth, leaving no part unclaimed. She had the urge to strip off her clothes and fuck him right here in the kitchen.

What was wrong with her?

Emerald felt like she was totally out of control. Jackson must have sensed her turmoil because he softened the kiss, no longer claiming but cajoling. Seducing. His hands slipped over her neck and shoulders. He traced her collarbone with his fingers before slipping downward. His hands came to rest just below her breasts. They were so close she could feel the edge of them every time she took a breath.

Desire coursed through her veins as she covered his thick wrists with her hands and pushed them upward. They both groaned when his palms covered the mounds of her breasts. Her nipples pressed hard against his hands.

Jackson's fingers stroked her breasts, circling her nipples without touching them. She moaned into his mouth, unable to keep the needy sound inside. She wanted his hands on her naked flesh, stroking, touching and kneading. She needed his hard cock inside her, filling her as he fucked her to completion.

He tore his mouth from hers and took a step back, dropping his hands from her. Emerald swallowed hard, wanting to yank him back against her, while at the same time, she was glad that he'd pulled back. She'd just met him this morning. This was all too much too fast. Obviously, he felt the same way.

He raked his hand through his hair and blew out a hard breath. "God almighty. That almost got out of hand."

"Yeah." Her voice came out as a sultry purr, so she cleared her throat, striving for a more even tone. "Must be the heat."

His eyes practically scorched her. "Oh, it's the heat all right."

She swallowed hard and turned away. Going to the refrigerator, she hauled out the pitcher of iced tea she'd made for lunch. The cool air bathed her skin but did nothing to diminish the heat flooding through her body. She needed that shower more than ever now.

He was seated at the table by the time she closed the refrigerator door, helping himself to the sandwiches. Unaccountably, she felt angry with him. How dare he recover his composure so fast? She was still shaking with desire. Plunking the pitcher on the table, she hauled out a chair and sat.

"It's going to happen. You know that?" She'd just taken a bite of sandwich when he spoke and almost choked on it. He thumped her on the back until she waved him away.

"Pretty sure of yourself, aren't you?" she asked as soon as she'd managed to swallow her food. After what had just happened, it was no wonder he was so sure. Still, it rankled her.

"There's no denying the chemistry between us. If you don't want it to happen, you should pack up your things and leave. If you stay, you're going to end up in my bed."

Emerald almost fanned herself, but managed to stop before she actually did it. Her eyes narrowed as her mind began to work. The anger that had begun to subside surged to life again. "You'd like me to run away, wouldn't you? I know you don't want me here. Erin told me that she'd all but forced you to give me a ten-day trial period. Was that what this was all about?" She motioned to him and back at herself. "You trying to scare me into leaving?"

If she'd thought he'd looked fierce before, it was nothing compared to the glare he shot her. It was a wonder she didn't melt and puddle beneath the table with the force of his anger.

He slowly pushed back his chair and came to his feet. Resting his large hands on the table, he leaned forward. Emerald resisted the urge to pull away. "I would never, ever, force myself on a woman, and I'd never use sexual attraction to try to frighten you or drive you away. If I wanted you gone that badly, I'd pack your belongings in your car and put you out of the house."

Every word was spoken softly, but still she flinched. She'd known as soon as the words left her mouth that they weren't true. She'd not only hurt his pride, but she'd insulted the man too.

He was as still as a statue as he continued. "If that's what you think about me, I want you gone when I get home. Rest assured, if you stay, I won't be bothering you with my attention again." Pushing away from the table, he turned on his heel and stomped out of the room. The door slammed shut behind him.

Emerald slumped back in her chair and took a deep breath. Her body broke out into a cold sweat. She'd thought for a moment that he was going to toss her out and she wouldn't have blamed him if he had. She'd learned a valuable lesson about the man though. His word was obviously his bond and since he'd promised his sister he would, he'd give Emerald her ten-day trial, even if he didn't want to.

Picking up her glass, she took a long swallow of the quickly warming tea. She also knew that there would be no more kisses in the kitchen. Not unless she initiated them. And if she did, she better be darned sure she was ready for an intense affair. Because once Jackson started, she was sure he wasn't stopping until they were both sexually sated. She'd end up spread across his bed, just as he'd said.

Funny, but the idea wasn't as frightening as it had been. Emerald had never indulged in an affair before. The two men she'd slept with each had been men she'd had a long-term relationship with. Her attraction to Jackson was undeniable and definitely something for her to think about.

Pushing away from the table, she gathered the dishes and piled them in the sink. Her appetite gone, she wrapped the sandwiches and put them in the refrigerator, along with the pitcher of iced tea.

Stopping, she leaned against the refrigerator door and took a deep breath. She was staying. Of that there was no doubt. She was going to have to apologize to Jackson too. What she'd said to him wasn't very nice and she knew in her heart that it wasn't true. There was no way he'd use sex to frighten her into leaving. He'd been just as caught up in the attraction between them as she had.

Pushing away, she decided to leave the dishes until she'd had a long, cool shower. She'd take the time to unpack and make up her bed with fresh sheets before tackling the rest of the house. She'd have to plan something special for supper. Jackson had barely taken a bite of his sandwich. He was going to be starving when he came home this evening.

She stopped in the laundry room long enough to haul one load of clothing out of the dryer and put the last load into the washer. From now on, she'd hang the clothing out on the line, but for today, there had just been way too much and she'd been in a hurry to get it all done. Helping herself to one of the clean facecloths and towels, she hurried to her room.

Feeling the heat pressing down on her, Emerald grabbed a change of clothing out of one of her suitcases before stripping off her sweaty clothing. Leaving them in a dirty pile on the floor, she headed for the shower.

# Chapter Four

ဆ

Anger was his constant companion all afternoon as Jackson threw himself into his work. Physical labor helped him burn off some of his sexual tension and cleared his mind. Still, he was semi-hard all afternoon, his cock reminding him of the soft feel of Emerald's body next to his.

Her breasts had been showcased to perfection in the tight red tank top she'd been wearing when he'd come in for lunch. Now he knew how supple and full they really were. Her nipples had been outlined against the fabric like two tight little berries. Fool that he was, he'd pulled away before he'd touched them.

"Damn it." He yanked off his work gloves and shoved them in his back pocket. The heat was starting to get to him. His skin felt prickly and tight. He took a deep breath and exhaled. Then he took another.

His stomach growled, reminding him that he hadn't actually eaten any of his lunch. A few bites of a sandwich didn't count. He glanced up at the sky and then at his watch. It was almost five o'clock. Early for him to be calling it a day, but suddenly he didn't care. His gut clenched as he climbed aboard the tractor and headed back toward the barn. Would she even still be there?

He honestly didn't know. She'd been as shaken as him by the hot flash of desire that had burned between them. Her lips were soft and when they'd parted for him, inviting him inside, he'd felt a fierce sense of satisfaction. He shuddered as he imagined those lips on other parts of his anatomy. His cock stirred yet again, letting him know what it thought of the idea.

"Get a grip," he muttered as he easily maneuvered the heavy vehicle. She was his housekeeper, his employee. That's if she was still even here. The thought of her being gone left him feeling slightly bereft, as if he might have missed something special. Something important. That just made him angry again. He barely knew the woman. There was no way she could mean much of anything to him.

He forced himself to drive straight to the barn and park the tractor safely away for the night before heading toward the house. He knew he was delaying the inevitable, but he did the rest of his chores first, as if that would somehow prove that Emerald meant nothing to him.

Flinging his gloves onto the seat of the tractor, he spun on his heel and stalked toward the house. He stopped, his heart pounding, as he realized her blue Honda Civic was still parked in the yard. She hadn't left. Relief flooded him even as he told himself not to read anything into it. She probably needed the job.

Still, he hastened his step, suddenly in a hurry to see her. He'd told her that she was safe from his attentions, and he'd meant it. But that didn't mean he'd turn her down if she wanted to turn her sights in his direction. After all, they were both mature adults. Erin hadn't told him how old Emerald was, but she was in her late twenties or early thirties for sure. More than mature enough to know her own mind.

Unsure of his reception, he quietly walked up the steps and eased the back door open. He could hear her voice as he stepped inside.

"I'm fine, sweetie. Really." She was standing with her back to him, staring out the front window while she talked on the phone. Her long curls were piled on the top of her head and anchored with some kind of clip. It exposed the long, slender line of her neck and back. The red tank top and colorful skirt were gone, replaced by jeans and a blue tank top. She looked good enough to eat and he had a powerful hunger growing inside him. Jackson wondered who "sweetie" was

41

and felt unaccountably angry that she could kiss him so passionately at lunchtime, yet sweet-talk some other guy a few hours later.

"No. I've got a job and a safe place to stay." She paused and sighed. "I miss you too."

His body quivered, his muscles all tensed as he stood there with hands fisted by his sides. Sweat made his shirt and jeans cling to his skin. He was jealous, he realized in a flash. And he had no right to be. Hanging his head, he rubbed the back of his neck, trying to loosen the tight muscles. Sure, they'd shared a kiss, but that was it. And he didn't really believe a word he was thinking. There was something between them. What it was, he wasn't quite sure. But it was powerful. And she'd felt it too. He knew she had.

"No!"

His head jerked up. Whatever the other person said had upset her.

"No." Emerald softened her tone as she continued. "I don't want Mom or Dad to know. There's no reason to bother them with this. I've got a safe place to stay while the investigator looks into things."

Relief surged through him. It wasn't another man, at least not one she was romantically involved with. It was either a brother or a sister. Then the rest of what she'd said registered in his brain. Investigator? Safe? What the hell was going on with her?

"No. Don't tell Derek where I am. I know he's upset, but he'll just have to get over it. Don't tell anyone. Listen, I've got to go. No, Sapphire, I don't need you or Topaz to come out here. You just be careful and watch out for yourselves. I know you've hired a bodyguard…" She broke off and nodded. "Tell Topaz I'll get back to work on the designs as soon as possible. I'll have some spare time to work in the afternoons and evenings once I get this place back in order."

She laughed and Jackson closed his eyes as the lilting sound made him shiver with desire. He leaned his back against the wall, content to wait and to watch her. She made a mighty fine picture talking to her sister. At least he assumed it was her sister. With a name like Sapphire, he didn't think that was that big a stretch to make. Now he just wanted to know who this Derek guy was and where exactly he fit into her life.

"No, the place isn't in too bad shape. It just needs a bit of elbow grease is all. Typical man." Jackson arched his eyebrow as she continued to talk. "I've really got to go, Sapphire. I'll call again in a few days. If anyone asks, you haven't heard from me and don't know where I am. Look worried and concerned." Emerald sighed as she turned around. She gasped when she saw him and almost dropped the phone. Her face paled but she recovered quickly. "Bye." She cut the call and stared at him, the phone clenched tight in her hand.

He pinned her with his gaze and spoke softly. "You want to tell me what that was all about?"

Emerald swallowed, her fingers digging into the phone. Jackson was leaning against the wall, looking totally relaxed, but she wasn't fooled for one moment. He was like a cobra ready to strike at any moment. His blue eyes were like lasers as they studied her. Tension swirled around him so thick she could almost see it.

"I had to make a call. I reversed the charges, so you don't need to worry about the bill." She'd forgotten to charge her cell phone the night before and hadn't wanted to wait to talk to her sisters. Besides which, after yesterday's call from her stalker, she wasn't sure she should use her phone. The stalker seemed to have no problem accessing her credit card charges—how hard would it be for him to trace her cell phone records?

How long had Jackson been standing there? What had he heard? She glanced at her watch. He was earlier than she'd expected. Damn her luck. She decided that the only thing to do was brazen it out. "Supper will be ready in about thirty minutes. You've got time for a shower." Acting nonchalant, she hung up the phone and went to the stove, turning on the oven. It wouldn't take long to heat the lasagna she'd already put in there or to bake the frozen rolls she'd found in the freezer.

He pushed away from the wall and she took a step back. In the space of a few hours, she'd forgotten just how large and potently male the man was. His shoulders looked incredibly wide as he propped his hands on his hips and stared at her.

Waiting.

She had the feeling he would stand there and wait until she spilled all her secrets to him. Too bad. She wasn't involving a complete stranger in her problems. Only trouble was Jackson didn't seem like a stranger.

"Emerald?" The way he said her name made her nipples pucker. The low rumble had goose bumps rising on her arms.

"What?" She wasn't volunteering anything.

One corner of his mouth kicked up in a smile and she could see the respect in his eyes. "Why do you need a safe place to hide? Why have you hired an investigator? And why don't you want your parents to know what's going on?"

Emerald wrapped her arms around herself. He'd heard pretty much everything. How was she going to get out of this without telling him what was going on? She could always pack her belongings and leave, she supposed. Yet she stayed where she was. She wanted to stop running and looking over her shoulder. She wanted to stay here. With Jackson. For the first time in weeks, she felt safe.

She shook her head as he came toward her. His big hands clasped her shoulders. "Look at me."

She tilted her head back, mesmerized by the mixture of emotions in his eyes. The lust was easily identified. Mostly because she felt it too. But there was concern and worry there as well. "It's nothing."

He shook his head and she had the distinct feeling she'd disappointed and hurt him with her words. "Why do you care?" she blurted out before she could stop herself.

"I'm not really sure." He stopped and thought, choosing his words carefully. "But I do. You're in some kind of trouble, aren't you?"

"Nothing I can't handle."

He gave a bark of laughter. "Independent and stubborn."

She felt her hackles rising. "You think I can't handle a difficult situation as well as you could just because you're male and I'm female?"

Jackson held up his hands in front of him in mock surrender. "I never said that."

She harrumphed. "You implied it."

He cupped her face with his hand and smoothed his thumb over her cheek. In spite of her resolve to stay strong, she found herself leaning into his gentle caress. "I didn't say that you couldn't handle it, just that there's no need to handle it alone." His thumb continued to glide over her skin. "Let me help you."

Emerald felt a lump of emotion clogging her throat. Tears stung her eyes, but she blinked them away. She forced herself to step away from him. His hand dropped back to his side. "I…I need to apologize for what I said at lunch. I know that you would never use this…" She waved her hand at him and then back at herself. "This thing between us to drive me away. I'm sorry that I even implied such a thing."

Jackson didn't speak for almost a full minute. She struggled not to fidget beneath his regard. She could almost see him processing everything. She knew the moment that he decided to back off. But she also knew it was only a temporary reprieve. He wouldn't let this drop.

"I'm going to get a shower. I'll be back in a few minutes." He strode to the kitchen door, but paused. "You'll still be here when I get back?"

She nodded, unable to speak.

He gave her a curt nod and then bounded up the stairs two at a time. Emerald slumped back against the counter. Most people wouldn't even have bothered to ask what was wrong. A lot more would have asked her to leave and take her problems with her. But not Jackson. He was the type of guy who would get involved. He was such a take-charge kind of man that, if a woman wasn't careful, she might find her entire life being managed by him.

Water began to run through the pipes, reminding her that she didn't have time to waste. Pushing away from the counter, she smoothed her damp palms over the thighs of her jeans. She opened the cupboard door and quickly grabbed plates and set them on the table. Cutlery and glasses followed.

When the table was set, she slid the rolls into the oven. They only needed fifteen minutes according to the package. Emerald was glad she'd found enough ingredients to make lasagna. It was a specialty of hers. She only hoped that he liked it. She'd have Erin's list tomorrow, so she'd have a better idea of what kind of meals Jackson enjoyed.

The coffeepot was already filled, so she flicked the switch to start it brewing. There hadn't been much for her to work with to make a dessert, but she'd found a can of peaches in the pantry. That would do for tonight, but someone had to go grocery shopping tomorrow. She already had a long list of staples that were needed. Plucking it off the counter, she scanned it one more time before placing it next to Jackson's plate. She'd have him approve it over supper. The mail was still stacked in three neat piles at the far end of the table, waiting for him as well. If she kept him busy, perhaps he wouldn't ask her about the phone call again.

"Keep on dreaming," she muttered under her breath as the water shut off upstairs.

It was all too easy to imagine Jackson naked and wet as he stepped out of the shower. His dark hair would be plastered to his skull, emphasizing the harsh planes of his face. His tanned skin made his blue eyes seem even bluer. His lips would be moist. Emerald licked her lips as she imagined tasting his mouth like she had early today. It would be hot and wet and overwhelmingly male.

She'd noticed that his jaw was dark with stubble. It would rasp against her skin as she kissed him. She wanted to smooth her hands over his shoulders and down his flat abdomen. And then lower.

Her breathing quickened and she felt the dampness between her thighs. He'd been aroused earlier. There was no mistaking the bulge in the front of his jeans. He hadn't even tried to conceal it. Unabashedly male, he was quite at ease with his body and saw no need to hide his desire for her. It was blatant and it was surprisingly a huge turn-on as well.

She made a sound of frustration and whirled away to check the food in the oven. Jackson Connors was occupying way too much of her thoughts. She had other things to think about, bigger worries to ponder. Somewhere out there was a stalker who wanted to take over her life and her. She shivered as she closed the oven door and leaned against the counter. It was much more pleasant to think about Jackson and her growing attraction to him than it was to think about her other problems.

She stood there, staring out the kitchen window while supper cooked. It was quiet here. There was no air-conditioning in the house, just the low whir of the overhead fan turning slowly. There was no traffic outside or planes overhead. As she listened, she could hear the happy twitter of a bird as it perched in a pine tree in the far corner of the front garden. The breeze was slight and it was warm. The sun was a giant fireball in the sky. Peace slowly seeped into her very bones. It felt... She didn't quite know how it felt, except to say that it felt *right* in some fundamental way. The town. The farm. Jackson. They all felt...*right*.

A sound on the stairs alerted her that her reprieve was over. Wiping a hand over her face, she took a deep breath and hauled open the oven door. If he was going to question her, then she wanted food. For the first time in weeks, she was actually hungry. Her stomach growled as she lifted out the pan of lasagna and carried it over to the table. She laid it on a potholder she'd dug out of one of the drawers.

Jackson hadn't spoken a word and the suspense was killing her. Emerald glanced over at him and almost groaned. His hair was wet and slicked back from his face. He was wearing a clean pair of jeans and a crisp white T-shirt. Shaking her head, she went back to the stove for the rolls. She'd just have to accept the fact that this man pushed all her buttons. Just one look at him and she was instantly aroused.

She caught a whiff of aftershave too, something earthy, like the man himself. She wanted to walk up to him and bury her face against his neck. But she knew where that would lead and she wasn't quite sure she was ready to go there. Emerald knew in her heart that getting involved with Jackson would not be a light affair. Not that she did light affairs, she reminded herself, but he would be different. He could break her heart if she let him.

"Can I do anything to help?" He chuckled as soon as the words left his mouth.

"What's so funny?" She slid the rolls into a basket and then placed them on the table.

Jackson shrugged, a self-deprecating smile on his face. "It's just that a year ago I probably wouldn't even have asked. It took Abel pointing it out and then Erin leaving to make me appreciate everything that she used to do around here."

Emerald pulled out her chair and sat, motioning Jackson to his seat. "So you're a bit of a chauvinist? Good to know that you're trainable." She groaned as soon as the words left her wayward mouth. "Not that I care or anything. I'm just the housekeeper."

He sat down and grabbed the serving spoon, heaping a large serving of lasagna on her plate before doing the same to his own. "You're more than just the housekeeper. Or you could be, and we both know it." The color of his eyes seemed to deepen. "And yeah, I'm definitely trainable."

She didn't say anything as heat suffused her body. Taking one of the rolls, she tore it apart with her fingers and then painstakingly buttered it. She laid the knife carefully on the side of her plate, knowing she was just delaying the inevitable.

Jackson helped himself to a roll and then began to eat. He took one forkful of lasagna and his expression changed, becoming one of sheer bliss. His chewing slowed as if he were savoring the food in his mouth. Emerald felt inordinately pleased.

His Adam's apple bobbed as he swallowed. "This is incredible." He scooped up another forkful and closed his eyes as he chewed. Emerald laughed. When he'd swallowed, he glanced over at her. "Don't laugh. I've been eating my own cooking for the best part of a year, except for when Erin's taken pity on me. This is amazing. If this is any indication of how you cook, I may not ever let you leave."

Just like that the tension was back between them. The hairs on the nape of her neck seemed to rise. If she got too involved with Jackson, she might not want to leave. Clearing her throat, she tried to make light of things. "Glad you like it. But since you were half-starved to begin with, I won't let your compliments go to my head."

He didn't bother to answer, but just kept eating. He had seconds before he bothered to speak again. Emerald began to relax again and savor her food. She really enjoyed cooking, but it had been quite a few years since she'd bothered with it. The faster Sisters' Jewels had grown, the harder she and her sisters worked. Seemed as if that's all any of them did these days. She loved their business, but she realized she'd lost any sense of balance in her life.

Jackson scraped his plate clean, laid down his fork and sat back in his chair. Folding his hands across his flat belly, he watched her. She'd known the questions were coming. It was only a matter of time. He'd actually shown more patience than she'd expected. The man was full of surprises. She still hadn't quite decided how much, if anything, she was going to tell him. "Go ahead."

He cocked his eyebrow at her. She braced herself for his barrage of questions about why she was here and why she had an investigator. Jackson's eyes narrowed as he sat forward. "I've got to know…" He paused, his eyes narrowing intently. "What possessed your parents to name you and your sisters after jewels?"

# Chapter Five

**ෂ**

It was so unexpected that Emerald laughed. Satisfaction flashed in his eyes and she knew that that was what he'd intended. Jackson was proving to be a much more complex man than she'd first suspected. He wanted her to relax so she'd spill more of her secrets. The man was diabolical and totally irresistible because, beneath the humor, she sensed that he really was interested in her, really wanted to know.

The lie had been bothering her since she'd first uttered it and it was time to come clean. "I lied to your sister."

All signs of humor fled as Jackson slowly sat up straight. Emerald had the urge to flee. Not that he'd done anything threatening, but menace poured off him in waves. This was not a man to cross. "About?" His tone was mild, but she wasn't fooled.

"Jones is not my last name." She paused and took a deep breath. "It's Jewel."

His eyebrows came together in a frown. "I don't understand. Why would you lie about something like that?" Some of the angry tension seeped out of him. He seemed more quizzical now than mad.

"My name is Emerald Jewel. My sisters are Sapphire Jewel and Topaz Jewel." She watched his face for recognition, but saw none. She could have saved herself a lot of headache by not lying in the first place. Seems as if he didn't have a clue who she was or who her parents were.

"You say that like it's supposed to mean something to me." He shook his head. "The names are unusual to say the least."

Emerald laughed. "I guess my ego was a bit too big. I was afraid that someone might recognize the name, and I'm trying not to attract attention."

Jackson pushed back from the table and ambled to the counter. He poured up two mugs of coffee and brought them back to the table, handing one to her. "Why don't we go out and sit down on the back porch and watch the sun go down?"

As Emerald took the mug from him, his fingers brushed against hers. She shivered. "Okay, but I want to put the dishes in the sink to soak first."

Jackson sighed as he plunked his mug down on the table and began to pile the dishes. "I'll help. The quicker we get this done, the quicker we can continue our chat."

Bowing to the inevitable, Emerald quickly put away what was left of the lasagna and rolls. Jackson eyed the plate as she covered it with plastic wrap and headed to the refrigerator. "You can have it for lunch tomorrow."

He laughed. "That obvious, am I?"

She shrugged but secretly was pleased by how much he'd enjoyed the simple meal. "There would have been salad too, but you didn't have anything in the house I could use to make one. I made a grocery list. It's on the table." She tugged open the refrigerator and popped the plate onto an empty shelf. "If you want to eat, you need to buy groceries."

"Erin usually runs into town a couple times a week. I'll have her take you tomorrow and show you around town. She can help you with the shopping and let you know what I like. Then next time, you'll be able to go on your own."

"Sounds good to me."

"I'll call her now." While Jackson used the phone, Emerald took the time to wash the dishes and stack them in the drain tray to air dry. She hated having dirty dishes sitting around. Jackson glanced her way and raised a questioning eyebrow. She just shrugged and continued to scrub the lasagna pan.

She listened with half an ear as he talked with Erin, hearing the underlying affection between them. She squeezed her eyes shut as tears pricked them. She missed Sapphire and Topaz so much and she'd only been gone a couple of days. The main problem was that she had no idea when she'd be able to see them again.

"I would have helped you with that." She jumped and almost dropped the pan. He'd finished on the phone and come up behind her when she wasn't paying attention.

He was so close she could feel the heat coming off his large body. She had an urge to lean back against him and rub her ass against his erection. Instead, she carefully placed the pan in the drain tray and pulled the plug in the sink. When the dirty water was gone, she cleaned the sink and then hung the dishcloth to dry. "I know."

Neither of them moved and then she thought she felt the slight brush of his lips against the top of her head. Then he was gone. Her knees felt weak, but she forced herself not to slump against the sink. Taking a deep breath, she turned and casually walked back to the table and picked up her mug of coffee.

"Erin said she'd pick you up at eight tomorrow morning. Better to get in and out of town early before it gets too hot."

"I'll be ready."

Jackson held the door for her, his body blocking most of the doorway. She had to angle her body to slide past him and her hip grazed his groin. He groaned and her hand shook, threatening to spill her coffee. She grasped the mug with both hands and quickly sat down on the top of the three steps that led from the yard to the porch.

Jackson eased himself down onto one of the two large patio chairs that sat just to the right. Emerald loved the covered wraparound porch. The view of the orchards and farmland from every side of the house was spectacular and it could be used pretty much year-round. "This porch needs a swing." She'd always wanted a porch swing and this two-story farmhouse just cried out for one.

"We have one. I just never bothered to put it up this year. Erin used it more than myself or Nathan did."

And Erin wasn't here anymore. Emerald could sense the thread of loneliness hovering just below his words. "You miss her, don't you?" She turned sideways, resting her back against the top post of the stairs so she could see him better.

"Yeah." He took a sip of his coffee and laid the mug on the wide arm. "I was more father to her than older brother. Both she and Nathan got married last year."

"Erin mentioned that."

He nodded and Emerald realized that he wasn't going to say any more about the subject. "Tell me about you and your sisters. Why did you think I'd recognize your name? Are you famous?"

Jackson said the last half jokingly, but Emerald didn't laugh. She nodded and then shook her head. "We're not famous, not really. But our parents are."

"Who are they, Emerald?" He kept his voice calm and low. A million questions were clamoring to be asked, but he wouldn't press her too hard. Not yet. He'd have his answers one way or another.

She sighed. "Moon and Aloysius Jewel were a popular folk duo in the late Sixties and early Seventies. They had hits like 'Under the Moon' and 'Sweet City Nights'."

Jackson was surprised and impressed. "I know both those songs, although I couldn't have told you who sang them."

Emerald nodded as she picked at a loose thread on her jeans. "They were really big for a few years, but then came disco."

She laughed and shook her head. The motion caused some of her black curls to slip from their anchoring clip and cascade over her shoulder so that one lock caressed her breast. Jackson longed to stroke that lock of hair and the nipple that it covered. He shook himself as he realized that Emerald was talking again.

"Long story short, Mom got pregnant with Topaz and they retired from touring. Dad found that he had a knack for managing money and making more and so they retired to upstate New York, bought a house and started a family."

Jackson knew that there had to be a lot more to it than that, but it was a start. Still, the question nagged at him. "Why the unusual names?"

Emerald smiled and it lit up her entire face. "Mom and Dad were hippies and they wanted unusual names for us. With a last name like Jewel, they decided to name us after the birthstone of the month we were born in. Topaz was born in November, Sapphire was born in September and I was born in May."

"That's..." He tried to find a diplomatic way of putting it. "Different."

Emerald chuckled. "It is that. I've just always been grateful that I wasn't born in March."

"Why March?"

"Would you want to be stuck with the name Aquamarine?" She laughed and it was overflowing with the love that she obviously felt for her family. Suddenly he was filled with a burning need to have that love for himself. He shook himself. What was he thinking? He was fine by himself here on the farm, and besides which, she obviously wasn't staying. She'd grown up amongst the rich and the famous. A daughter of music stars. He was a farmer.

Emerald was clutching her stomach, she was laughing so hard. "I often wonder what they would have done if they'd had boys instead of girls."

It boggled the mind. Jackson just sat back and enjoyed the sight of Emerald laughing. She was so beautiful that she took his breath away. "I'll bet you met lots of famous people growing up."

"Sure." She was still smiling as she leaned back against the post again and took another sip of coffee. "There were always people coming and going. Plus, Mom and Dad would do the occasional guest appearance on some television special or award show. They still write songs, but now they just let other singers do them. Mom jokes that she's too old to be on the road, but honestly she looks as beautiful now as she did in the Sixties. Maybe even more so."

"You must take after her then."

Emerald glanced away, but not before he saw the telltale blush on her cheeks. "Thank you."

"Do you and your sisters sing?"

"Lord no. We all love to sing, but we didn't want that kind of life. We made a record a few years back as a present for our parents. They loved it, but some record executives started pressuring us to cut a real record and go on tour." She shook her head. "I know that a lot of people would give anything to have that kind of opportunity, but it's not what we wanted."

Jackson's supper was churning in his gut. "What did the three of you want?"

"Sisters' Jewels." She said it with such pride that he smiled.

"Okay, I'll bite. What is Sisters' Jewels?"

"It's our company. It belongs to me, Topaz and Sapphire. We started it all on our own about five years ago. It's an upscale boutique in New York that sells accessories for women. We sell specialty journals, stationery, greeting cards, scarves and jewelry and we're thinking about expanding into purses as well."

"So you work in the shop?"

Emerald shook her head, sending her loose curls bouncing all around. "Only part-time. Topaz is the brain behind the day-to-day running of the boutique. She got a degree in business, so she handles that aspect of Sisters' Jewels. Sapphire designs and makes the jewelry we sell. Her work is amazing."

Jackson could sense the closeness between her and her sisters and he understood it. After all, he and his siblings had worked side by side for years to make the farm a success. It built a deep bond that could never be broken. He sat back in his chair, slightly amazed at that revelation. He'd been feeling slightly abandoned these past few months, even though he'd been extremely happy for both Erin and Nathan. But he realized now that nothing could break the close bond that they'd formed during all those years they'd spent working alongside one another. It was a good feeling. Life might change, for better or worse, but the strong bond with his siblings would never diminish.

"What about you?"

"I'm an artist. I do all the designs for the journals, greeting cards and stationery. I'm also just starting to design fabric for making scarves and that new purse line I mentioned. I've also been thinking about including extras like lipstick cases, makeup bags…stuff like that." She ducked her head as if she were almost embarrassed to be talking about herself.

"I'd love to see some of your work."

"You would?" He could see she was genuinely surprised.

"I wouldn't have said so if I didn't."

"I don't have anything new to show you." Her smile faded and she looked pensive. "I've been in a bit of a creative slump the past three or four months. It's been especially hard the last two."

He sensed that they were starting to get to the crux of the problem. He wanted to ask her about her work, but there would be time for that later. Right now, he needed to know why she'd felt the need to leave the job she adored and the sisters she loved and run all the way to an apple farm in Maine. "What happened in your life, Emerald?"

His heart skipped a beat when she looked up at him. Her dark brown eyes were filled with worry and fear. "Someone is stalking me."

Jackson was out of his chair in a flash. Emerald jerked back and knocked over her mug. Coffee spilled over the deck and she jumped up to keep it from seeping into her jeans.

He grabbed her arm to keep her from toppling off the steps. Her skin was soft beneath his hand, but he could feel the slight trembling that engulfed her. He drew her slowly into his arms and wrapped them around her. Her heart was thudding so hard he could feel it against his chest. "You're safe here."

She gave a bitter laugh that made his heart twist. "I'm not sure I'm safe anywhere."

As much as he wanted to go on holding her in his arms, he needed to find out exactly what was going on. Why this woman had become so important to him in such a short time, he didn't know. She just was.

Settling back onto the chair, he eased Emerald down on his lap. Instead of trying to get away, she snuggled closer. That alone told him that she was more than a little upset and distracted. He might not have known her for long, but one thing he did know for sure was that she had an independent streak a mile wide. Otherwise, she'd be tucked away on her parents' estate with a ton of bodyguards rather than leaving her family and heading out on her own. "Your parents don't know about this?" He already knew the answer, but he wanted her to tell him everything.

When she shook her head, her hair brushed against his face. He wanted to bury his face in the thick mass and just inhale her sweet scent. Tucking a stray lock behind her ear, he waited as she marshaled her thoughts. "No, they don't know. They're traveling in Europe right now and I didn't want to bother them." She rubbed her hands over her jeans in a nervous gesture as she gave a rueful laugh. "That's not totally true. If Daddy knew, he'd lock all of us up on the estate and we might never get out again." Emerald tipped her head up so that she was looking straight at him. "Daddy's a mite protective at times."

Jackson found himself drowning in her liquid brown eyes. He cleared his throat. "I don't blame him for that."

She laughed. "Thankfully, Momma is there to keep a tight rein on him. Otherwise we might all still be living at home."

He could tell she was trying to work up to the issue at hand. "Tell me what happened."

She sighed. "It started out innocently enough." As she sat there on his lap, the entire story spilled out of her. The flood of presents that gradually escalated from the harmless to the perverse. The tampering with her e-mail account and the problems it caused for Sisters' Jewels. And finally, the wedding dress and black cuffs that had been delivered to her apartment and the note that had been tucked in with it.

She shivered and he wrapped his arm tighter around her. "What do the police say?"

Emerald shrugged. "They're looking into it and checking leads, but there really isn't much to investigate. This guy hasn't given them much to go on. They're leaning toward the theory that it's a crazed fan of my parents."

"What do you think?" He rubbed his hand over her back, doing his best to comfort and soothe her.

She scrubbed her hand over her forehead. "I honestly don't know. I guess it's easier to believe that it's some crazy stranger rather than someone I actually know. But..." She bit her lip and turned her head away.

He captured her jaw in his hand and gently turned her face back toward him. "But?"

"But it seems more personal than that." She peered out over the yard. "It's so quiet here."

"Yes, it is."

"I like it. You can really see the moon coming up in the sky. The air is fresh and clean and you can hear yourself think."

They sat in silence for a few minutes. Jackson's mind was mulling over what she'd told him and what she hadn't.

"He called me."

Jackson took a deep breath, biting back the surge of anger that shot through him. "Since you got here?"

She shook her head. "No. When I was on the road. He called me on my cell phone. It was a new phone I'd just gotten before I left the city. Only Topaz and Sapphire were supposed to have the number."

It was a battle, but Jackson forced his body to stay relaxed when he felt anything but. The urge to find this guy and beat him to a pulp was almost more than he could stand. But right now, Emerald needed him to be calm. "So this guy knows his way around computers and electronic equipment."

"Yeah. He also knew where I'd stayed the night before. I knew then that he was tracking my credit cards."

Knowledge flooded through Jackson. "That's why you took this job."

Emerald glanced up at him and nodded. "I needed a safe place to stay, where no one could find me while the investigator I hired looks into things."

"This investigator any good?" Jackson was filled with the unreasonable urge to go to New York and check things out for himself. Which was totally crazy. He wasn't an investigator. He was a farmer. But he did know several people who might be able to help him.

Emerald nibbled on her bottom lip. Jackson realized that it was a nervous habit. He smoothed his thumb over her lip, soothing the abused bottom lip. She jerked but didn't pull away from the small caress. "He's very good. My father has used him in the past for other things. I figured my sisters would be safer if I left town. I mean, this person seems to be fixated on me, not them."

He realized that she was looking for some kind of reassurance that she'd done the right thing. "You said that they have a bodyguard?"

"Yes, one each. And they're keeping their activities to a minimum."

"Then they should be fine."

Emerald sighed, her warm breath brushing across his face. "That's what I thought too."

Jackson shifted, trying to get more comfortable. Having Emerald in his lap was having a predictable effect on his body. He did his best to ignore the erection pressing against the zipper of his jeans. "Have you made a list of men you know for the police to check out?"

She stiffened in his arms, but he continued to rub her back and arms and she gradually settled back. "Yeah. It was hard though. I mean, I know these people. Or at least, I think I do." She buried her face in her hands and took a deep breath. "I don't know anymore."

"What about that Derek guy you mentioned on the phone?"

Emerald shook her head. "He's a friend—the son of my parents' former manager. No, that's not quite true. He's more like an overbearing older brother. I've known Derek since we were both kids. He's a successful promoter for big-time musicians and movie stars. Appearance and success mean a lot to him. He'd never do anything to jeopardize what he has."

"What about the rest of them?"

His anger built slowly as she told him about her ex-boyfriend, Beau Vater, who just happened to run his own computer software company. Then there was Fred Kirby, who was a delivery guy by day and computer geek by night. Finally, there was the odd assortment of acquaintances, people she came in contact with through work and friends of her sisters.

"What about the investigator?"

"Dane Hatcher? What about him?" Her brows were drawn together as she frowned. "He's not very happy that I disappeared without telling him. Apparently he raked both Sapphire and Topaz over the coals for not contacting him immediately."

Jackson's hackles rose immediately. "He knows your father, your family. It would be easy for someone like that to trace phone records and credit cards, maybe hack into your e-mail account." He shrugged when she continued to frown, his mind working furiously. "Makes sense that if you were having trouble you'd turn to an investigator you knew and trusted."

"I never thought of that." She chewed on her bottom lip and Jackson barely swallowed back a groan. The urge to sooth the small hurt with his tongue was almost overwhelming. "He's probably just worried about me."

"How old is this guy?"

"Mid to late thirties, I think. Maybe a bit older." Her eyes widened and she sucked in a breath.

"What?" He continued to smooth his palm up and down her spine, as much to relax himself as to soothe her.

"I just thought of something." She rubbed her hands against her jean-clad thighs. "He asked me out about a year ago, more than once. I turned him down."

Jackson swore under his breath. "Tomorrow, I want you to sit down and write out all you know about these guys, including Hatcher, and if you can think of any reason why any, or all, of them would be angry with you or possibly hold a grudge of some kind."

"I already did that for the police." She stared at him, slightly bewildered by his request. "Well, I included everyone except Dane."

"Yes, but I know some people who can do a bit of poking around as well. Very discreetly." Jackson was already planning to call Nathan and Abel tomorrow morning as soon as Emerald left to go shopping with Erin.

"Who? And why would you bother?" Her innocent question stopped him cold.

He cupped her face in his hands and gently skimmed his thumbs over her cheeks. He'd known her less than twenty-four hours, but already it was as if she were a part of him, a part of his existence.

One section of his mind was yelling at him to walk away, to protect himself from the hurt that was bound to come by getting involved with her. Emerald would be going back to her life as soon as the stalker was caught. New York, her sisters and their company were her life.

Another part of him already knew it was too late. He was already involved. Emerald was special and he knew that if he walked away from what might happen between them, he would always regret it.

And yet another piece of him knew that he could never walk away from her, knowing that she was in danger. His overriding instinct was to protect her at all cost.

She was shifting restlessly in his arms and he knew he'd been silent for way too long. "Who? My brother and brother-in-law. Nathan is in law enforcement and Abel has contacts everywhere from his years as a crime writer." He paused, trying to find the words to make her understand. "Why? There is something between us, Emerald. Something I can't explain, but I can't deny it either. Whether it goes anywhere or not, it's there. I could no more walk away from you now than I could walk away from Erin."

"But I'm not your sister. I'm not related to you at all."

Jackson barely swallowed a groan as her hip pressed against his throbbing erection. "Believe me," he gritted out between his clenched teeth. "I know."

# Chapter Six

ఴ

Emerald was still trying to digest the fact that this virtual stranger not only was willing, but seemed adamantly determined to help her when he bent his head and brushed his lips across hers. Soft yet firm, they skimmed her bottom and then her top lip. Her mouth parted on a moan and his tongue slipped inside. He tasted of coffee and some hot, male essence that enticed her to give more.

Her fingers crept up the front of his shirt, digging into his wide shoulders for support. She felt lightheaded, as if she were floating on air as she returned his kiss.

His hand stroked over her hip and belly, coming to rest on her torso just beneath her breast. She sucked in a breath, willing his hand to move higher, but he just rested it there as he continued to plunder her mouth. It got harder to breathe, so she tore her lips from his, gasping for air.

Jackson nibbled a path down the line of her jaw and neck. She groaned when he nipped the sensitive skin at the base of her neck where it met her shoulder. The edge of his hand barely grazed the bottom of her breast, but her nipple puckered tight in anticipation. She shifted restlessly, her fingers opening and closing over the firm muscles of his shoulders. She wanted more. Much more. But it was way too soon for that. Wasn't it?

As if he could read her thoughts, Jackson raised his head, his blue eyes smoldering with desire. "If you don't want this, then now is the time to go inside." She could feel the pulse of his erection beating against her hip. "We can forget that this ever happened."

She bit her lip and swallowed hard. That would be the smart thing to do. The safe thing to do. The sensible thing to do.

Emerald couldn't wrench her gaze away from his face and she felt herself falling deeper into his amazing eyes. A lock of his reddish-brown hair tumbled down across his forehead and she tenderly brushed it back. He closed his eyes as if he were savoring her touch. His skin was much darker than hers, tanned from years of working under the sun and in the wind. Taken individually, his blunt features weren't overly handsome, yet they suited his face perfectly, a reflection of the inner man.

It might not be smart or safe to give in to the physical attraction blooming between them, but deep in her heart she knew she would always regret it if she walked away without sampling it.

Her mind made up, she pushed away from him. His hands tightened around her for the briefest of moments before falling back down to his sides. He said nothing as she rose gracefully to her feet and shifted to stand in front of him. His eyes widened and his nostrils flared as she placed first one knee and then the other on the seat cushion, straddling his lap. She lowered herself so that she was sitting on his thighs facing him.

"You're sure?" His voice was rough and it made her stomach clench. She nodded, unable to verbally answer him. "Good." Satisfaction tinged his reply as his large hands cupped her ass and tugged her closer.

The movement caused her jean-clad mound to press against his erection. Even though they were both fully clothed, Emerald could feel the heat of him against her. Her panties were already damp and getting wetter every second. She rose up on her knees, rubbing her sex against his shaft. They both groaned.

Jackson tugged at the bottom of her tank top, pulling it from the band of her jeans. His hands slipped under the material to rest against her stomach. She sucked in a breath as he continued upward. This time he didn't stop until his hands were wrapped around her breasts. Her nipples stabbed at his palms through the thin satin of her bra. It felt good, but it wasn't enough to have him touching her—she wanted to feel him beneath her hands.

Grabbing a handful of his shirt, she tugged it upward. Jackson released his hold on her long enough to take over the job, practically ripping the shirt from his body and tossing it aside. "Your turn, sweetheart." Although a sense of urgency surrounded them, he took his time, inching up the fabric of her shirt to reveal a strip of bare skin. Her breasts rose and fell with each deep breath she took as he slowly exposed her pale blue satin bra.

By the time he got her top over her head, they were both panting heavily. His fingers skimmed the satin straps, moving downward and over the lace edging of the cups. "You are so damn beautiful." Her nipples puckered under his lustful gaze. His thumb just barely grazed the hard nub and she whimpered as her sex clenched painfully.

Reaching out, she ran her hands over the large expanse of his chest. The muscles rippled beneath her fingers as she explored him. A neat thatch of hair covered the center of his chest between two flat brown nipples. Leaning forward, she flicked at one with her tongue. His hands tightened over her breasts as he gave a guttural groan. His cock flexed against her mound and she gave in to the need to press herself more fully against him. She wanted to be totally naked, to feel every hard plane of his body against her softer curves. There was something about this man that brought out the elemental female within her. She wanted to claim him as hers and have him claim her in return.

Giving his nipple one final lick, she sat back up and allowed her fingers to trail down the silky line of hair that bisected his torso before disappearing into the waistband of his jeans.

Jackson gave a low growl as he buried his face in her cleavage. Finding the front closure, his fingers gave a quick flick and the satin cups fell away, exposing her. Plumping the full mounds in his hands, he held them as his lips moved closer to one taut nipple.

Emerald practically held her breath as he got close enough for her to feel the heat of his mouth against her skin. He carefully traced the outline of her areola with his tongue. Then he did the same with the other one.

"Jackson," she gasped as she tangled her fingers in his hair, trying to tug him closer.

"Mmm," he responded, flicking his tongue out to taunt the tight peak.

Her thigh muscles tightened as she rubbed her mound against his rock-hard erection. "More," she demanded.

She cried out as he opened his mouth over her breast and took her nipple inside. His tongue stroked over it, softly at first and then with increasing firmness. "Yes," she groaned as she pushed her breast more firmly against him.

He captured the tip with his teeth and carefully tugged. Emerald shook with desire. She was on fire for him. Her fingers flew to the opening of his jeans, pulling at the button and zipper. It was his turn to groan when she freed his erection from the confinement of his jeans. She shoved aside his underwear and then he was in her hand. Hot. Hard. And hers.

Her palm slid over his length before she closed her hand around him. His skin was warm and soft, but what was beneath it was pure steel. The plum-shaped head was wet, and as she watched a pearly bead of liquid seeped from the slit. She used her thumb to spread it over the top and Jackson groaned again, his hips jerking upward. He was thick and long and she could only imagine how good he'd feel buried deep inside her. Her pussy wept with need for him. She was wetter than she'd ever been in her life.

Jackson gave one last gentle tug on her nipple before releasing it. Tilting his head back, he took a deep breath. The thick column of his neck was exposed and she couldn't resist leaning forward to lick it. He tasted salty and hot. She imagined his cock would taste the same. "You taste so good." His shaft jumped in her hand in response and she laughed.

He swore as his hands made quick work of the fastenings of her jeans. He had the zipper down before she knew it and slid his hand inside. His fingers slipped beneath the satin of her bikini underwear, brushing the curls of her mound. But he didn't stop there. He kept going until he was touching the slick folds of her labia. "You're so wet." There was wonder and pleasure in his voice. "I've got to see you." He removed his hand and shoved at her jeans and underwear.

Emerald wanted to feel his naked flesh against hers. Squirming backward, she managed to get one foot on the porch floor and then another. Wobbling slightly, she stood, her bra tangled around her arms and her jeans and panties down around her hips. She reached for her bra.

Jackson could barely breathe as Emerald reached for the strap of her bra. He wasn't sure if she was going to get dressed or get naked. His breath came out in a whoosh as she slid the thin straps over her shoulders and then the scrap of pale blue satin fell onto the deck.

Damn, she was gorgeous. Her breasts were large and full, perfect pale mounds tipped with rosy nipples. Her waist dipped inward, but her hips curved out generously. She was all woman and, for the moment, she was his. He couldn't look away as she reached behind her head and pulled the clip away. Some of her hair had already slipped away from the holder, but now the rest of it tumbled down around her back, so dark against her creamy skin.

Her hands gripped the waistband of her jeans and she shoved them down her hips and thighs. Quickly, she toed off her sandals and pushed the jeans over her calves and feet, kicking them away. She stood in front of him clad only in a tiny piece of blue fabric masquerading as underwear.

Every muscle in his body was tight. His cock throbbed insistently, begging to be inside her delectable body. Jackson swallowed hard. As much as he wanted her, he wasn't sure now was the right time. She was feeling vulnerable and emotional and he was the only one here to reach out to. He'd hate to make love to her tonight only to have her regret it in the morning. That didn't mean that he couldn't make her feel good though.

"Come here." He barely recognized the rasping tone of his own voice.

Emerald shook her head, making her sassy curls bounce. "Not yet." She hitched her fingers inside the waistband of her bikini underwear and pushed. She shimmied her hips and the fabric fell down around her ankles.

Jackson could only stare at the perfection in front of him. The black curls covering her mound glistened with the evidence of her arousal. He wanted to see all of her. "Show me." He patted the arm of the patio chair. "Put one of your feet up here."

He'd surprised her. He could tell by the way her body jerked and her breathing increased. She licked her lips nervously. He could see the fear and arousal in her eyes. Just when he thought he might have pushed her a bit too far, she slowly raised her foot and perched it on the arm of the chair. It opened her up to him, but not enough.

"I want to see all of your pussy, sweetheart. I'll bet it's wet and hot and the same color as your rosy nipples."

She was panting harder now and he could see the confusion in her eyes.

"Put your hands between your legs and spread yourself so I can see you." When she hesitated, he leaned closer. "Please."

Her hands skimmed over her belly and then down into the vee of her legs. She pulled back the folds of her labia and he could see her wet, pink sex. Reaching out, he traced his fingers over her sensitive flesh. She pulled away and then pushed closer. Jackson sat forward and flicked his tongue over the tight nub of nerves at the top. Emerald whimpered, the sound skipping along all the nerve endings in his body, setting him on fire.

Taking his time, he inserted one long finger into her tight channel. The muscles contracted around him. He watched Emerald as he pushed deep. Her head tipped back and she sighed, her hips tilting forward to take him. He pulled his finger all the way out and rimmed the opening with the tip.

"Jackson." She barely breathed his name, but he heard the underlying need, the fire in that one word. She swayed and he caught her as she stumbled. Her hands flew out to steady herself as he drew her back down onto his lap. When he had her settled and facing him once again, he cupped her face in his hands and kissed her.

She opened completely to him, giving him all that he asked for and more. His hands slid over the curve of her neck, across her delicate collarbone and down her sides. He palmed her breasts, kneading them gently as his mouth consumed hers. Their tongues touched. Dueled. Mated.

His cock was throbbing so hard he was surprised he hadn't come. His balls were drawn up so tight to his body they hurt. But he wanted more. He wanted Emerald's pleasure. Wanted—no, needed—to see her come.

He left her sweet mouth and sat back, sucking air into his starving lungs. He allowed his hands to slip lower over the curve of her hips. The lushness of her ass called to him and he couldn't resist giving it a quick squeeze. Someday he wanted to take her from behind so he could hear the smack of his flesh against the plumpness of her ass as he fucked her.

Emerald's hands felt so good against his flesh as she touched his shoulders and chest. But when her hand reached lower, he grabbed her wrist. His fingers wrapped easily around it, stopping her from reaching her goal. Her eyes flew to his. "If you touch me, I'll come in your hand. I'm hanging on by a thread here."

Surprise and then pleasure lit her face and then she smiled. Jackson barely stifled a groan. It was time to finish this before he lost all control. Sliding one hand between her thighs, he didn't hesitate as he pressed two fingers inside her. Emerald gasped, making her breasts jiggle with each breath she took. Her pussy was so hot and tight he thought his cock might just blow. He gritted his teeth and tried to think about something else, anything but the beautiful, giving woman curled so trustingly in his arms.

"Touch yourself," he rasped. "Play with your nipples. You know that they're aching to be touched and petted." Leaning forward, he nuzzled one of her breasts before licking the tip. He sat back and feathered his thumb over her swollen clit as he worked his two fingers in and out of her pussy. "Do it," he whispered.

She licked her lips and then brought her hands up to cup her breasts. They overflowed her smaller hands, but she squeezed and rubbed them, gradually touching her nipples with her fingers.

"That's it," he encouraged. "Pinch them." He withdrew his fingers from her channel and lightly pinched her clit. Her hips jerked forward, her eyes glazing over as she tugged at her nipples.

Jackson thrust two fingers back inside her. He wanted it to be his cock buried inside her, but not only was it too soon, he suddenly realized he didn't have any protection. He hadn't needed any in quite some time. The older he'd gotten, the less he'd indulged in meaningless affairs. There was no way he was making love to Emerald without it.

Emerald was panting harder now, her hips moving quickly against his fingers as he thrust them in and out of her pussy. Dampness coated his fingers as her muscles tightened around them. He could feel she was close. A light sheen of sweat covered her body, making her glow in the last rays of the day. Her head was tipped back, exposing the curve of her neck. Her lips were parted and they looked slightly swollen and moist from their earlier kisses.

Sweat rolled down his back as he continued to work her with his fingers. He pressed on the hard nub of her clit as he started to insert a third finger into her molten core. Emerald stiffened and then jerked forward. Her climax hit her hard, making her entire body heave. Jackson kept his fingers moving as she cried out his name. His hand was wet with her desire by the time he finally withdrew it. He gritted his teeth as he pulled his fingers from her, wanting to bury himself in her sweet depths.

She slumped against him and he cuddled her close. Her mound was pressed tight against his cock and he could feel her throbbing against him. The smell of sex seemed to sit on the warm, still evening air. Jackson had never been so aroused in his life, yet he was oddly content as he held Emerald tight against his chest. The sounds of the evening that had all but disappeared in the haze of passion started to seep back into his consciousness.

He began to hear the calls of the birds as they flew from tree to tree in search of an evening meal. The bees hummed gently as they flitted from flower to flower. The sun was low in the sky, partially sunk below the horizon. It glowed a fire red as it gradually faded from sight. The wood of the chair was warm against his back and the woman in his arms was soft, her delectable body draped almost bonelessly across him.

Jackson contented himself with just rubbing his hand across her back and shoulders. His own breathing calmed and his cock, while still erect, at least wasn't in danger of erupting at an inopportune moment. Gradually, Emerald stirred and pushed away to sit up in his arms. She looked sleepy and sated and incredibly sexy with her hair tumbling around her flushed skin.

She also looked slightly bewildered. "You didn't..." She broke off and looked down at his erection.

"No, I didn't."

"I don't understand."

Jackson sighed, wishing she'd stayed curled in his arms a while longer. "I don't have any protection and it's too soon."

Her eyebrows came together. "Too soon?"

He kept rubbing her back, willing her to understand. "You're in a vulnerable position right now and feeling emotional. I didn't want to take advantage."

The flush of sated desire was quickly turning into anger. He could see it in the way her entire body stiffened. Her voice was low and controlled but throbbed with hurt. "Let me get this straight. It would be taking advantage of me to sleep with me, but it's not taking advantage to have me strip naked and make me come outside on a patio chair." Her voice got louder with each word and he winced. When she put it like that, it sounded bad.

"I just wanted to make you feel good."

Stiffly, she climbed off his lap and grabbed her clothing, holding it in front of her. "I don't need your pity."

"Pity," he yelled. "I don't feel pity for you. If anything, I feel pity for me. I'm the one with the raging hard-on."

She sniffed, tilting her chin up as she glared down at him. "That's your own fault. I think you're just too afraid to be vulnerable. It's okay for me to be totally exposed to you, but you don't want to risk the same in return."

Jackson froze in place. Was she right? Was he afraid to risk opening himself up to her so soon? No! No, he assured himself. He was being thoughtful, trying to be sensitive, and look where it got him. "That's not true. I wanted to touch you, to taste you, more than I've ever wanted any woman. And I'll always be grateful for the gift you just gave me here. The last thing I wanted to do was to make love to you here tonight and have you regret it in the morning."

73

Uncertainty filled her face as they simply stared at one another. Finally, it was Emerald who broke the connection between them. "I'm going to bed." Without another word, she hurried into the house. He caught a glimpse of her lush ass before the door closed behind her with a resounding thump.

Jackson slumped back in the chair and closed his eyes, wondering exactly what had gone wrong. He didn't know how long he just sat there thinking about everything, but by the time he dragged himself out of the chair, darkness had claimed the land. He tugged his jeans up around his waist but didn't bother to zip or button them as he followed her inside, closing and locking the door for the night.

He strode over the closed door of Emerald's room and laid his hand on the door. He stood there for long seconds, trying to decide what to do. Sighing, he dropped his hand, turned and walked away. His footsteps were heavy as he climbed the stairs and headed for the bathroom and a cold shower. It was going to be a long night.

Emerald lay curled in a ball on top of her bed as she listened to Jackson finally come into the house. He'd been out there so long she almost got up to check on him. She still wasn't sure how she felt about what had happened between them.

Her body was still thrumming with the aftereffects of her orgasm and she squirmed to get more comfortable beneath the thin sheet that was draped over her naked body. She hadn't been able to bear the thought of putting on a nightgown. Her skin still felt extremely sensitive. Even the sheet was almost too much.

She'd let down her guard and made herself vulnerable to Jackson while he'd held part of himself back from her. Maybe she should be glad at least one of them had some common sense. She hadn't even thought about protection and there was just no excuse for that, especially not in this day and age.

She'd felt his presence outside her bedroom door. Could almost feel his indecision as he hovered there. She'd had to bite her lip to keep from calling out to him. Part of her wanted to comfort him and another part of her was warning that he could hurt her. She could easily lose her heart to him if she wasn't careful.

When she'd finally sensed him leave, she didn't know what she felt exactly. Slightly bereft. Partially relieved. She was a mess of emotions. With all the other troubles she had, a romantic entanglement was the last thing she needed. It had been an incredible experience, one she'd never forget, but it couldn't happen again. After all, she wasn't going to be here that long.

And why that thought depressed her, she didn't know. Her life was in New York, not here. She heard water running through the pipes and knew that Jackson was taking a cold shower. She could use one of those herself. But she didn't move. She just didn't have the energy. The morning would be time enough to shower.

The water cut off and she thought she heard his footsteps as he walked to his bedroom. Then there was silence. With her window wide open, she heard what she thought might be an owl. It was so quiet here compared to New York.

She yawned and closed her eyes. It had been a long, strange day.

# Chapter Seven

ജ

Emerald sighed deeply as the farmhouse faded from view.

"That was a deep sigh. Anything wrong?"

She turned to find Erin glancing her way, concern on the other woman's face. "No, I'm fine. I just didn't sleep well last night."

The truth was she'd hardly slept at all. She'd drifted off to sleep but had spent the entire night waking up almost as soon as sleep claimed her. Strange noises had made her heart pound, and when she hadn't been thinking about her stalker, she'd been imagining Jackson naked upstairs in his bed. And that thought was more than enough to keep a woman awake all night long.

"You'll settle in." Emerald wished she felt as confident as Erin sounded. "That is, if Jackson doesn't scare you off."

"What do you mean?" Oh God, did Erin suspect what had gone on between her and Jackson last night? Her heart began to pound. Had she seen something? They'd been naked together on the back porch, of all places. Well, she'd been naked. Jackson had still been partly dressed.

Erin just laughed. "I figured if the mess and Jackson's grumpiness hasn't driven you off yet, it's not going to."

Emerald took a deep breath and forced herself to relax. Of course no one knew what happened last night. It was her imagination working overtime this morning. She hadn't been sure how she was going to face Jackson this morning, so she'd gotten up early, made a pot of coffee and cooked breakfast. When Jackson came downstairs, she'd served up bacon and eggs and then hurried upstairs to start cleaning.

It had worked for the most part. He'd left her alone until just before he left the house at seven o'clock. She'd sensed him behind her and had turned off the vacuum cleaner. The look he'd given her had been filled with a combination of exasperation, lust and some other emotion she couldn't quite place. But there had been a distinct tenderness in his blue eyes when he'd placed his hands on her shoulders.

"You can't hide from me or from what's happening between us forever, Emerald." He'd rubbed his thumb across her bottom lip, making it tingle. "We don't have to deal with it until you're ready, so there's no need to hide from me."

She'd bristled at the suggestion that she was hiding until she realized that it was the truth. She hadn't wanted to face him last night and that was cowardly. Still, she'd felt the need to deny it. "I'm not hiding."

"Good. Then we don't have a problem, do we?" He'd bent down and brushed a gentle kiss across her lips. Her nipples had tightened immediately and she'd parted her lips, but he was already backing away. "Good morning." His husky voice had made her shiver, but she'd quickly shaken off the sexual lethargy that had threatened to descend upon her.

"Did you go over the grocery list that I left on the table?" She desperately needed to get things back on a businesslike setting.

He'd stared at her as if he knew exactly what she was doing, but thankfully he didn't call her on it. "Yeah, I checked it. Erin will let you know if there's anything else you need. After this trip you should be able to handle it on your own. Just tell them to put it on the farm tab. With Erin there to vouch for you, there should be no problem. I'll call in to the store later and tell them that you can charge groceries there until I tell them differently." He'd hesitated, but then a determined look settled over his face and he squared his shoulders. "I don't know how much money you have or if you need anything. If you do, just get it and charge it to the farm."

Once again his generosity had overwhelmed her. She'd opened her mouth to thank him, but he was already plowing ahead.

"Don't get all riled up. I know you're proud and you've got money that you can't access. Think of it as an advance on your salary."

Emerald had almost smiled when she'd realized that he'd expected her to argue with him. "Okay."

That had seemed to surprise him. "Okay. Good." He'd dragged his hand through his hair as he puffed out a deep breath. She realized that he wasn't any more comfortable than she was this morning. He'd just been hiding it better. "Did you make the list of names I asked you?"

She had. When she hadn't been able to fall back to sleep early this morning, she'd turned on her light and made a list as he'd asked, even remembering to add her investigator's name and phone number at the top. It was similar to the one she'd given the police and Dane Hatcher, except that list hadn't included information about the investigator himself. Reaching into the back pocket of her jeans, she'd pulled out the folded list. Jackson had taken it from her, his fingers barely grazing hers. But that simple touch had been enough to set her heart racing.

"Erin will be here in an hour. I'll see you when you get back." At that, he'd leaned down and pressed another kiss on her lips. This one was firmer, but it was still over before she'd had a chance to even think about participating. Jackson's boots had clunked down the stairs and she'd heard the back door slamming shut behind him.

Sighing, she'd touched her fingers to her lips. When she'd realized what she was doing, she'd shaken herself, finished vacuuming the hallway and hurried downstairs to clean up after breakfast and get ready for Erin's arrival.

She hadn't seen Jackson when she'd left. He must have already been out working somewhere in the orchards.

"You sure you're all right?" Erin's voice jolted her back to reality.

"I'm sure." She glanced out the window and was surprised to see they were almost to town. She'd been quiet all the way in. "I'm sorry I'm not better company this morning." Erin had been nothing but kind to her and she didn't want the woman to think she didn't like her.

Erin just smiled. "No problem. I'm sure you're just beat after yesterday."

Emerald laughed. Erin wasn't one of those women who tried to sugarcoat things where her brother was concerned. "You've got that right. The downstairs has been put to rights, but now I've got to tackle the upstairs. Other than the bathroom and Jackson's room, there shouldn't be much to do but vacuum, dust and change the sheets on the beds." Just thinking about Jackson's bedroom had her stomach doing somersaults. "The kitchen was the worst of it."

Slowing the truck, Erin turned into a parking lot on the edge of town. The big sign in front of it proclaimed it the Stop and Shop Grocery. Even at this early hour, there were quite a few vehicles parked out front.

"I've got a list that Jackson approved, but he said that you'd let me know if there's anything else I need."

They undid their seat belts and both climbed out of the truck. Emerald started to lock her door, but Erin stopped her with a breezy, "No need to lock your doors here." It was strange for a city girl to walk away from an unlocked vehicle, but kinda nice too.

The day was already starting to warm and promised to be another scorcher. Emerald had opted for a simple flowing skirt in a floral print, contrasting green tank top and a pair of flat sandals. She'd wanted to look nice for her first trip to town, but she'd also wanted to be comfortable.

"I love your necklace." There was no mistaking Erin's sincerity as they strolled across the paved parking lot toward the entrance of the store.

"Thanks. My sister made it."

"Really?" Erin reached out and touched the intricate silver twists that were interspersed with malachite, citrine and quartz beads. "She's incredibly talented."

"Yes, she is." She felt like a fraud for lying to Erin about her real name and why she was there, but this wasn't the time or the place to explain things.

The automatic doors slid open as they approached. Erin grabbed a cart and Emerald pulled one out and followed her inside the store. She sighed as the cool air hit her and then shivered. The hairs on the back of her neck fluttered and she glanced around. She felt as if someone were watching her. She bit her lip nervously and hitched her purse closer to her body.

Then she saw an elderly lady watching her. Emerald almost laughed aloud the relief was so deep. Of course people were staring at her. She was a stranger in their small town and she was with someone they probably all knew. They were curious about her was all. There was absolutely nothing for her to worry about. No one from her *real* life knew she was here. She hadn't even told her sister exactly where she was. It was safer for everyone that way.

Hurrying, she caught up with Erin at the first aisle. Taking her list from her pocket, she focused on her shopping. The quicker that was done, the quicker she could get back to the safety of the farm and Jackson.

Jackson strode toward the house as he heard the truck pulling up. He'd called his brother and brother-in-law first thing this morning and asked them to come over as soon as Erin and Emerald were gone. Neither man had asked why, but both of them had promised to be there. It was good to have family.

Abel had no sooner parked his truck behind the house than Jackson heard another vehicle approaching. When the police cruiser came into sight, he knew it was Nathan. Abel climbed out of his vehicle and they both waited for Nathan.

"Morning," Nathan called as he climbed out of his official vehicle. He was dressed for work and Jackson knew that his brother had already been up for hours. Since his wife, Carly, ran the local diner, she was up at the crack of dawn each day to go to work. Abel was also an early riser and that was why Jackson didn't feel guilty about calling either one of them.

"Come on inside." He turned the handle and shoved at the door. It didn't budge. That was strange. The door didn't usually stick. He pushed at it again, but this time harder.

"What's wrong with the door?" Nathan peered over his shoulder.

Jackson shrugged. "It was fine when I opened it this morning." He jiggled the handle again and then leaned his head against the door and started to laugh.

Abel leaned against one of the porch posts and watched with interest. "What is it?"

"She locked the damn door."

"The new housekeeper?" Abel started to grin.

"Yeah. She's a city girl. Hang on. I left my bedroom window open." Walking around the porch, he stopped at the front. He quickly climbed up on the railing, grabbed the roof of the house and swung himself up. In no time, he'd scuttled across the roof to his window and shoved it open enough to squeeze inside. He was still grinning when he unlocked the back door and let the other men inside.

"You want some coffee?" He strolled back to the counter and already had the carafe filing with water.

"I wouldn't turn down a cup." Nathan pulled out a chair, sat down and kicked his long legs out in front of him.

Jackson quickly filled the coffeemaker and set it to brewing. Both men had already made themselves at home and were waiting for him to tell them why he'd called them here.

He pulled out his own chair and sat, marshaling his thoughts. Where to begin? The clock on the wall ticked loudly. Jackson glanced over at it, remembering the older one that had been broken in a fight between himself and Abel about a year ago. He shook his head. So much had changed since then. And he was also wasting time.

"You know that I've got a new housekeeper." He decided the best thing to do was to jump right in. Abel nodded and Nathan inclined his head. "Either one of you could have warned me," he added wryly.

Nathan grinned, his eyes sparkling with humor. "What would have been the fun in that? I just wished I could have been here when Erin told you."

Jackson ignored his brother and slanted a gaze at his best friend who just sat back with a satisfied smile on his face. "Don't look at me," Abel protested. "I didn't want Erin mad at me. You might be my best friend, but I'm not doing anything to upset Erin these days."

Jackson sat forward. "Erin's all right, isn't she?" He remembered that she'd almost passed out in the kitchen yesterday morning. It was amazing to think that that had happened only twenty-four hours ago. So much had changed in his life since then.

"What's going on? Is Erin okay?" Nathan eased upward from his chair.

"Erin's fine." Abel motioned Nathan back to his seat. "If I tell you, you have to promise not to say a word about it. Not to Carly or to Erin. She wants to tell you herself."

Nathan nodded, concern plain on his face.

"We're going to have a baby." A huge grin split Abel's face. Nathan just stared at him in disbelief, his mouth hanging open. Abel laughed. "She's pregnant."

"A baby." A slow smile curved Nathan's lips. "I'm going to be an uncle." He jumped up and offered his hand. "Congratulations, man. Damn, I hope she tells Carly today or I may not be able to hide it from her."

Abel grinned as he pumped Nathan's hand. "I'll make sure she calls Carly later today."

It took a few more minutes for the men to remember that Jackson had called them there for a specific reason. By then the coffee was ready, so Jackson poured up three mugs and carried them back to the table.

"You know I've got a new housekeeper," he began again.

"You already said that once, brother. We know it's a shock, but you gotta get over it." Nathan saluted Jackson with his mug before taking a sip of his coffee.

"What you don't know is who she is or why she's here." Jackson saw the spark of interest in both men's eyes as he began to outline the basics of what Emerald had told him, including the truth about her name.

Abel's eyes widened at one point and he whistled. "I remember The Family Jewel. That was what they were called. My mom had a couple of their records. They're probably still over at the house."

Nathan sat forward, his blue eyes narrowing as Jackson continued. "You sure she's telling you the truth and not yanking your chain? You don't know this woman at all and she already admitted to lying about her name."

Leave it to Nathan to be cynical and logical. Jackson understood his brother's concern. Heck, he had concerns himself, but deep down in his gut, he knew that Emerald wasn't lying to him. "She's running and she's scared."

Nathan nodded and pulled a notebook out of his pocket and began to scribble notes. "What did she tell you? Any suspects or leads?"

Jackson yanked the sheet of paper out of his pocket and handed it to Nathan. He took it, scanned it quickly and paused occasionally to jot more notes into his notebook. When he was done, he handed the note to Abel. When Abel was finished with it, he folded it. "Can I keep this for today? I'll want to do some searches online and check with some folks I know in New York."

Jackson nodded and the knot in his gut began to loosen. "I was hoping you'd say that."

"I'll let you know as soon as I find out anything."

"She shouldn't have gone to town." Nathan tucked away his notebook and drained the last of his coffee, plunking the mug back on the table.

"Why? No one knows she's here." Jackson hadn't thought there would be any danger in Emerald going into town with Erin.

"And you want to keep it that way. She's a stranger, Jackson. She's going to stand out like a sore thumb and it won't matter what last name she's using, her first name is so distinctive. If anyone asks about her, all the locals will be able to point in this direction."

"Damn." Jackson jumped up and headed toward the door. "I gotta go get her."

"Wait." Nathan was hard on his heels. "You go in there like that and folks are really going to suspect something is up. Let me handle this." He looked thoughtful for a moment. "We need a plan."

Abel drank down the last of his coffee and rose from the table. "Got anything in mind?"

Nathan scrubbed his hand across his jaw. Jackson could practically see the wheels in his mind turning. "What we need is a very public scene in which Emerald quits working for you and leaves town."

"I don't want her to leave." Jackson's chest tightened at the mere thought.

Nathan shook his head and Jackson realized that he was being totally irrational. "She won't really be leaving."

His brother was staring at him strangely and Jackson knew Nathan suspected there was more to the story than he'd told them. Too bad. He wasn't about to talk about the instant attraction he'd felt to Emerald the moment he'd laid eyes on her.

"We just want folks to remember that she left and if we do it right, that's what will happen." Nathan crossed his arms and glared at his brother. "Then we'll all come back to the farm and figure out where to go from there."

"It's a stupid plan." Jackson just wanted to jump in his truck, find Emerald and bring her back to the farm.

"No," his brother countered. "It's a good plan and, at the moment, it's the only one we've got."

Jackson wanted to object, but deep in his gut he knew his brother was right. That didn't mean he had to like it though. His muscles were tight, his body coiled for action, but all he could do was stay here at the house and wait.

Nathan turned to Abel. "You drive Emerald's car to town. When we find her, I can clue her and Erin in on what's going on. She can quit publicly and be seen driving away in her car. I can follow her back here and she can hide the vehicle in the barn until this is over. Unless it's a rental, and then we can just return it and be done with it."

"I don't think it's a rental. Let me see if her keys are in her room." Jackson felt like an intruder as he pushed open the door to Emerald's room. It smelled like her. Some kind of light floral scent that lingered in the air. He breathed deep as he checked the top of her dresser and the nightstand. The bed was made, but he could see the slight indentation in the pillow where her head had lain. Unable to resist, he picked up the pillow and sniffed. His cock stirred. Jackson swore and tossed the pillow back onto the bed. He paused and straightened it, smoothing his hand over the soft fabric before turning and stalking back out the door.

"She must have her keys on her."

"No problem." Abel took his empty mug to the counter and laid it in the sink. "I can hotwire it."

Nathan laughed. "I didn't hear you say that. I'm going to go sit in my car and pretend you have keys and permission to take that vehicle."

"If you arrest me, I'm going to tell Erin it was all your idea anyway. I'm just a helpful bystander." Abel hustled out the door.

"I know it's hard, but it's best if you stay here." Nathan put a hand on Jackson's shoulder. "And if you ever need to talk about this…"

Jackson nodded and rubbed the back of his neck, trying to ease the knotted muscles. "Thanks, man. I appreciate this. All of it."

"That's what brothers are for." Nathan slapped his brother on the back and then headed out.

Jackson followed him, not surprised that Abel was already sitting in the car with it running. The large man looked squashed behind the wheel of the smaller car, and in spite of the seriousness of the situation, Jackson couldn't resist the chuckle that bubbled up inside him.

"Never say that I wouldn't do anything for you," Abel griped as he rolled down the car window.

Jackson leaned against the car. "I really appreciate this."

Abel became serious immediately. "It's no problem. I'll start digging for information as soon as I get home, starting with the investigator she hired. You said that she knew him before this started?"

"Yeah. That's what she said. He'd done some work for her father. He'd also asked her out and she turned him down."

"Hmm. I'll keep that in mind. Could be nothing. Could be something. Hopefully, I'll be able to eliminate some of the suspects fairly quickly."

Jackson could see the sense of that. "That would be a great start."

"Good enough."

"Hey," Nathan called out from his car. "You ready?"

"They were only going for groceries and then coming home so it should be easy to find them." Jackson stepped back from the car.

Nathan laughed. "Going for groceries never just means going for groceries. They may go to a few other stores and stop for coffee as well."

Jackson glanced at Abel who shook his head and sighed. "I can see we're going to have to educate you about the finer points of woman-speak."

Jackson grinned. "Go on. Get out of here. Some of us have work to do."

Nathan tooted his horn and led the way. Jackson watched both vehicles until they disappeared from sight. He rubbed the back of his neck again and swore. He wouldn't be happy until Emerald was safely back here with him.

He scuffed his boots in the dirt as he headed to the barn. He hadn't been thinking when he'd sent her to town. It hadn't even occurred to him that just having her visible in town could put her in danger. Granted, it was a long shot, but not one he was willing to take. He only hoped that she agreed to Nathan's scheme and didn't just decide to take off for good.

Every muscle in his body tightened in protest. He forced himself to breathe and to relax. It wouldn't help anything to get himself worked up about what might be. The only thing that mattered was that he knew Emerald would have to come back to the farm, if only to get her things. Once she was here, he was sure he could convince her to stay and let him help her.

In the meantime, some physical labor would help him work off his worry and anger. Right on time, a pickup rumbled up the driveway. Andy Mercer was here for his truckload of alfalfa. Loading up the large bales would keep his body and mind occupied.

Still, he glanced down the road as the truck pulled up alongside the barn. He wouldn't feel settled until he knew Emerald was safe.

He needed this done quickly and the truck out of here before the group returned from town, but he had to act like this was just any other normal day. Taking a deep breath, he forced a smile on his face and greeted the other man. "Morning, Andy."

# Chapter Eight
ℰᴖ

Emerald followed Erin into Jenny's, the local diner. They'd finished up their grocery shopping quicker than she'd expected. Erin was nothing if not efficient. When she'd asked Emerald if she wanted to go for a coffee, there was no way she could resist. She liked the other woman, plus, if she were honest with herself, she was hoping to learn more about Erin's big brother. She knew she should be cautious, but for the first time in several months, she felt free and safe and wanted to celebrate that fact, even if was just with a cup of coffee.

Jenny's was like a thousand other diners scattered across the country. It was clean and homey and filled with locals eating breakfast and gossiping. Several people called out to Erin as they passed and she returned their greetings. Must be wonderful to know everyone in the community, Emerald mused.

It was a far cry from the hustle and bustle of New York. The city was alive with a vibrant energy all its own. There were museums, cultural events, shows and shopping galore. It was what had attracted her to New York in the first place—the never-ending energy and fast-paced life.

The town of Meadows was entirely different. No one here seemed to be in too much of a hurry, including the waitress. Everyone was kicked back, chattering and enjoying the morning. It was…nice.

Erin led the way to a booth seat and slid onto the vinyl-covered bench. Emerald sat down across from her and plucked the menu from behind the napkin dispenser. Before she'd even had time to crack the cover on it, the waitress ambled over, coffeepot in hand and began to fill the clean mug in front of

Erin. "Morning, Erin." With short brown hair, blue eyes and a round face, the woman was pretty in a girl-next-door sort of way.

"Morning. Emerald, I want you to meet my best friend and sister-in-law, Carly. She's married to Nathan, who you haven't met yet. Carly, this is Emerald, the new housekeeper I hired for Jackson."

Carly stuck out her free hand. "Pleased to meet you." Emerald shook the other woman's hand, noting the keen look in Carly's eyes.

"Likewise." Emerald was used to being scrutinized by people and it didn't bother her. Not too much. Besides, this was only friendly curiosity, which was to be expected considering she was now working for a member of the family.

"Coffee?" Emerald nodded and Carly filled her mug. "What will you ladies have this morning? If you don't want breakfast, there's fresh apple, lemon meringue and peach pie as well as oatmeal and chocolate chunk cookies."

Erin groaned. "I gotta start watching what I eat."

Carly's mouth dropped open. "Whatever for? You never have, so why start now?"

The other woman laughed. Emerald sat back and enjoyed the byplay between them. They reminded her of her and her sisters. A pang of envy flashed through her, followed swiftly by sorrow. She missed her sisters. Used to working with them every day, it was hard to not be able to see them or talk to them.

"I'm starting to put on some weight."

Carly scowled. "So what? You can handle a few extra pounds with your height."

Erin's eyes twinkled. "I'm going to be putting on a lot more pounds in the next six months."

The coffeepot hit the table with a thud. "Do you mean? You're…" Carly stared at Erin, who nodded. Carly squealed and the next thing Emerald knew, both women were standing up in the diner, jumping up and down, clutching at each other. Erin had mentioned yesterday that she was pregnant. Emerald hadn't realized that not many other people knew about it yet. But from Carly's reaction, this was obviously news to her.

"You ladies disturbing the peace?" Emerald glanced over at the deep male voice to find a uniformed deputy scowling at them. As she watched, he took off his mirrored sunglasses and hooked them in the front of his uniform shirt. Damn, he was big. His large hands were propped on his waist, emphasizing the leanness of it. His brown hair was cut short and his blue eyes were shrewd as he sized her up. He looked vaguely familiar although she knew she'd never met him.

Carly released Erin and jumped at the man, who caught her easily in his arms. Nathan. This had to be the brother she hadn't met yet. "Erin is pregnant." A huge grin split his face, making him look rather handsome and reminding her even more of Jackson. Emerald blinked.

"Is that so? Congratulations." He shifted his wife easily to one side, still hanging on to her as he hugged his sister with his free arm.

"You already knew," his sister accused as she hugged him back.

Nathan shrugged, totally unrepentant. "I just came from Jackson's. I promised to act surprised."

The women laughed and Nathan released his wife when another customer called out to her. "I'll be back." Carly grabbed her coffeepot and hurried off.

"You got time for a coffee, Nathan?" Erin scooted back into her seat.

"Sure." He sat down next to his sister, pinning Emerald to her seat with his laser stare.

"Hi, I'm Emerald." She held out her hand and found it engulfed by his. He didn't hold it for long, but still she was nervous. He knew something. She could feel it in her bones.

"Nathan Connors." He picked up his sister's coffee and took a sip, never taking his gaze off her. The tension mounted around them.

Erin stared from one to the other. "What's going on?"

Nathan's eyes bored into her. "Are you going to tell her or will I?"

Emerald closed her eyes and sighed. She really didn't want to do this in public. "This might not be the best place to do this."

He shook his head. "It's the best place. There's been a slight change of plans."

Her stomach clenched and the small amount of coffee she'd drunk began to stir in her belly. She swallowed hard, but before she could ask any questions, Erin's husband strode up to the table.

Abel nodded to her and then smiled at his wife before returning his attention to Nathan. "It's parked right out front. I'll be waiting outside." He leaned over and planted a quick kiss on his wife's lips before heading out again. He called out and waved to a few folks as he left.

"What was that all about?" Erin demanded. "What the heck is going on?"

Emerald licked her suddenly dry lips. "This has to do with me, I'm afraid." Squaring her shoulders, she faced the woman she was beginning to think of as a friend. "I lied to you about my last name and about why I'm really here."

Bewilderment flashed across Erin's face, quickly followed by anger and disappointment. "I see," she said slowly.

"No, you don't see," Nathan cut in. He leaned against the back of the seat and rested his hands on his belly. The pose was deceptively relaxed. Emerald could see his eyes were continually moving around the diner, assessing the patrons.

He was obviously leaving the telling of her story up to her. She didn't know whether to be grateful or pissed off. He'd dropped this little bomb and was now leaving it up to her to pick up the pieces. Sighing, she knew she had two choices. She could either just get up and go, knowing that she'd have to pack her things and leave the farm or she'd have to explain.

She closed her eyes on a flash of pain. She should have known that it was all working out too easily. And, truthfully, what right did she have to drag these people into her problems? They were nice folks. Good people and they didn't need the ugliness that had invaded her life invading theirs.

"This was a mistake. I'm sorry." She pushed away from the table and grabbed her purse. "I can't stay here." She could see surprise flash on Nathan's face, while Erin just looked concerned. "Thanks for everything you've done for me."

Nathan surged from his seat and stared down at her. "So you're just leaving your position as housekeeper with no notice at all?" His voice wasn't loud, but still it carried, filling the diner. Emerald could sense the other patrons watching them.

"Yes." She didn't know what else to say. Really, there was nothing else to say. She knew now that she had to leave. She was better off not involving innocent people in her problems. Her heart began to throb painfully at the thought of leaving Jackson, but she ignored it. She'd only met the man yesterday. She refused to believe that he could mean so much to her in such a short span of time.

"Well then, your car is waiting out front for you. Don't let us stop you if you want to leave." Nathan's voice was cold and, Emerald freely admitted, intimidating.

She whirled on her heel and stalked toward the door with her head held high. She would not cry. She wouldn't, she promised herself, blinking back tears. She heard people whispering behind her, but ignored it. This town would forget all about her and by tomorrow she'd be old news.

She managed to get out through the door and, sure enough, her car was there. She had no idea how that had happened as the keys were in her purse, but she didn't question it, not when she needed the transportation. A large hand fell onto her shoulder and she whirled around, gasping as she knocked it away.

Nathan stood behind her with Erin right next to him. "Are you okay, Emerald? I don't understand what's going on." Emerald couldn't bear the concern in Erin's eyes. She'd lied to this woman and still it seemed she cared.

"I'm fine."

"We'll follow you back to the farm." Nathan's authoritative voice cut through her misery. It dawned on her then that he was a local cop. She couldn't blame him for wanting a known liar off his brother's property. Was it illegal that she'd given them a false name? She hadn't signed any documents or anything.

Still, it stung to be treated like a criminal. "Afraid I'll steal the family silver on my way out the door?"

Erin gasped, but Emerald was past caring. Her mind was already scrambling. Where would she go? What would she do with little to no money? She'd have to risk going to an ATM and then hightail it to another state. She didn't have much choice with a maniac on her trail.

Sliding into her car, she dug in her purse for her keys and shoved them in the ignition.

She didn't even check her rearview mirror as she drove. She knew that Nathan was probably following her in his police cruiser. And wasn't that embarrassing. She was being run out of town by the local cops.

She laughed, the sound rough and loud in the confines of her small car. She bit her lip to keep from crying at the pain that filled her. It wasn't fair what was happening to her, but no one ever said that life was fair. She'd have to suck it up and do what needed doing.

She braked at a stop sign and just sat there, contemplating just turning left instead of right. She had her purse. There was no need for her to really return to the farm. She could buy what she needed and send for her things in a few days when she was settled. Her laptop was the only thing of value that she truly needed, but she could do without it for now. It wasn't as if she was doing much work these days.

Her palms were sweaty, so she wiped them on the folds of her skirt. Left or right. Her mind said left, but her hands went back on the wheel and turned right. She wanted to see Jackson one more time, to at least get the opportunity to say goodbye and thank him for his offer of help. She could understand why his brother wouldn't want her here. He was a cop, and she'd not only lied, she'd brought a heap of trouble with her too. People took care of their own. She understood that.

Swiping at her eyes with the heel of her hand, she sniffed back her tears. "Stop that. You're no worse off than you were two days ago." Except she felt worse off. Jackson had touched something deep inside her and now there would be no opportunity to explore that. Not that she was sure she even would have, but now she'd never find out.

Shaking her head, Emerald sighed. She was really losing it. She had a stalker after her, she was being run out of town by the local law and she was worried about a nonexistent relationship with a man she'd just met.

By the time the farmhouse came into view, she had herself back under control. Her early years in the limelight had taught her how to bury her feelings in front of others. Drawing on that training now, she took a deep breath and blanked all emotion from her face. With any luck, Jackson would be working out in the orchards and she wouldn't have to deal with him. God, she was being perverse. She wanted to see him and yet she didn't.

The choice was taken out of her hands as Jackson was waiting on the back steps when she pulled up. He was wiping some grease off his hands, a large red toolbox sitting next to his feet. Emerald drank in the sight of him as the police cruiser pulled in behind her, followed by Erin's truck.

Sighing, she wondered if she should even bother turning off her car. In the end, the need to conserve gas made her shut off the ignition. The silence was almost deafening. "You can do this," she muttered as she got out of the car and headed toward the door. She kept her eyes on the door, ignoring Jackson.

"Emerald?"

She almost stumbled as he spoke her name. He reached out his hand to steady her, but she jerked away. She could hear the underlying concern in his voice and suddenly she wanted to turn back the clock to last night, to experience the closeness they'd shared. This time she wouldn't let him stop without making love to her. No! She shook herself. It was better that it hadn't happened. She was sure that, if it had, those memories would haunt her forever.

Her hand was on the screen door and she tugged, but it wouldn't open. She could feel Jackson's large body behind hers. Looking up, she could see his hand planted firmly on the door, keeping it shut. She should never have come back here. She should have taken her opportunity when she'd had the chance and just left.

"Will someone tell me just what the heck is going on?" Erin stomped up the steps and stood beside Emerald.

She sensed Jackson's stillness behind her. "Just what the hell happened in town?" She could feel the vibration of his chest against her back, he was standing so close to her.

"I'm just doing what I should have done last night. I'm leaving." Her voice sounded rough to her own ears. She cleared her throat, knowing she had to get through this quickly. "I'll just pack my things and go."

"You're not going anywhere," he growled. His muscled forearm wrapped around her waist and he shifted her so she was standing to one side. Yanking the door open, he practically pulled her inside.

She could hear everyone else piling in behind them. She wanted to yell and scream and cry. Instead, she pushed his arm away from her and sent up a prayer of gratitude when he released her. Turning, she cocked an eyebrow at him, ignoring Nathan, Erin and Abel as they ranged around the room.

His brows were drawn together in anger as he stared at his brother. "What happened?"

Nathan leaned against the kitchen counter and crossed his ankles. "Slight change of plan. Emerald decided that she was leaving instead of talking, but we accomplished what we set out to do. Everyone who was at the diner knows she quit without notice, and better still, they saw me following her out of town."

"Good." Jackson's reply made her heart ache. She was so sure that he'd felt something for her beyond lust, that they had some connection. It was hard to realize that it was all on her side. "Don't worry." He laid his hand on the small of her back. "It's all for the best."

She swallowed back her bitter reply. "I'm sure it is. I'll just pack and be gone in five minutes."

He gripped her shoulders, practically forcing her to look at him. "Where do you think you're going?"

"Anywhere but here." She shot Nathan a glare before returning her gaze to Jackson. "Which I'm sure will make some people very happy."

"You're not going anywhere."

She shook her head. "I don't understand what's going on. You just said that you're glad that I quit and I'm leaving."

"No, I didn't."

"Ah, Jackson." Nathan's smooth tones interrupted them. They both turned and scowled at him. "She doesn't know about the plan."

"What plan?" As she spoke, Jackson swore, practically drowning out her words. She was totally confused and her head was beginning to pound.

"Sit down, sweetheart." He herded her to a chair and she sat. She felt sweaty and too lightheaded to object. He crouched down in front of her and took her hands in his. "I'm sorry about this. I'm not quite sure what happened in town, but we had to make everyone there think that you were leaving for good."

"I don't understand." She wanted to smooth the worry lines away from Jackson's face, but she kept her fingers clasped in her lap.

"I put you in danger." He tucked a stray curl over her ear, the tender action raising goose bumps on her arms. "Until Nathan pointed it out, I didn't even stop and think that your first name and your looks are very distinctive. Anyone who saw you in town while you were shopping would remember you. It didn't occur to me that you and my sister would go gallivanting all over town."

"It wasn't all over town." The need to defend Erin rose up inside her. "We only went the grocery store and the coffee shop." Even as she said it, she realized that he was right. This was a small town and she was a stranger. Erin had introduced her to a few people at the grocery store and she knew she would be a source of gossip for them. It was a natural thing for them to do.

Just because she was in a small town and her stalker didn't know where she was for the moment didn't mean that she was safe for good. Her stalker had already proved to be smart and resourceful.

Jackson nodded. "Exactly. At this moment, half the county probably knows you up and quit without notice." He gave her an almost apologetic smile. "The other half will know by suppertime."

She couldn't suppress a chuckle. "I guess you're right."

Nathan pushed away from the counter and strolled over to the table. "I'm sorry about how that went down. We figured you'd tell Erin what was going on and then I could let you know about our plan. You surprised me when you just got up to leave. I had to improvise."

"You were just going to leave?" She could see the hurt on Jackson's face, but she didn't back away from it.

"Yes." She cupped his face in her hands. "Look, I lied to you when I got here, and I brought a lot of problems into your life. You're good people and I wouldn't blame you for not wanting me here."

"We settled this last night." He was so close to her now, she could smell him. The scent of sweet grass, clean sweat and pure male filled her nostrils. God, she wanted to bury her face against his shoulder and just breathe. Her nipples tightened and her pussy clenched, remembering just how good he felt against her, naked flesh to naked flesh. His eyes flared and he leaned closer.

She pushed away her growing arousal and tried to focus on the situation at hand. "No, we didn't." Her voice sounded unusually low and husky to her ears. Knowing there was nothing to be done about it at the moment, she plowed forward. "Not really. You have a family that loves you and I can understand if they didn't want me anywhere near you, given my problems."

"Will someone tell me what's going on right now?" Erin's voice broke the connection between her and Jackson. It was just as well. She was becoming aroused in a roomful of people and that was totally embarrassing. Jackson covered her clenched hands with one of his and gave her a squeeze before he stood. As succinctly as possible, he outlined her situation to his sister.

When he was done, Erin reached across the table to her. Reluctantly, Emerald unwound her white fingers and took the other woman's hand. "You poor thing. I'm sorry for what you had to go through, but the men are right. The best thing for you to do is to stay here until you know something."

These people were amazing. She glanced over at Nathan, less certain of him than of the rest. He was impossible to read. He tipped his head to one side, staring at her. "If you'd turned left at that stop sign, I would have turned on the siren and hauled you back."

His gruff assertion made her smile, even as her eyes widened. He'd known she was thinking about running. This man would be a formidable enemy and an unshakeable friend. She was glad that he seemed to be on her side.

"Erin and I are going to take off. I want to get started researching those names that Jackson gave us this morning." Abel stood and peered thoughtfully at her. "I'll also want a list of every male that you've come in contact with in the last six months. Everyone from the kid at the local deli to your dry cleaners. Anyone is a possible suspect."

Emerald nodded. "My investigator has a complete list. I'll get it from him rather than try to recreate it from scratch."

"I'm not sure you should talk to him right now. He hasn't been cleared as a possible suspect."

"That's crazy," she protested, vigorously rubbing her hands up and down her arms. "Dane isn't a stalker."

"You sure enough to risk your life?" Abel's stark reminder sent a chill down her spine. "He was interested enough in you to ask for a date."

"Yes, but that was months ago." God, would this nightmare never end?

Nathan, who been silently listening to her and Abel, added his two cents' worth. "Maybe you should call him."

"Are you out of your mind?" Jackson took a threatening step toward his brother.

"No, I'm not." He held up his hands to placate Jackson. "Just listen for a second. I called it in and had one of my people do a quick search. So far this Hatcher guy checks out. Let Abel talk to him. He's known for his investigative work and it's less likely to piss Hatcher off than getting a call from the local police." Nathan turned his attention to Emerald. "If he's not the stalker, the work he's done on the case would be a big help. If he is the stalker…" Jackson swore, but Nathan ignored him and continued. "If he is the stalker," Nathan repeated, "then he'll probably show up here fairly quickly and we'll be waiting for him. Any stranger will stand out like a sore thumb, unlike in New York City where it's easy to blend in."

Emerald nibbled on her bottom lip. Her stomach was churning. There was no use in lying to herself. She was scared. But more than that, she was sick of running. She wanted her life back. "Okay."

"I've already got his number from the list you gave Jackson." Abel hauled out his cell phone and handed it to her. "If you could just give him a quick call and let him know it's okay to talk to me, I'll handle things from here."

Emerald took the phone and dialed. Her head was spinning with how fast everything was moving. Less than a half an hour ago, she thought she was totally on her own. Now she was surrounded by people who wanted to help her. And she'd only just met them. Overwhelmed by their generosity, she barely kept it together as she spoke to Dane. Well, he yelled and she listened.

"What the hell were you thinking?" She could hear the barely suppressed anger in his voice as he continued, "Do you have any idea what I went through when you didn't answer your phone? I contacted your sisters and they told me they didn't have any idea where you were."

The man obviously wasn't pleased that she'd taken off without telling him. Her stomach lurched. Did that mean he was the stalker or was it just honest concern for her? Emerald no longer knew. When Dane finally wound down, she told him why she'd called. Once she'd made the introduction, Abel took the phone and strode outside to talk to the other man.

Erin stood and came around the table. Leaning down, she hugged Emerald. "Try not to worry too much. Everything will work itself out."

Emerald sensed her hesitation. "It's okay. You can ask me anything you want to."

"I don't mean to pry, but I'd love to see more of your work if you wouldn't mind. The business you run with your sisters sounds absolutely fascinating."

The normalcy of the question almost shattered Emerald's composure. She could see the genuine interest in Erin's face. "I'd love that." She made up her mind then that the next time she talked to her sister, she'd ask her to send out a box of samples. It occurred to her that it might be easier to get Dane to pass the message along. After talking to Abel, her location was no longer a secret from him. In his profession, it wouldn't take him long to trace the call. "If you'll excuse me, I want to talk to Dane before Abel hangs up." Pushing out of her chair, she went outside with the rest of them following her. So much for privacy.

She motioned to Abel just as he was about to hang up and he handed her the phone. Walking several feet away, she whispered her request to Dane who promised to pass it along to Topaz for her. Satisfied, she hung up the phone, walked back and handed it to Abel.

"I'll call you as soon as I know something."

"I appreciate all your help. I don't know if it will do much good, though, if it really is just a crazy fan of my parents. I don't believe the stalker is Dane and it's definitely not Derek. I've known him since we were kids. And it's not Fred." Emerald shook her head. "Fred is kind to everyone. He always brings us flowers on our birthday..." Her voice trailed off.

Abel shrugged. "We'll eliminate as many suspects as possible and go from there."

"Flowers are something that your stalker likes to send you too," Jackson pointed out to her before turning to Abel. "Check it out."

"Her investigator is already on it, but I'll double-check," Abel assured him.

Erin gave her a quick hug. "I'll see you soon." Then Abel and Erin walked back to their truck.

"The groceries," she called. She had completely forgotten about them. They'd been sitting out in the hot sun for quite some time. She hurried down the steps, thankful that Erin had had the foresight to bring along a cooler to pack the perishables in.

It didn't take the men long to cart all the groceries into the kitchen and then Abel and Erin headed home. Nathan lingered behind as they stood on the porch and watched the truck fade into the distance. "I'm sorry again for what happened at the diner, but it couldn't be helped."

Emerald crossed her arms across her chest, but nodded. "I understand." And she did. Nathan was the sort of man who would do whatever needed doing, even if he didn't particularly like it. He and his brother were much alike. They were both dependable men. Good men.

He turned to Jackson. "Park her car in the barn."

"Will do."

Nathan nodded and headed for his vehicle. "I'm sure Carly will want to come out in the next day or so after I explain the situation to her."

Emerald wasn't quite sure what to say or do, so she inclined her head. "That's fine."

Then Nathan was gone and she and Jackson were alone on the back porch. The heat was like a living thing between them, making the air heavy and humid. Now that the others were gone, Emerald felt unsure and awkward with him. The sweet connection of last night was nowhere to be found.

"Emerald?" She turned away from the question she heard in his voice. Knew that he felt the same tension that she did. Arousal was there, low in her belly, but she ignored it. Now was not the time or the place. Her emotions were too all over the place.

She started to walk away, but came to a quick halt. Her throat ached as she swallowed up the emotions that suddenly swelled. Her heart beat heavily as she took a step forward and then another. Hanging from heavy hooks at one end of the porch was a white swing. Reaching out, she touched the thick chains that held it up and remembered that when she'd driven up, Jackson had just finished working on something.

She whirled around. "You put up the porch swing?"

He came toward her slowly. She noticed the way his jeans clung to his thick thighs, the way his T-shirt strained at the shoulder seams, and the heavy stubble on his chin. He hadn't shaved this morning and it made him look dark and dangerous as he stopped in front of her. "I did."

"Why?"

He cupped her chin in his hand and leaned closer. "Because I thought you might like it." His lips grazed hers and she parted them without thought. His eyes closed and she stared at his thick, dark eyelashes. They looked so soft against the ruggedness of his face that she wanted to touch them.

He pulled back and stared down at her, tracing his thumb over first her top and then her bottom lip. She shivered, her nipples pebbling against her bra. Jackson heaved a sigh and leaned his forehead against hers. They stood like that for several minutes, neither of them wanting to break the mood.

Finally Jackson stepped back. "I'll move your car."

"All right." She missed his presence next to her already.

"I'll be back in time for supper."

She nodded.

"You'll be here when I get back?"

"I will."

He nodded and then strode across the porch and down the stairs. He didn't look back as he climbed in her chair and drove it toward a smaller barn just beyond the big one. Emerald slowly eased herself down onto the porch swing. Pushing off with one foot, she let it swing as she pressed her fingers against her still-tingling lips.

# Chapter Nine

**જી**

Emerald was pulling a roast chicken out of the oven when the back door opened. She didn't even bother to turn around. It was just past five o'clock in the evening and Jackson's boots had made their familiar stomping sound as he'd climbed the few steps to the back door. She'd only been here a week, but already she found herself listening for the sound of his footsteps in the evening.

The screen door opened and he stepped inside. He brought with him the smell of summer and sweaty male. Emerald busied herself with laying the roaster on the counter then checking the pots on the stove. Anything to keep herself from going over to him and burying her face against his shirt.

"That smells great." His voice was so close she knew he was standing right behind her. He didn't touch her, yet she could feel the heat from his large body practically surrounding her. "I'll be down as soon as I shower."

"That's fine." She was proud of the way that her voice didn't wobble. She sounded steady and matter-of-fact. She raised the lid on the pot of carrots and gave them a stir with her fork. She could sense him hovering behind her, undecided, but a second later the air stirred and he was gone. His footsteps echoed as he took the stairs quickly.

She all but slumped against the kitchen counter and took a deep breath. Ever since her first night here, she'd made it a point of keeping her distance from Jackson. And boy, it hadn't been easy. That first night had been too intense and her common sense had forced her to take a step back and examine the situation. She'd been ready to climb into bed with a man she'd barely known. That just wasn't like her at all.

With everything else that had happened, the last thing she'd wanted to do was get into a relationship, so she'd backed off. She'd sensed Jackson's impatience and confusion, but he'd accepted the fact that she wasn't ready or willing to pursue the attraction between them. But that resolve was weakening as each day went by.

The more she got to know Jackson, the more she liked him. He was exactly what he seemed to be—loyal, honorable, hardworking, earthy and sexy as all get-out. He had a quick wit and a dry sense of humor that appealed to her. She'd never seen him lose his cool or his temper, but she hadn't heard him laugh either, although when he turned his smile on her, she felt lightheaded. The man was good-looking in a rugged sort of way, but when he smiled, he was something special.

Rather than abating, the attraction she felt toward him was growing as each day went by. He hadn't made any overt moves toward her, but he was always touching her. Small touches. The graze of his finger over her cheek, the firm squeeze of his hand over her shoulder, the brush of his muscular body against hers.

She sighed as she lifted the chicken onto a platter and began to carve it. There was really no reason why she couldn't or shouldn't let nature take its course. Sex with Jackson would be spectacular. Of that, she had no doubt. If they came together physically, it would be explosive. No, that wasn't why she was holding back. It was the emotional attachment that worried her.

Emerald had never slept with a man she hadn't been in love with. It just wasn't in her nature to take these things lightly. The fact that she was seriously considering sleeping with Jackson told her that she was already in over her head when it came to him. She worried her bottom lip with her teeth as she spooned up carrots, mashed potatoes and corn onto their plates. She was already half in love with the man.

Wrapping her arms around her waist, she hugged herself tight. As if her life wasn't confused enough at the moment, she had to go and add something like this on top of it. Shaking her head, she picked up the plates and placed them on the table. The shower had gone off and Jackson would be here any moment.

By the time she'd placed the platter of chicken on the table, she could hear him on the stairs. Taking one last look to make sure that everything was in place, she slipped into her chair just as he strode into the kitchen.

"Everything smells great." His hair was still damp and brushed the back of his denim shirt. The sleeves of the shirt were rolled back to reveal darkly tanned forearms sprinkled with dark hair. His fingers were thick and long, his palm broad. They were strong, capable hands and she remembered all too well what they felt like against her skin.

Sucking in a deep breath, she picked up her fork. "Thanks."

They ate in silence, the only sounds the scrape of their utensils against the plates, the clink of their drinking glasses as they sipped iced tea and their deep breathing. Finally, Emerald couldn't take it any longer. "Tell me about the farm." In the week she'd been here, she'd barely ventured beyond the yard.

Jackson finished chewing and swallowed. He laid his fork down and sat back. She could tell she'd surprised him with her willingness to talk. He'd tried the first few days she was here, but she'd shut him down. Now she was feeling badly about that. He'd only been trying to be friendly and put her at ease, but she'd been feeling too raw and had just wanted to be left alone.

"What do you want to know?"

She shrugged. "Everything."

One corner of his mouth kicked up in a grin. His jaw was covered with evening stubble and a lock of hair tumbled over his forehead. The collar of his shirt was open, exposing his strong throat and neck. A tuft of hair peeked out from between the parted fabric. It gave him a roguish look, like a sexy pirate.

His blue eyes stared intently at her, making her squirm in her chair.

He leaned back and linked his hands over his flat belly. She swallowed and laid her fork down on her plate. She couldn't eat with him watching her so intently.

"This farm has been in my family for several generations. My grandfather owned it first and then my father."

"And now it's yours." She marveled at having such a family legacy.

"Not quite mine." He looked thoughtful. She could tell he was picking his words carefully. "It belongs to the three of us — me, Nathan and Erin. Our father never liked the farm, never truly wanted it or us. Our mother died when Erin was just a kid and he just went through his days until I was eighteen. I knew he was going to sell the farm and I offered to buy it from him. At first he laughed."

Emerald couldn't look away from Jackson. She could sense his underlying pain even though his words were matter-of-fact. She thought about her own parents — so loving and giving — and couldn't even imagine what it must have been like for Jackson and his siblings. She and her sisters had known nothing but love and acceptance and encouragement. They'd been very lucky.

"Then what happened?" she prompted after he went silent.

"He agreed to give it a go and moved to Florida. The three of us worked like dogs and finished paying off the farm a few years back."

Jackson was the oldest, so she knew he'd born the brunt of the workload on his shoulders. She could also tell from the way he was shifting in his seat that he didn't want to talk about this subject any longer. "So, tell me about the farm itself. What kind of apples do you grow?"

He tilted his head to one side, watching her, gauging her reaction. "We grow about fifteen varieties, including your more popular Macintosh, Ida Red, Golden Delicious, Red Delicious and Courtland." Sensing her genuine interest, he kept going. "We're all organic. That's the first thing I changed after I took over the farm sixteen years ago. Took a while and a lot of hard work, but we're now certified organic."

That was smart of him, but then, she'd never doubted Jackson's intelligence. "Erin mentioned something about alfalfa and blueberries."

He nodded. "We own the orchards and a few more acres of land, but we also lease Abel's land from him. Have for years. Erin cultivated blueberry fields on her own and has a U-pick operation that's been doing real well the past few years. She convinced me to take a few acres of the orchards close to her crop and designate them as U-pick as well. That way folks can come and pick apples and berries. She takes care of that end of the operation. The rest of the orchards are harvested and bagged or pressed to make cider. We sell a lot of them at the small stand that Erin set up to sell berries and apples to those who don't want to be bothered with picking them themselves. The rest are sold to local stores. I also grow fields of alfalfa and hay and sell it to local farmers as feed and bedding for the animals."

Emerald was fascinated. "It really is a family operation."

"Sure is. We all work hard, especially from late August to late October. Erin convinced me to put in a pumpkin patch a few years back, so now we have a U-pick pumpkin patch that's busy in October."

"How do you handle it all yourselves?" The sheer amount of physical work was daunting.

"We do the bulk of the work ourselves, but we hire local kids, mostly students looking for extra money, in the late summer and fall. For a few weeks, it gets real busy around here."

So far, she hadn't seen anyone but Jackson and his family. She couldn't imagine that much activity around the place. "Wow."

Jackson chuckled. "Yeah. It can get pretty crazy around here. But don't worry, most of the activity takes place away from here. We put in another road a few years back and that's where we built the fruit stand. That way, we get a lot of drive-by traffic, especially on the weekends. Although, by the end of September, the barns will be filled while we're waiting for buyers to come and pick them up."

Now she knew where Jackson got all those hard muscles. His work was incredibly physical. "What are you doing now while you're waiting for the harvest?"

"Watching for pests and disease, mowing the orchards, checking on the other crops." He shrugged. "There are always a million things to do."

"You love it, don't you?"

A slow smile slid across his face. For the first time since she'd met him, Jackson appeared relaxed and happy. "Yeah, I do. There's no other life for me."

She nodded. She'd already known that, sensed it, but now he'd confirmed it. If she got involved with Jackson it would be a short-term affair. His life was here and hers was back in New York with her sisters. But it would be an affair to remember for a lifetime.

"What about you?"

She shook off her thoughts. "What about me?"

He chuckled and the sound made her stomach clench. "Tell me about your work. About Sisters' Jewels."

She picked up her glass and took a sip of iced tea, wondering where to begin. Laying her glass on the table, she made a decision. "Maybe I can show you instead." She pushed away from the table and disappeared into her room for a moment. When she returned, she had a box in her hands. "This came day before yesterday. I didn't go outside," she hurried to reassure him when he frowned. "The mailman left it on the back step and I got it after he left."

"Good," he nodded. "We can't take any chances."

Her heart stuttered when he said *we*. "Well, in any case, my sister sent along a few things." She opened the box and pulled out some of the items inside. There were journals covered in ornate designs, including their signature jewel ones. Each journal cover was designed around the birthstone of that month. The color of the ink and the design itself were all focused on the birthstone and the corresponding flower. There was even a semiprecious birthstone set into each journal cover. These were one of their most popular sellers.

Emerald pulled out greeting cards with figures of ancient goddesses and some with Middle Eastern designs. There was stationery in various colors, including a perfume collection they'd done. The scented paper filled the air with the smells of rose, vanilla, jasmine and lavender.

There were also a few pieces of jewelry that Sapphire had designed. Emerald planned on giving one of the necklaces to Erin.

Jackson was just staring at the mound of merchandise she'd piled on the table. "Well, what do you think?" She hadn't been this nervous since the first day they'd opened the doors on Sisters' Jewels. For some reason, Jackson's opinion was very important to her.

He pushed his chair back and stood. Coming around the end of the table, he reached out and touched one journal, then another. His long fingers gently traced the designs on all the items. Emerald almost groaned. She wanted his fingers on her, touching her skin. Her nipples tightened almost painfully as she watched him flick one of the stones set into the cover of a journal. Between her thighs, her sex clenched and her panties dampened.

"I think," he began huskily, "that you're an incredibly talented lady." He picked up one of the journals and turned it over. His eyes widened at the discreet price tag on the back. "People must really like this stuff."

The butterflies in her stomach settled a bit and she laughed. Only a man would call these amazing items stuff. "We do okay."

He laid the journal back on the table and rubbed his hand over the back of his neck. He seemed tenser than he had been. She could almost feel him pulling away from her even though he was standing right next to her.

"I had no idea you were so talented." He cupped the side of her face in his hand and she swayed forward, wanting to be closer to him.

"Thank you," she whispered as his mouth moved closer to hers. She went up on her toes, unable to wait. She moaned when his lips touched hers. It had been too long and she'd missed this, wanted this with all her being.

Jackson forgot all about the worry gnawing at the pit of his gut as his mouth brushed against Emerald's. He'd been dreaming of kissing her again, ever since that first explosive night. Truthfully, he'd been doing more than just thinking about kissing her. His imagination had run the whole gamut from slow to fast, from gentle to rough and everywhere in between.

He wanted to peel off her clothes piece by piece and savor every inch of her sweet flesh. He wanted to tear her clothes from her body and fuck her until they were both screaming with release. She had him so wrapped up in knots he didn't know what he wanted. The one thing he did know was that he wanted Emerald and he'd take her any way he could get her.

His tongue stroked across her upper lip and then he nibbled on her plump bottom one. She whimpered and he wrapped his free arm around her back, urging her closer. His cock was thick and full as he pressed it against the soft swell of her belly. He groaned as she pressed against him. He'd hardly slept this past week, his nights spent lying awake, thinking about having Emerald beside him, on top of him and under him. His testicles ached they were so full and tight.

She'd pulled back and he'd respected her wishes, even though it had almost killed him. But now she was here and she wasn't trying to get away from him. If anything, she was trying to get closer. Her hands fisted in his hair, tugging his mouth closer. He slid his tongue past her lips and barely stifled a moan when she sucked on it.

He forgot about the remains of their supper on the table, forgot about the fact that she wasn't here to stay. His daydreams about her remaining with him were shattered the moment he'd seen her work and what people were willing to pay for it. She was too talented to bury herself in the middle of nowhere on a small family farm. But still, he could have her. If only for the time she was here.

His heart beat heavily and he ignored all the warnings in his brain. This woman was already under his skin. It would hurt when she left, regardless, so he might as well take whatever he could get, whatever she would give.

He pulled back and stared down at her. Her face was flushed, her lips red and pouty from his kisses. Her hair was piled on her head, but several long, black tendrils had come free of the knot. He hooked his finger in one of the curls, watching in fascination as it wrapped around him. Her dark brown eyes were wide and uncertain, but beyond that he saw the need, the same deep need that filled him. She wanted him. His body clenched and he lowered his head again.

The phone rang shrilly, shattering the moment. Emerald jumped back so quickly that she would have fallen if he hadn't caught her. She stumbled against him and then smacked him in the nose with her head when she jerked away.

Swearing, Jackson reached out his hand and snagged the phone. "Connors," he barked into the receiver. He turned to Emerald and barely swallowed another curse. She had her arms wrapped so tight around herself that her knuckles were white. She was once again closing herself off to him. "It's your investigator."

She stumbled forward and took the phone. "Dane?" She stood there listening and nodding for a minute and then hung up the phone.

"Well?" Jackson was in no mood to be pleasant. His dick was as hard as a spike, his balls throbbed and there was no relief in sight. And on top of that, he wanted to know what Hatcher had to say. No matter that Nathan had investigated Dane Hatcher thoroughly, Jackson didn't trust the man. In this profession, he knew what to do to hide his tracks. The fact he didn't trust the man had nothing to do with the fact that Hatcher had asked Emerald out.

She shook her head. "There's no news. He's still working, but so far, everyone on the list is checking out okay."

Jackson nodded. It was no more than he'd expected. Unless the stalker was Hatcher himself or he was stupid, and he hadn't been so far, he wouldn't have left any obvious clues. They might never find him unless he made some mistake or came after Emerald, either here or when she went home. She couldn't stay away from her life indefinitely and Jackson was afraid that the stalker was counting on that, waiting patiently for her to return home.

That got him to thinking. "Do you know anything about self-defense?"

She appeared startled by his abrupt change of subject. "Not really." She started to pile the supper dishes. "I mean, I know as much as most women. Don't walk in the shadows or on sparsely populated streets, keep your keys between your fingers as a weapon, don't wear your purse slung over your shoulder if you can avoid it." She laid the dishes on the counter and faced him. "Why?"

"Because this might not be over before you have to return home." She paled, all the color leaching from her face. Jackson didn't want to scare her, didn't want to be the one to frighten her, but he was also realistic. "This stalker might just wait until you return."

As he watched, she squared her shoulders and nodded. "I've considered that."

"You need to learn some basic self-defense. It can't hurt and might help." He paused and then plowed ahead. He'd started this so he might as well finish it. "I can show you some moves."

"Really?" He could tell from the look on her face that she was intrigued. He was just glad to see some of the color returning to her cheeks.

"Yeah. Nathan's had a lot of training over the years and I've sparred with him out in the old barn. He can probably give you a few more pointers than me, but I could get you started." His mind was sorting through what he knew, what would be of the best use to Emerald.

"You'd do that for me?"

He crossed his arms over his chest and frowned. "Of course."

"Of course," she repeated, shaking her head.

The room was closing in around Jackson. He'd almost swear he could smell her arousal even though that should be impossible. His body ached, his mind was racing and his heart was pounding. He had to get away before he did something they both might regret. "I'll be out in the barn if you decide you want some pointers."

Shoving the door open, he stepped out into the night. The air was still thick and the sun had a few hours before it sank below the horizon. Ignoring the pair of robins that flew past him, Jackson stalked to the old barn, thankful for the punching bag that hung from the rafters in one far corner. He'd set up the workout area years ago when he and Nathan were still in their teens. He'd never needed it as badly as he did tonight. If he didn't work off some of his tension, he'd explode.

# Chapter Ten

ഩ

Emerald watched Jackson retreating through the screen door. She leaned against the doorframe, admiring the way his long legs ate up the distance between the house and the barn. Realizing that she was just standing there ogling his fine butt, she made herself turn away and finish clearing the dishes from the table.

Both Jackson and her investigator were right about one thing—the stalker might just decide to outwait her. Dane was working hard, but there were no obvious clues pointing to any one person. Several of the men were being more rigorously investigated, including her ex-boyfriend and Fred, the delivery guy, but that was mainly due to their proximity to her and their skills at computers. In the meantime, Abel and Nathan were still investigating Dane and the rest of the men on the list.

As she thought, she washed and dried the dishes by rote, her mind wandering. It really wouldn't hurt for her to learn some basic self-defense moves. She probably would have taken a class or something if she'd stayed in New York. It had absolutely nothing to do with wanting to spend more time with Jackson. Really, it didn't.

Grimacing, she hung the dishtowel up to dry. Who was she trying to kid? She wanted to be with Jackson. She was more drawn to him than any other man she'd ever met and it wasn't just because of his exceptional good looks, although they certainly didn't hurt. She loved the way he was with his family. If he didn't see them, he at least talked to them on the phone every day. He was responsible and hardworking and there was no pretension about him. What you saw was what you got. Her parents and sisters would like him.

"Don't go there," she muttered to herself as she wiped her hands over the legs of her jeans. She was nervous, which was ridiculous. She'd just go out to the barn and get a few pointers from Jackson about self-defense and that would be that. If they happened to share a kiss or two, all the better.

"You're losing it, Emerald." Pushing the door open, she hurried down the steps and across the yard before she talked herself out of this. She had to make a decision, and soon. She couldn't keep pulling him toward her and then pushing him away. That smacked of being a tease and that wasn't something she was particularly proud of. Her emotions were just so all over the place.

"Maybe physical release is what you need," she told herself as she neared the barn. She snorted as her mind immediately jumped to picturing her and Jackson locked in a tight embrace that had little to do with learning defense techniques.

Grunting sounds followed by the rhythmic thud of fists assailed her as she crept to the opening of the barn. She hadn't been in here yet, but she admitted to being curious. It was a large building, older than the newer ones that Jackson had told her were used to store the apples during the harvest. This older one was used mostly as temporary storage for alfalfa and hay.

Making her way inside, she inhaled deeply. The scent of fresh-cut hay assailed her nose. It tickled her senses and made her smile, but that smile quickly faded as she strolled to the far end of the structure. The area was more like a large stall, but it had obviously been set up as a gym of sorts. There were free weights as well as a bench with a bar and more weights. But that wasn't what Jackson was doing. No, Jackson had his shirt stripped off and was pounding on a punching bag that hung from a heavy beam.

He hadn't noticed her yet, so she was free to watch and admire him as he feinted to one side, his fist shooting out to strike the bag. She swallowed hard as she leaned against the wall. She'd seen men that were more handsome, but never one who was so elemental. Testosterone practically oozed from his pores as he continued to work the heavy bag.

A bead of sweat trickled down her spine and her breathing deepened. The muscles in his back rippled and shifted with every move he made, reminding her once again of just what a large and powerful man he was. The waistband of his jeans dipped just below his navel, exposing his bellybutton. His lightly furred chest was glistening with perspiration and she wanted to run her hands over the hard ridges of muscles in his abdomen.

She must have made some kind of noise because he dropped his hands suddenly and spun around. His nostrils flared and his eyes narrowed, but he made no move to come toward her. Jackson swiped his forearm over his forehead and then sucked in a deep gulp of air. Rolling his shoulders, he stepped away from the bag.

"You come for a lesson?" He grabbed a towel that had been laid over the top rung of the stall and rubbed it over his face.

Emerald took that moment to compose herself. Or at least try to. Her heart was racing, her body all but shaking with a growing need that she could no longer deny. "Yes." She swallowed the lump in her throat. "I came for a lesson."

His head snapped up at the double entendre, but he was all business as he strode to the center of the small room. "Come here."

The roughness in his voice made her nipples pucker and she almost groaned aloud. Now was not the time for this. But her body ignored her and she could feel her panties getting damp as she walked toward him. "What do you want me to do?" He seemed to freeze at her husky whisper, but then he shook himself.

"Stand in front of me with your back to my chest." She did as he asked. His large frame dwarfed hers, but she didn't feel afraid. No, what she was feeling was just as basic but totally different. Rather than wanting to get away, she wanted to lean against him. She wanted him to wrap his arms around her and hold her close. She wondered if she'd spoken her thoughts aloud when his muscled forearms came around her waist and across her collarbone.

"Now," he instructed, tightening his grip on her. "If a man grabbed you like this, what would you do?"

Emerald tugged at his arm with her hand, but it was like a steel bar across her chest. There was no way she could move it. She lifted her heel and stomped down on his foot, but ended up only hurting her own. Her sneakers didn't make a dent in his work boots. Frustration set in and she began to struggle in earnest.

"That's no good." His voice was brisk. "I'm much larger than you and stronger. We have to assume that your attacker will be too. You can't beat him or me in a battle of strength. You have to go for the weak points." He kept up a steady commentary as he continued to hold her almost effortlessly, her puny attempts to escape him having absolutely no effect.

"What weak points?" Frustration was giving way to anger. Her life had been turned upside down by some unknown man. She had done nothing, yet he was systematically trying to destroy her life and her.

"If you can get a hand free, go straight for the eyes. Don't hesitate or think about it, just do it. The throat is vulnerable as well."

She gritted her teeth. "That doesn't help me at the moment." If she were facing him, she would have gladly taken one of his suggestions. "Let me go?"

"No. You have to get free. Use your head, Emerald. Your hands are locked down around your waist. What can you reach on a man that's vulnerable?"

Without thinking, she fisted her hand and drove it backward. Jackson jerked away, and her hand grazed his thigh, barely missing his groin area. She spun around, panting hard with anger only to find the idiot grinning at her.

"That's my girl." Pride filled his face as he circled her. All her anger dissipated under the warmth of his smile and she suddenly felt inordinately pleased with herself.

"You could have head-butted me as well." He danced from side to side like a boxer as he reached out and tagged her on the shoulder. "So, you want to try it again? I'll grab you from the front this time and you try to get away."

"I don't want to hurt you."

He laughed in her face and that roused her competitive spirit. How she wished she'd taken martial arts classes years ago so she could flip him onto his arrogant male butt. All those art lessons had helped her career, but they wouldn't do a thing for her in this situation.

"Think you're tough, do you?" he taunted as he continued to reach past her raised hands and tap her on the shoulder.

She tightened her fists and narrowed her eyes. Oh, he was going to pay for that. She swung out with one hand and as she did so her foot hooked in the floorboard and she stumbled. Jackson dropped all pretense of sparring with her and reached out to catch her. With him off guard, she put her head down and rammed him with all her strength. He yelled and started to tumble. She had a momentary flash of pleasure at tricking him but it was short-lived. As he fell, he didn't release his hold on her and she began to fall.

Shrieking, she stuck out her arms to catch herself, but there was no need. Jackson wrapped his arms around her and took the brunt of the fall himself. He grunted as he struck the wood floor and then rolled, tucking her beneath him. When she opened her eyes, she was flat on her back on the dusty floor with Jackson looming over her. He propped himself up on his elbows, pressing his pelvis against hers. She could feel his erection against her and the anger she'd felt shifted into a different sort of heat.

"You did that on purpose," he accused.

"You're darn right I did." She tried to look tough, but it was hard. She knew that she was probably covered in dust. Besides that, her hair had come down from its knot and was tangled around her face, her top was untucked from her jeans and she couldn't suppress the grin that threatened.

Jackson looked at her, threw back his head and roared with laughter. It was so infectious that she started to giggle. She pinched his sides in an effort to get him to move off her. The man weighed a ton and breathing was getting difficult.

He didn't let her go, but he rolled with her again so that he was on the bottom now and she was sprawled across him. He pressed his hand against her ass, pushing her mound against the hard ridge in the front of his jeans.

They both moaned. Emerald arched inward, wanting to feel more of him against her. She nuzzled his bare chest, flicking out her tongue to taste his warm flesh. The hand on her butt tightened and became more of a caress as he began to knead it through her jeans.

"I want you." The starkness of his words stopped her cold. She shivered even though she was so hot she thought she might burst into flames any moment. There was no denying that she wanted him too.

She raised her head and lost herself in his pale blue eyes. Never in her life had a man looked at her with such lust and longing. There was only one answer she could give.

"Yes."


Jackson shook his head to make sure he wasn't hallucinating. He'd dreamed of having Emerald draped across him, her body flush against his. But never in his wildest fantasies had he imagined them rolling around on the floor of the barn. He was an adaptable man though, and he'd make do.

No way was he risking taking her back to the house and giving her time to change her mind.

Still, the words tumbled from his mouth. "Are you sure?" He could have kicked himself, but he had to be sure. The last thing he wanted was for her to have regrets in the morning.

"I'm sure." Dust streaked her flawless skin, her hair was tumbling wildly around her shoulders, her mascara was slightly smudged and there was a light sheen of sweat covering her face and arms. He'd never seen a more beautiful sight in his entire life.

He wanted to eat her up and make her scream her release before he took her. He licked his lips in anticipation. She parted her lips as he cupped the back of her head and brought her mouth down to his. Snaking his tongue out, he tasted her plump lips before slipping inside to stroke her teeth and beyond. He could feel the heat from her mound through both layers of their clothing. Damn, she was hot.

Although his body was screaming for release, he took his time, leisurely exploring her mouth. He loved the taste of her—sweet with a hint of spice. There was a wild side to this woman that she kept mostly under wraps, but it came out in her brightly colored clothing and funky jewelry. Tonight she was wearing jeans, but her top was a bright splash of purple and around her neck was a collar of brightly colored stones. He had no idea what half of them were, but they glittered against the silver of the necklace.

Her wild side also showed up in her work. The beauty of her work amazed Jackson and he'd only seen a small sample of it. His arms tightened around her. He knew he couldn't keep her with him forever, but she was here now and that's all that mattered.

He broke the kiss and sat up, shifting her in his arms as he did so that she was left sitting on the floor as he rolled to his feet. Reaching down, he pulled her up and walked her backward until her back hit the heavy bag suspended from the ceiling.

Her eyes were like thick, dark chocolate, filled with a slumberous longing. Her face was flushed, her lips moist. His hands shook as he reached out and tugged the end of her shirt over her head. She raised her arms and allowed him to slip the garment from her body. He let it drop, instantly forgotten.

She was wearing a purple bra, much the color of lilacs. He traced a finger over the edge of the lacy cup. It was so feminine that he was almost afraid to touch it with his work-roughened hand. Emerald sucked in a breath as his finger dipped into her cleavage. His thumb grazed her nipple, which was already puckered into a tight bud.

"You're so responsive." He cupped her lace-covered breasts with his palms and squeezed them gently. She leaned forward, pressing herself tighter into his hands. He had to see her, had to touch her soft skin. Memories of the night on the porch had haunted his dreams and he had to see if it was as good as he remembered.

It was better.

He opened the front clasp and pushed back the cups. With the harsh light from the bare bulb shining on her, he could see every sweet inch of flesh he'd revealed. Her breasts were large and firm and tipped with rosy nipples that just begged to be tasted.

Groaning, he leaned down and captured one turgid peak between his lips and tugged. She gasped and dug her fingers into his scalp. He used his teeth to gently scrape her sensitive flesh before laving it with his tongue.

Her hands slid over his neck and shoulders, her fingers curling into his biceps for support as he tasted first one breast and then the other. When he finally pulled back, both her nipples were glistening. He blew on them and they tightened even further. Her chest was rising and falling with each breath, making her breasts sway enticingly.

He reached for the snap of her jeans, his eyes never leaving her face. She made no move to stop him. Instead, she swayed forward. That was all Jackson needed. He went down on one knee in front of her and quickly removed her right sneaker and sock and then did the same with the other one. Even her bare feet were sexy. They were slender and delicately arched, and each toenail was painted a pale shade of purple. He wanted to nibble on them. But that was for another time. Right now, he had to see her naked.

The more civilized part of him knew he should take her inside to a soft bed. But the male animal inside him was screaming at him to take her now, to claim her and put his mark on her. His hands went unerringly back to the opening of her jeans. He yanked the zipper down and slipped his hands inside. Leaning forward, he pressed open-mouthed kisses against her belly, which was smooth and gently rounded.

Her sex was covered with a ridiculously small scrap of fabric and lace that matched her bra. He pushed her jeans down around her ankles but left the panties in place. "I'll bet your panties are wet, aren't they?" He traced the creases of her thighs as he watched her.

She leaned back against the heavy bag, her breasts swaying, her nipples moist, and nodded. His cock was hard and ready, but he wanted more from her. He wanted to hear her cries of pleasure as she came, feel the heat of her release against his mouth and hands before he took her.

He pulled her jeans away from her feet and then stood. "Jackson?" She licked her lips and reached for him.

He captured her hands, wrapping his fingers around her wrists and raised them over her head. The motion lifted her breasts invitingly. He pressed her hands against the rope holding the bag in place. "Wrap your hands around this." He released his hold on her and waited. Her fingers trembled slightly, but she grabbed the rope and held on tight. "Don't let go," he told her as he took a step back.

With her bra pushed back, the purple framed her breasts. She looked soft and extremely feminine spread against the heavy punching bag. She'd make one hell of a picture, he thought as he examined her. His fingers itched to hold his camera. Not that he'd ever share the explicit photo with anyone. It would be for his private collection. "Spread your legs." He nodded in satisfaction as she widened her stance. Emerald was fairly tall for a woman, but she still had to stretch to keep her grip on the rope.

The pressure of his jeans was killing him, so he plucked open the button and pushed the zipper down. His cock sprang forward. He was glad now that he hadn't bothered with underwear after his shower. Emerald's eyes went straight to his erection, causing it to swell even more than he thought possible. His testicles were heavy and full, but he wasn't ready to give them relief. Not yet.

Reaching into his back pocket, he pulled out a condom. He'd been carrying it around ever since that first night with Emerald. He wasn't going to be caught unprepared again. Tearing open the packet, he pulled out the condom and smoothed the latex over his swollen shaft. Emerald made a purring noise that had his entire body clenching.

Condom in place, he fell to his knees in front of her, using his wide shoulders to part her legs even more. With his face so close to her pussy, he could smell her heat, her desire for him. Like an aphrodisiac, it drew him closer.

He slid one long finger between her legs, feeling the wet fabric of her panties. She groaned and arched her hips toward him. He was finding it difficult to think, to breathe. All he wanted was to taste Emerald.

Grasping the thin strap in his hands, he tugged. Fabric ripped and the remainder of her panties fell down one supple leg to pool around her ankle. Jackson swallowed hard as the dark curls came into view. They glistened with her moisture, evidence of her need for him.

He parted her with his fingers, staring at the slick folds of her vulva. She was pink and flush and swollen with need. Her delicate clitoris was peeking out from beneath its hood, demanding attention.

Leaning forward, he pressed the tip of his tongue against her clit. Emerald moaned and undulated her hips toward him. He murmured his pleasure against her as he sucked the delicate bud between his lips.

His fingers glided over her slick folds. He couldn't believe how hot and wet she was. And it was all for him. Heady with desire, he pressed two fingers into her slit, not stopping until they were buried as deep as they could go.

"Jackson," she panted. He felt her body straining toward him, but she didn't let go of the rope. She held on tight, allowing him to do with her what he would.

Blood pumped heavily through his veins, his muscles clenched, his body swelled. He slipped his fingers out of her heat and then thrust them deep again. All the while, he sucked and flicked the tight bundle of nerves at the apex of her thighs.

He felt her tightening around his fingers and knew she was close. "Come for me," he whispered, blowing against her heated flesh. Burying his face between her thighs, he licked and sucked as his fingers pumped in and out of her pussy.

"I'm coming," she gasped a second before her entire body bowed. Her inner muscles clamped down tight around his fingers. Needing to be inside her to feel her orgasm, he pulled his fingers out of her tight channel and surged to his feet. Grasping her waist, he guided his cock to her opening and pushed. It was a tight squeeze as her muscles were rhythmically clenching around him. The delicate flesh was swollen and still pulsing with her orgasm. She cried out his name again.

"Wrap your legs around me." He hooked his hands under her thighs to help and she locked her legs tight around his hips. Her heels dug into his butt and he sank deeper into her. The heavy bag swayed as he leaned against it. Emerald shrieked and Jackson locked his legs to keep from falling.

Burying his face against her throat, he breathed deeply. Sweat, hay and sex permeated the air. He loved that fact that she didn't mind getting down and dirty with him in the barn. Bending his knees slightly, he then stood, thrusting himself to the hilt. Her wet heat surrounded him and Jackson cursed the fact that he had to use a condom. Although, he probably would have lost all control if it had been flesh against flesh and he wasn't ready to come just yet.

As he drove into her again, the bag swayed, knocking him off balance. Emerald gasped and grabbed his shoulders, releasing the rope. This wasn't going to work. As if sensing his dilemma, Emerald whispered in his ear as she peppered his neck with kisses. "What about a bale of hay or something?"

He grunted as he lurched away from the bag, still keeping his arms wrapped tight around Emerald. "Too scratchy. I don't want anything to mar this sweet skin." He nuzzled her neck, nipping lightly at the base.

"We have to do something," she wailed as she rubbed her breasts against his chest.

She was right about that. They were both close to coming. He could feel the tightening of her pussy around his cock. His testicles were drawn tight against his body. He needed to thrust. Hard. Now.

He glanced around and made his decision. Like a drunken fool, he staggered to the edge of the room. It wasn't a room, really, but an old stall that he and Nathan had converted into a workout area. He wanted to lean her against the low wall and fuck her hard, but he was afraid that she might get splinters. The wood was old and rough, and the last thing he wanted to do was hurt Emerald.

He had a plan, but first he had to extricate himself from her hot depths. And that wasn't going to be easy. Leaning her against the wall, he waited until he was sure she was steady before slowly pulling away from her. He had to grit his teeth to keep from losing it there and then. The last thing he wanted to do was come prematurely.

Emerald moaned as Jackson pulled his cock from her. "No." She wanted him inside her, stretching her. He was so hard and hot and she wanted to feel him thrusting into her.

"Have to," he growled. His face was harsh in the artificial lighting, as the sunlight didn't reach this far into the barn. She could see the strain on his face as he struggled to keep it all together. She was hanging by a thread herself and she'd just had one orgasm.

"What," she panted heavily, "can I do?"

He didn't answer, but turned her so she was facing the low wall. When he wrapped her hands over the edge, she understood. Leaning forward, she stuck out her ass and spread her legs. "Now, Jackson," she pleaded. She wanted to be joined with this man, to feel his orgasm within her, to bring him the kind of mind-blowing pleasure that he'd given her.

Between her legs, she ached with a growing need. Cream leaked from her core and trickled down her inner thighs. Her breasts ached for his touch. They felt heavy as she leaned forward.

His hairy thighs tickled the backs of her legs and she quivered as the broad head of his cock was pressed just inside her slit. His large, roughened hands slid up her sides and around to cup her breast. "Now," she moaned, digging her fingers into the wood railing for support.

"Fuck, yes," he hissed as he drove deep with one heavy thrust. He was thick and long and she took every inch of him into her. He stretched her inner muscles, filling her completely. If she hadn't been so prepared, it might have hurt. But instead, it felt gloriously right.

His fingers toyed with her nipples, pinching them lightly. Sensation flowed from her breasts to down between her thighs where she ached with a growing need. Sweat dripped from her temple and she could feel the slickness of Jackson's chest against her back.

This was no pleasant tumble in bed. Emerald thought she'd known what real desire was, but now she knew that what she'd had before had only been the tip of the iceberg. This was real and elemental. It was messy and noisy. And she loved it.

As Jackson began to thrust, the sound of his stomach hitting her ass filled the space around them. Sex, musky and real, permeated the air like some rich perfume. She could smell the remains of Jackson's spicy aftershave mixing with the remnants of her floral soap. Masculine and feminine. Dark and light. They came together over and over, one dominating, the other yielding, both giving and receiving pleasure.

His hips hammered against her, driving his cock into her waiting pussy. She'd never felt so filled, so needy in her life. Clenching her jaw, she met each heavy thrust, pushing her bottom back to meet him.

"Harder." She wanted more. Needed more.

One of Jackson's hands slid down her belly and between her thighs. He didn't break his rhythm as he fingered her swollen clit. His other hand continued to tease and torment her taut nipples.

Emerald felt as if she were a wire pulled too tight. "Jackson," she screamed as he rammed himself deep one final time. She felt the pulsing of his cock as he came and it set off her own orgasm.

Her entire body shook and shuddered as she came. Liquid flooded her core as tears filled her eyes. For the first time in her life, she bitterly resented the need for a condom. She wanted to feel the rush of her lover's release and the wet heat as it filled her. Still, it was amazing. His body jerked and heaved against hers as he gave several short thrusts. His hands finally fell away from her and he leaned heavily against her back.

Her knees began to buckle. Jackson swore as he lowered them carefully to the ground, still buried deep within her. She rested her head on the plank floor and sighed. She was dirty, sweaty and sticky, but she felt wonderful. Two orgasms in such a short period of time were practically unheard of for her. And never had they been so intense.

Jackson stirred behind her and they both groaned as he pulled his now semi-erect cock from her still-pulsing body. She collapsed onto the floor, rolling to her side and watched as he staggered to his feet. He dug a tissue out of his back pocket and removed the condom, wrapping it inside. Then he hitched up his jeans.

It was only then that she realized that he was still mostly dressed and she was naked. Well, almost naked. She didn't count her bra that was still tangled around her upper body or the necklace wrapped around her throat. What was left of her panties was crumpled on the floor over by the punching bag. They must have fallen off when she'd hooked her legs around him. Her jeans and top were in a heap on the floor.

His eyes were unreadable as he leaned down and scooped her off the floor. She wasn't a small woman by any means, but he was so strong, he did it as if she weighed nothing at all. Holding her tight, he strode from the barn. "My clothes," she protested.

"I'll get them later," he promised. The sky was still light when he stepped outside the barn, but barely. The sun was just sinking below the horizon. Totally unconcerned about her nakedness, she relaxed against him as he carried her to the house. His heart was a reassuring heavy thud beneath her cheek. She felt totally sated and absolutely safe as he elbowed his way in through the back door and up the stairs.

"We'll get you cleaned up first."

"First?" she questioned as he bypassed his bedroom and went straight to the bathroom.

He let her legs slide down his arm until her feet were flat on the floor. She stared up at him and was instantly ensnared by the look of pure lust shining from his eyes.

"I'm not done with you yet."

Her toes curled into the tile flooring and heat suffused her body. Maybe she wasn't done either.

# Chapter Eleven

ಐ

Emerald stretched in bed, ignoring the slight aches and pains that rippled throughout her body. They were nothing compared to the pleasure that Jackson had given her last night.

Once again, he'd surprised her. She'd thought for certain they'd make love in the shower. Instead, he'd taken his time, washing every inch of her body, paying special attention to her breasts and between her thighs. She'd returned the attention, stroking his chest, cupping his testicles and wrapping her wet, soapy hand around his stirring erection. By the time he'd patted her dry with a fluffy white towel, she was so aroused she thought she'd scream.

Jackson had scooped her into his arms and carried her back to bed. Their first time in the barn had been quick and almost out of control. This time had been slow and measured. He'd taken his time, kissing and touching every part of her — her arms, neck, torso, hips, thighs and legs. No part of her had been missed.

Then he'd sheathed his cock with a condom and slowly eased into her waiting heat. With his arms braced on either side of her, he'd rocked them to completion. Her orgasm had been deeper and more satisfying than she'd expected.

Once they'd both recovered, Jackson had hauled her into his arms and tucked her against his chest, holding her as they drifted to sleep. She'd stirred once during the night, turning away from him. He'd followed her, wrapping one arm around her waist and cupping her breast. His other arm was tucked under her head. She'd been totally surrounded by him.

She was alone in bed now though. The sheets beside her were cool and the room seemed emptier somehow. Emerald rolled over and squinted at the light peeking in through the curtains. Groaning, she sat up, resting her elbows on her knees. The sheet slipped, but she barely noticed as she scrubbed the sleep from her eyes.

A quick glance at the old-fashioned wind-up alarm clock sitting on Jackson's nightstand told her that she was already late. It was past eight o'clock. Jackson had probably been up and gone for hours. She'd been looking forward to having breakfast with him.

Shrugging, she scooted to the end of the bed and sat there taking inventory of her body. Yes, she ached, but she felt good too. Better than good. Already her body was beginning to thrum with energy. She glanced around, but there was no sign of her clothing. Wrapping the sheet around her, she padded downstairs.

A white sheet of paper sat in the center of the table and she stopped to read it. Sure enough, Jackson had left her a note. "Hope you slept well," she read aloud. "You looked too peaceful to wake. Coffee is ready. Took lunch with me, so I'll see you at supper." He hadn't even signed it. Yet she held it to her chest like some lovesick schoolgirl. Shaking her head at herself, she started to ball up the paper. The moment the sheet began to crinkle, she stopped, sighed and laid it on the table, smoothing it out. Then she folded it carefully and carried it into her bedroom.

Her clothing was folded neatly on the end of her bed, and she sent out a quick thank-you to him for remembering to bring them in from the barn. The last thing she wanted was Erin, Abel or Nathan finding them. Quickly, she tucked her note away in her nightstand drawer and picked up the clothing to dump them in the bathroom hamper.

As she sorted out her clothing, she made a mental note to make sure her bra was in the upstairs hamper and not under Jackson's bed. She had no memory of what had happened to it last night. Speaking of underwear, hers were missing. They weren't with her jeans and top. Not that they were of much use anymore. Jackson had ripped them from her body last night.

She shivered at the memory and her core began to throb. Groaning, she slammed the lid on the hamper. He'd probably just tossed them in the garbage, but she'd have to remember to ask him about them later. Right now, a quick shower was what she needed to clear her head. Then she'd get to work.

She had to change the sheets on Jackson's bed. After that, she had to run the vacuum over the floors, clean the bathrooms and do a couple of loads of laundry. By then it should be lunchtime. Emerald wondered if Jackson was avoiding her, but decided against it. This was a working farm and this was a busy time of year for him.

She'd take her free time this afternoon and do some of her own work. The past few days, she'd had some ideas floating around in her head. It was time to see if they would translate on paper into a usable design. After that, she might seek out the swimming hole that Erin had told her about. From the feel of the air, it was going to be another hot and sticky day.

Jackson walked softly through the woods, his boots not making a sound on the ground. Stopping, he crouched slowly and raised the camera to his face. Peering through the lens, he framed the shot. He took several photos in quick succession as the robin made quick work of the worm that it held tight in its beak. It had been sitting on a large, flat boulder and if he got the shot he'd wanted, it was definitely one he could sell at the gallery.

Pleased, he stood and stretched. He should be working. Lord only knew there was plenty to be done, but after he'd eaten the sandwiches he'd packed for his lunch, he'd felt restless. Part of it was that he missed Emerald. He should have just gone back to the house for lunch, but he'd felt the need to spend some time alone to think about what had happened.

He hadn't had many serious relationships in his lifetime. Working the farm and practically rearing his younger siblings had precluded that. While other young men had been going to college and sowing their wild oats, he'd been predicting crop yields and worrying about how to find the money for new sneakers for Erin and clothes for Nathan. Their father hadn't cared so the job had fallen to him.

Not that he'd minded. He loved his brother and sister and the farm. Nothing was too much to sacrifice for them. He'd had his share of women. Usually, though, they had been the type of women who were only looking for a good time and not a lasting relationship.

Those kinds of couplings had left him cold and unfulfilled and he hadn't bothered with them the past year or so. A man could do just as much with his own hand as those kinds of one-night stands could. Still, he'd felt the sting of loneliness, especially after Erin and then Nathan had married and moved out.

He'd never thought about a wife and kids of his own. Well, not in a lot of years. Those dreams had been put on the backburner for someday. Now he was thirty-four and he'd all but given up hope that those things would ever happen for him.

Then Emerald had walked into his life.

She'd brought life and vibrancy back to his home. With her funky tie-dye skirts, colorful T-shirts, unusual jewelry, brilliant smile and her sense of humor, she'd charmed him completely. He'd fallen hard before he'd even realized what was happening. All he'd known was that her laughter made him laugh and her smile made his chest ache.

Reaching into his back pocket, he drew out a scrap of fabric and stared at it. The fragile purple garment was already torn beyond repair, but he hadn't been able to bring himself to toss out her ruined panties. Instead, like a lovesick fool, he'd folded them and tucked them in his jeans pocket. It was like having a piece of her with him all day.

Boy, he had it bad!

Sighing, he shoved Emerald's panties back into his pocket. Already it was hard to imagine the farm without her here. And that was the problem.

Resuming his walk, he kept one eye open for photo opportunities as his thoughts wandered. He knew himself well enough to know that Emerald was special. He'd never wanted a woman the way he wanted her. Last night had been incredible. His cock stirred. He'd taken her twice within the span of an hour and he could have taken her again. The only thing that had stopped him was that Emerald was tired and sore. It had been enough for him to tuck her into his arms and have her sleep with him.

He'd never spent an entire night with a woman before. Usually they'd gone back to her place and he'd left long before dawn. When he was younger, he'd made out in his truck. But never before had he taken a woman in his own bed, in his home. He'd kept his liaisons private from his home life. Now he wanted to do the opposite.

Deep down, he wanted Emerald to love the place so much that she'd never want to leave. Hell, he wanted her to love him. He rubbed his chest with his free hand. His heart ached even as his loins tightened. He was very much afraid he was already in love with her. And that could only lead to heartache. For as much as he wanted her to stay, he knew that she'd have to leave. She was a city girl with a career. She had too much talent not to use it.

A twittering sound interrupted his thoughts and he glanced to his right. He managed to get a shot of a crow sitting on the limb of a dead birch tree before the bird took flight again. When he reached the edge of the meadow, he stopped and crouched down low. Wildflowers were in bloom and several bees and butterflies were flitting from flower to flower.

Patiently he waited and managed to get about a dozen shots that had potential. He wouldn't know until he got them developed, and that took a while as he always sent them away to get them done. No one in town knew about his sideline business, and that was fine by him. He was a private man and saw no reason for everyone to know his business. And part of him couldn't believe the prices that some folks were willing to pay for his photos.

It had been a while since he'd taken part of a day and just indulged himself in his second passion. Yes, he loved the farm, felt the call of the rich earth in his blood, but photography had fed a part of his soul that had almost dried up before he'd discovered this hobby. It had started about a year before Erin had married and he'd taken to it like a duck to water, reading every book he could find on the subject and experimenting. It had come so easily to him, it was almost as if he'd done it before and was just remembering how. He had an eye for framing a shot. At least that's what the gallery owner who'd contacted him had told him.

He'd needed this time to himself. Time to think. Time to just wallow in the farm and in nature without having to work. On a working farm there were really no days off, especially this time of year, but he'd needed to recharge his batteries. Last night had given him a lot to ponder.

He was realistic enough to know that Emerald wouldn't stay forever. He could step back and put some distance between them or he could take advantage of the time that she was here. Those memories would have to last him a lifetime, because as sure as he was standing here, he knew he'd never feel the same way about any other woman as he felt about Emerald. There was something about her that made him wanted to grab her tight and yell *mine*.

It was probably too late to pull back from her, and there was no way he was letting her leave until he knew the threat to her was over. His hands tightened into fists and he swore as the expensive camera in his hand protested. He forced himself to relax, but it wasn't easy.

He realized that he'd already made up his mind. There really was no choice. He'd take whatever Emerald would give him and cherish their time together. When it was over, he'd find the strength somewhere inside him to let her go.

Swiping the sweat from his brow, he decided that he needed to cool off before he went home. He was close enough to the old swimming hole to take a quick dip. Then he'd head home and maybe sweet-talk Emerald into a quick afternoon romp between the sheets.

The swimming hole was technically on Abel's land, but they'd all used it as kids and teenagers. Jackson hadn't been here in about a dozen years. He shook his head. Where the hell had the time gone? His life had become too much about work and survival and less about living. Somehow, having Emerald around was bringing him back to life again.

He had her to thank for that, even though it would hurt like hell when she left. But there was no going back, and truthfully, he didn't want to. It felt good to be really alive again.

The splash of water caught his attention and he crept forward. If his sister and her husband were fooling around at the pond, he didn't want to interrupt them. As he reached the edge of the trees, he raised the camera and peered through the telephoto lens for a better view. Nobody used this place much anymore as it was on private property. But maybe a few of the teenagers that Erin had hired were taking a break. Although at two in the afternoon, that wasn't likely.

There was only one person. Jackson could barely make out the top of a head as it disappeared beneath the water. He waited patiently and was rewarded a few moments later when she reappeared. It was definitely a woman. She was naked from the waist up and he saw her perfectly. Recognition made his heart skip a beat.

Emerald was skinny-dipping.

Like a water nymph, she stood waist-deep in the pond and slicked her wet hair out of her face. She was wearing no makeup, her skin glistening in the afternoon heat. He swallowed and focused his lens, getting a closer shot. His fingers longed to take a photo, but he couldn't, wouldn't without her permission. This was one picture he'd never share with anyone, but he'd give almost anything to have one for his private collection. Something that he could hold and look at long after she was gone.

Beads of water caressed her skin like a lover's touch. One poised on the edge of her nipple and he longed to lick it away. Her breasts were very sensitive. He loved to draw those pouty nipples into his mouth and suckle.

His jeans were uncomfortably tight, but he didn't move, totally enthralled by the picture she made in the lens. She laughed as she fell back into the water, disappearing below it, only to reappear a few seconds later. When she dove deep, her long legs briefly appeared and then were gone. Jackson wondered if she was wearing panties or if she was totally naked.

His hand went to his back pocket where her pale purple panties resided. He drew them out and held them to his cheek, sniffing them. They smelled like her—hot and spicy with a touch of floral. The real thing was only a handful of steps away.

Returning the panties to his pocket, he hesitated. Should he leave her alone or join her? He already felt like a damn voyeur watching her through the lens of his camera. She surfaced again, slicking back her hair. In spite of the cooling water, her skin appeared flushed. Her hands rested lightly on her belly and then slowly slid upward.

Jackson gulped air into his lungs as her fingers hesitated just below her breasts. "Higher, baby," he whispered. His cock was throbbing, but he ignored it. There was no way he could take his eyes off her as he waited to see what she'd do. "Touch yourself," he murmured, encouraging her even though she couldn't hear him.

Her hands cupped her breasts and gently squeezed. "Oh, yeah. That's it, sweetheart." His testicles tightened and he barely swallowed a groan. He was in agony, but he couldn't stop watching Emerald. She was beautiful, so natural, like a goddess of nature as she rubbed her fingers across her puckered nipples. Her head was thrown back and her hair hung in wet tendrils, clinging to her back and shoulders. Her long neck was exposed to his hungry view and her back was arched, pushing her breasts upward.

Her arm grazed the side of her breast as her hand slipped across her collarbone and throat. Her head turned slightly away from him. His finger pressed down automatically on the shutter.

The noise sounded loud in the silence of the day and he took a step backward, stepping on a twig. The snap echoed across the clearing. Emerald gasped and sank beneath the water. Swearing under his breath, Jackson sauntered forward, or at least tried to. His gait was as stiff as his erection.

"What are you doing here?" Her voice was shrill as she glared at him. "You frightened the life out of me."

"I'm sorry." He really was repentant, but she looked so damn adorable when she was angry, he couldn't really be sorry he'd seen her, only that he'd frightened her.

Her eyes went unerringly to the camera that now hung from his neck. "You were taking pictures?"

"Yeah." He shrugged.

She stared at him, searching his face. "Did you take any of me?"

He didn't even think about lying to her. "I never meant to, but I couldn't resist taking one. It's nothing that I'd ever show anyone else," he quickly reassured her. "But with the play of light on the water and you turned slightly away, you looked like a mystical nymph rising from the depths. The way the shot is framed, your identity is protected."

Emerald stared at him, then at the camera that he'd automatically grasped in his hands. "You're a serious photographer, aren't you?"

He looked down at his feet and then out over the water before giving one single nod.

"Why does it bother you to admit that?" Water rippled and his head snapped up. She'd stood in the water and pulled her hair forward to cover her breasts. Her skin was sun-kissed, her dark brown eyes were deep pools of desire. Before he'd realized what he was doing, he'd raised the camera, adjusted the lens and snapped several shots.

He swore and lowered the camera. "I'm sorry." He scrubbed his hand over his face. "I didn't mean to do that."

She crossed her arms over her chest. "Talk to me." Her soft voice soothed some of the tension from him. He felt his shoulders relaxing even as the ache in his groin intensified.

"No one knows, okay?" He kicked at the dirt and sighed. "It started as a hobby, but now I'm selling some in a gallery in New York."

"Really?" She appeared delighted.

"Yeah."

"But why doesn't anyone else know?" She seemed perplexed.

"I'm a farmer, damn it." He tugged the camera strap over his head and laid the camera carefully on Emerald's clothing, which was folded neatly and placed on a rock in the shade.

"That doesn't mean that you can't be an artist too."

Jackson shook his head. "I don't want to talk about it. I have something more important to ask you." He took a step closer.

"Okay."

Sweat rolled down his spine as he walked to the edge of the water. "Are you wearing panties or are you naked?"

# Chapter Twelve

ॐ

Emerald stared at Jackson. He was self-conscious about his photography even though she could tell it meant a lot to him. She was no expert, but that camera he was using was no cheap piece of equipment. He'd sunk serious bucks into it, and for a man like Jackson, that meant that he was deadly serious about it.

She wanted to talk more about his artistic career, but one look at his closed-off expression told her that wouldn't be happening. Not now. That didn't mean that she wouldn't pursue it later though. She could be tenacious when she wanted something.

He took a step closer to the water, the intensity in his blue eyes scorching her bare flesh even hotter than the sun was already doing. She licked her lips in anticipation. Jackson had too much responsibility and he'd had it for far too long. He needed to play and she was just the woman to make that happen.

Batting her eyelashes at him, she smiled coyly. "Why don't you come in and find out?"

The corners of his mouth kicked up in a slow grin. "I think that I will." He ripped his white T-shirt over his head and tossed it next to her pile of clothing. "How did you find out about the swimming hole?" He unlaced his boots and pulled them off one at a time, dropping them to the ground near his feet. His socks followed.

"Erin mentioned it to me. She said I could use it any time I wanted." The more male flesh he exposed, the harder it was getting to pay attention to the conversation. She'd seen him naked, but somehow this was different. Out under the harsh rays of the sun, there was no hiding anything. For either one of them.

His torso was bronzed from hours of working under the unforgiving sun. His muscles rippled as his hands went to the fastenings of his jeans. Quickly, he skinned his pants over his thighs, taking his plain cotton briefs with them. Kicking jeans and underwear aside, he stood there and let her look her fill.

She licked her lips, her skin tingling from the heat of the sun and pure anticipation. His cock stood straight up from its dark nest of curls and his testicles looked heavy and full. He was totally aroused and wasn't ashamed to show her. He propped his hands on his hips and it emphasized the sheer magnitude of his shoulders, his tapered torso and lean waist. Legs spread apart, feet planted on the ground, he was masculinity personified.

Her nipples were puckered into tight buds that ached, and her breasts rose and fell with each deep breath she took.

"I watched you touch yourself." Jackson's low voice caressed her skin, raising goose bumps on her arms.

It took her a second to realize what he was talking about. She could feel the heat on her face and knew it was more than just the sun making her blush. Still, she tried to brazen it out. "Did you now?" She was thirty years old, damn it. There was no need for her to be embarrassed.

"I liked watching you." His voice deepened to a husky growl as he took a step toward the edge of the pond. "Do it again. Touch yourself for me."

She shivered beneath the intensity of his stare, her nipples tightening in anticipation. Taking a deep breath, she placed her hands low on her belly and then slid them upward. Her hair still hid most of her breasts from view so she took a moment to push it out of the way.

Jackson grunted his approval, taking another step. Water closed around his feet and ankles.

Emerald cupped her breasts in her hands and rubbed her thumbs over her straining nipples. The air around her was heavy and thick with heat and expectancy. The continuous low buzz of the insects faded away as he took another step toward her. Her belly clenched and she felt a throbbing ache begin to pulse deep within.

He moved steadily toward her, not stopping until he was standing right in front of her. She was a tall woman at five foot eight, but Jackson was several inches over six feet. He made her feel almost petite and she was very aware of her femininity and the differences between them. Her pulse quickened.

His large body shaded hers and she had to blink so that her vision could adjust. He leaned down, his lips grazing the swell of her breast as he continued lower. Her hands, still cupping her breasts, tightened in reflex. He blew over her tight nipple. "That's it," he crooned. "Offer yourself to me." His tongue flicked over the nub, teasing it, tormenting it. "Give yourself to me."

There was no thought of denying him. She wanted him to the point of madness. Heat flooded her core and she was surprised that the water around them wasn't boiling or at least steaming. She made a low sound deep in her throat that he took as agreement, drawing her nipple into his mouth and suckling.

Emerald tipped back her head and closed her eyes. She swayed in the water, almost weightless. Needing something to anchor herself, she slid her hands over his strong forearms, across his shoulders and neck, until her fingers were tangled in his hair. Gripping him tight, she held him to her as his mouth continued to pleasure her breasts. First one and then the other.

"Jackson," she groaned. She wanted more. Needed more. Her fingernails dug into his scalp as he carefully grazed her breast with his teeth before tugging gently on the swollen tip.

His large hands cupped her ass, squeezing and caressing as they moved around her hips. "Spread your legs," he instructed as his fingers kneaded the front of her thighs.

She shifted her feet apart and had to bite her lip to keep from crying out as the cool water rushed between her legs. A gasp escaped when his fingers parted her and began to caress the slick folds. Without hesitation, he slipped one finger inside her. Her hips swayed toward him. One finger became two as he continued the in-and-out motion in a steady, unhurried rhythm.

"Jackson!" she cried almost mindlessly as he suckled her breasts and fucked her with his fingers. The heat of the day wrapped around her in a thick blanket, blocking the harsh realities of the world, at least for the moment. The pond water lapped around her belly, a cool caress.

Jackson's mouth and fingers coaxed her forward, leading her closer and closer to orgasm. This man barely had to touch her and she was ready to explode. Her skin tingled as the heat built within and without. His fingers stretched the delicate muscles within as he stroked deep, finding the sweet spot as he withdrew. His thumb stroked the hard nub of nerves at the apex of her sex.

Emerald gasped, her breath coming harder and faster. Her toes curled into the small stones lining the bottom of the pond. Her entire being was stretched tight and ready to snap. A low keening sound broke from her lips as she shattered. Her inner muscles convulsed and her body shook as she came. Heat and relief flooded through her veins, making her blood thicken.

Carefully, Jackson withdrew his fingers and straightened. She clutched him tight, not wanting him to leave her. His cock was hard and hot against her belly as he pulled her close. His arms came around her and she felt his lips against her forehead.

Smiling, she blinked away the lethargy threatening to swamp her and looked up at him. His face was a mask of unfulfilled desire, yet she could see the pleasure and satisfaction in his eyes. Jackson was a very giving man and now she wanted to give back to him.

He lifted her suddenly and she automatically wrapped her arms and legs around him. Jackson groaned as the head of his cock brushed against the heat of her pussy. She squirmed until the tip was positioned at the opening and pressed down. About an inch slipped inside her. Just enough to tease her and make her moan.

"I don't have any protection with me." Jackson began to slosh back to shore, each step driving him a bit deeper inside her. She bit the inside of her mouth to keep from screaming. Her head was spinning from the combination of heat and building desire. She'd just orgasmed, but already she could feel the familiar ache low in her belly.

Burying her face in his shoulder, she sighed, knowing that he was right and they couldn't take a chance. It was hard though. Sometimes being a responsible adult sucked.

He carried her easily, which was quite a treat for a woman of her size. His strength astounded her. He was always so careful with her that it was easy to forget just how powerful he was.

She couldn't quite swallow back the moan of disappointment as he lifted her off him. She unhooked her feet from around his waist and her legs slid down his flanks to hit the soft grass underfoot.

The coolness of the shaded trees felt good against her hot skin. She sighed when he released her, thinking he was getting dressed. But instead, he shook out the towel that she'd brought with her and spread it on the ground. Lowering himself to it, he reached out and captured her hand, tugging her down beside him. He sprawled out on the ground and lifted her so that she was straddling his waist.

Emerald pressed her hands against his chest for balance. This position had potential. She'd wanted to touch him, to pleasure him in the same way he'd done for her. This was too good an opportunity to pass up.

His skin was warm beneath her fingers, and as she stroked upward, she felt the ripple of muscles beneath them. The man really had an incredible chest. His waist was lean, his torso banded with the classic six-pack and his shoulders were wide. He had just the right amount of hair on his chest to be sexy. She tangled her fingers in it as she continued to caress him.

Leaning forward, she brushed her lips against his. His tongue swept out to lick at her mouth and she parted her lips, inviting him inside. Their tongues tangled as their kiss deepened. He tasted so good. Hot and masculine with a touch of peppermint.

One hand cupped the back of her head, tilting it slightly to give him a better angle to kiss her. The other cuddled her ass, kneading the white mounds. He did seem to enjoy touching her there.

The tip of his cock nudged her behind, reminding her of what she planned to do. It was all too easy to get lost in the magic of Jackson's kisses and forget about everything else. And that she wasn't about to do.

She broke away from his lips and kissed his strong jaw. It was the middle of the afternoon, but already she could feel the bristles of his beard against her skin. She worked her lips down the strong column of his neck and across his collarbone as she shifted lower.

Jackson dropped his hands back to his sides and she raised her head. "I'm all yours, baby." Usually, she didn't like when men called her baby, but the way Jackson said it made her pussy clench with need.

She smiled as she lowered her head again. She planned to make him groan and squirm before she let him come. She lapped at one flat brown nipple before doing the same thing with the other. A deep rumbling sound rose from deep in his chest. He sounded like a big cat purring.

Emerald continued to kiss a path over his chest, stopping to swirl her tongue in his navel. He sucked in a breath as her hair brushed over his belly and then lower. Intentionally, she blew on his cock as she allowed the long, curly strands of her black hair to wrap around it.

His fingers tangled in the mass and he tugged. "I'm too close," he panted. "You keep that up and I'll come."

"We wouldn't want that to happen, now would we?" she all but purred.

Jackson gave a bark of laughter. "You minx."

She shrugged. "You've had your fun. Now it's time for me to have mine." Not giving him a chance to reply, she licked a wet path from the base of his shaft right to the tip. Jackson's hips jerked and he groaned.

Capturing his balls in one hand, she began to stroke them gently. He widened his legs to give her better access. Pleased, she gripped his cock with the other, letting her fist slide up and down the hard length.

"Emerald," he growled in warning.

She allowed her hand to encircle the head of his erection, her thumb spreading the liquid that seeped from the tip. "You're so hard and so soft at the same time. I can feel your cock pulsing in my hand." It matched the heavy throbbing between her own thighs and she wished that one of them had thought to bring a condom.

"Come here." Jackson gently tugged on her hair to get her attention.

"No. I want my turn." She glared at him even as her body was screaming at her to do what he wanted.

"You'll still get your turn," he promised, his eyes hooded with desire. "But I'll get mine too."

She arched one eyebrow, giving him a quizzical look, not quite understanding what he wanted. When he tugged again, she sighed and gave his scrotum one final squeeze before releasing him and sitting back on his thighs.

He patted his tummy. "Sit here." She started to scoot up, but he shook his head. "Face away from me."

She climbed off him and turned away before mounting him again. Her face flamed as she realized that he was getting an unobstructed view of her pussy. Sitting back on her heels, she waited.

"Bend forward." All of a sudden, she knew what he wanted. She'd never done this with another man before, but the possibilities were exciting. She felt his hand on the center of her back, urging her forward. His hands cupped her hips and he tugged her back until her pussy was close to his face. Anticipation filled her as she felt his breath on her inner thigh.

Licking her lips, she stretched forward, capturing the tip of his cock in her mouth and sucking.

Jackson thought he might lose it when, without warning, Emerald sucked the tip of his cock into her mouth. Her warm heat enveloped the head as she swirled her tongue around. Her fingers closed around his shaft and she began to stroke him as she lapped at the tip.

Gritting his teeth, he switched his focus to her. He had a perfect view of her pussy and he wasn't going to pass up this opportunity to explore and indulge himself. Using his fingers, he spread her wide. Her folds were slick from her last orgasm and with her building desire.

She was pink and hot and he blew gently against her slit. Emerald groaned, the vibrations wrapping around his cock. His entire body tensed as he struggled to keep from coming. It was too soon. He wanted to make sure that she came with him when he finally let go.

Keeping her folds spread wide with one hand, he used the other to explore. Starting at her ass, he trailed one finger down the cleft of her behind. She shrieked and jerked her head up when he rimmed the tight, puckered hole. She gasped for breath as he teased her, pressing his finger in slightly before moving on.

Her head dropped back to his groin and he swallowed back a curse as her breath feathered his shaft. Her hair tickled his scrotum and it was all he could do not to tumble her from his body and fuck her until they both screamed. He hadn't bothered to put a condom in his pocket this morning. He hadn't thought he'd need one. He damn well wouldn't make that mistake again.

Emerald caught her breath and nuzzled his hard length before taking him into her mouth again. He'd had other women suck him off before, but at the moment he couldn't remember one single time. It had never felt this fucking good. Everything with her was deeper and richer than it had been before.

Her tongue stroked the pulsing vein that ran the length of his cock before curling around the head again. She gripped him in her hand and began to pump in earnest as she began to move her head up and down his shaft, taking him deeper with each downward stroke.

Breathing deep, Jackson turned his attention back to her, sliding two fingers past the tight muscles guarding the opening of her pussy. He felt the slight resistance as he pushed beyond it to her heated depths. As he withdrew, he widened his fingers, letting one of them stroke the top of her cunt as he pulled it out. She moaned. The vibration made his balls draw up tight against his body.

Sweat trickled down his forehead and into his hair. Both their bodies were slick with perspiration as they drove toward completion. Jackson didn't want it to end but knew that he couldn't stop it from happening. He was too far gone to pull back.

Lifting his head, he flicked his tongue over her clit as he inserted a third finger inside her sheath. Using his thumb, he rimmed the tight opening of her ass before pressing it inside.

Emerald's hand tightened around his cock, her mouth sucking hard. He felt her inner muscles begin to spasm around his fingers, indicating the onset of her release.

Jackson yelled as he came, his hips jerking upward. His cock pulsed in her hand and mouth as he spilled himself into her. She continued to draw on his shaft and he thought his head might explode with the intensity of his orgasm.

He couldn't think, could only feel as Emerald sucked him dry. His hands fell away from her body, landing with a thud on the ground. He could see and feel the liquid seeping from her core. Pleased, he couldn't resist lapping at her pussy. Emerald choked out a cry as she released him and buried her face against his groin.

Jackson's head fell back against the soft ground and he stared up at the sky. The sights and sounds of the day began to seep back into his consciousness. Everything looked more vibrant, from the blue of the sky to the green of the trees overhead. He could hear the insects buzzing, the occasional blue jay screeching and a crow squawking. The fragrance of the grass and wildflowers tickled his nose, intermingled with the scent of sex and the unique smell of Emerald.

As he lay there with her draped across him, he was startled to realize he was smiling. He felt more content than he had in...well, he didn't know when. All he knew was that Emerald made him happy. He felt more satisfied with everything in his life when she was with him.

She sighed and mumbled and then raised her head. When she lifted her leg to move, she almost hit him in the head. Deciding he'd better take charge if he didn't want anything important damaged, he lifted her off him and then rolled to his feet.

She just blinked like a sleeping, satisfied cat as he curled his arms beneath her and picked her up. She settled trustingly against his chest, nuzzling his neck. Emotion surged up within him and tears pricked his eyes. To cover it, he walked straight into the pond and fell backward with Emerald still clasped tight in his arms.

When he surfaced, she sputtered and laughed at him, her smile making his heart turn over. No matter what, he wouldn't let anything happen to this special woman. And when the time came, he'd let her go with no regrets, no matter the cost to him.

# Chapter Thirteen

## ✂

Emerald sighed as she sat back in the large, cushioned patio chair and sipped her iced tea. The glass was damp with condensation, as the heat still had not abated. She and Jackson had gone for a quick dip in the pond and then had dressed and come home. They'd said little between them, but there hadn't really been any need for words. There was a connection between them that went deeper than that and with each moment she spent with Jackson it seemed to grow stronger.

She rubbed her finger along the rim of the glass, wiping the condensation aside. Her life had taken some very strange turns lately, and not many of them good. But one thing she couldn't regret was coming to the small town of Meadows and finding Jackson Connors.

The air was heavy and still, blanketing the farm in its heat. Emerald had no idea when this heat wave was going to break, but she hoped it was soon. Jackson hadn't said anything, but he had to be worried about his crop. There hadn't been any rain in about ten days and the ground was cracked and dry. What little grass there was around the house was brown with patches of green. The few flowers scattered around the patio were fine because she'd been watering them.

The screen door was pushed open and Jackson ambled out, glass in hand. He was shirtless and shoeless, wearing only a pair of faded jeans. He had a folder stuck under his arm and she could see the wariness in his eyes as he lowered himself into the chair next to her.

She laid her glass on the porch floor beside her chair. On their stroll home from the pond, he'd agreed to show her some of his photos. Emerald had to admit that she was curious to see his work, especially since she knew it wasn't something he'd shared with anyone else.

She wiped her hands on her tank top, sensing Jackson following her movements with his eyes, staring at her nipples where they pressed against the thin fabric. There was a built-in bra, but it didn't help. Seemed that whenever she was around him, her body had a mind of its own. She held out her hand.

Almost reluctantly, he handed her the folder. She had to tug slightly to get him to release it, and when he did, he quickly turned away, looking out over the rows of apple trees in the distance.

Emerald turned back the cover of the folder and stared at the first image. It was stark in black and white and showed the orchard in the dead of winter. Or rather, it pictured one particular tree. The branches were gnarled, the bark rough and dark in sharp contrast to the pristine white of the snow. There were no tracks, no dirt, no sign of life in the thick layer of snow.

It was breathtaking.

Taking her time, she flipped over the photo to reveal the one beneath it. This one was in full color. A squirrel was seated on a log, nut clasped tight in his tiny paws. His face was turned inquisitively toward the camera.

The next one was of the same apple tree from the earlier black-and-white shot. This one was full color and showed the tree in bloom. Apple blossoms covered it as the sun shone down upon it. The sky was an impossible shade of blue that could only be caught in that rare split second in nature.

On and on it went. One photo after another revealing sheer artistic talent. It wasn't just the subject matter, but the way it was presented. It was, she knew, Jackson's unique vision. It gave her an insight into the man and how he viewed the land he owned and worked. There was a depth of love and respect that was unmistakable.

She knew then that he'd never leave here.

Her heart ached as she came to the last picture. It was sunset from the porch she was sitting on. The vibrant colors of red, yellow, green, aqua and blue were all there as if painted by the hand of God. She'd never seen anything quite like it.

She closed the folder slowly and let it rest in her lap. She could feel the tension from the chair next to her. Turning slowly, she stared at Jackson, shaking her head. His lips firmed and he reached out for the folder. Her hand covered his, stopping him from taking the folder.

"I've never seen anything this beautiful in my life." Her voice was husky with emotion, but she meant what she said. "No, that's not quite right." She struggled to find the correct words. "They're more than merely beautiful. They're compelling. They evoke emotion. God, Jackson." She gripped his hand tight, her nails digging into him. "They're incredible."

One corner of his mouth quirked up. "All of that," he teased.

She could tell he was uncomfortable with her praise and trying to make light of it. She wasn't having that. "Yes." She stared defiantly at him. "All of that and more. Whatever they're paying you, it's not enough."

Jackson's gaze softened, his hand slipping out from beneath hers as he cupped her jaw. Leaning forward, he touched his lips to hers. Unlike the tempest of passion at the pond, this was gentle, a kiss complete in and of itself rather than a prelude to sex.

Her bare toes curled into the plank floor beneath her feet. Her whole body seemed to sigh and relax. Being with Jackson felt right in a way that nothing else ever had in her life, except maybe her artwork. It was scary and exhilarating at the same time.

"Thank you," he said simply and sincerely as he sat back. He stroked the curve of her jaw with his thumb before sitting back in his chair. She noted that he left the folder in her lap.

He sprawled in his chair, extending his long legs in front of him. His hands were resting lightly on his flat, tanned stomach and even at rest his biceps were huge. He was the picture of relaxation, yet she could see the slight tightening in his jaw and the tension in his muscles.

He turned his head and a lock of hair fell onto his forehead. He swiped it away with his hand, raking his fingers through his hair. It wasn't overly long, but it was sexy. At least she thought it was. His blue eyes seemed even brighter against the dark tan of his skin. "When are you going to show me more of your work?" There was almost a challenge in his tone, as if he felt vulnerable and needed her to reveal a part of herself as well.

Without a word, she got up and handed him the folder before walking inside. In her bedroom, she grabbed her computer and went back outside. Jackson's head jerked her way as she stepped back out. Ignoring him, she perched on the arm of his chair, turned on her laptop and brought up the files of her last collection. She plunked the machine in his lap so he could look his fill.

Her last work had a Middle Eastern flair to it, the colors and designs inspired by that ancient culture. Sapphire had taken her cue from it and created some lovely and exotic earrings, necklaces, chokers, bracelets, anklets and belly chains. The journals had been crafted with vibrant covers that would have fit quite nicely in some ancient desert palace. The cards and stationery had depicted some of the ancient gods and goddesses of the various cultures. Topaz had commissioned an entire line of specially scented candles and incense to be crafted especially for their store. It had been expensive, but it had been well worth it. The line had been a huge success and it was now a standard that they kept in their store year-round.

Jackson scrolled though the files, examining each and every piece. When he was done, he gave her a questioning look. She nodded, knowing what he wanted without him having to ask. He opened another folder and began to scan.

This was from the original Sisters' Jewels collection. Each piece focused on the birthstone of the month. "This is all incredible." She could hear the sincerity in his voice as he opened yet another folder and another. The last five years of her work was on there. She'd loaded it all on before she'd left home on the run. Not knowing how long she'd be gone, she'd wanted to have it all on hand in case she wanted to refer back to something she'd already done.

He opened a new file before she could stop him. They both froze. His hand seemed to tremble as he scrolled though the work. Or maybe it was her who was shaking. Her stomach was in knots and she nibbled nervously on her bottom lip.

"This is new."

It wasn't a question, but she answered him anyway. "Yes." In the past few days the ideas had started flowing again. She put it down to the fact that she felt relaxed for the first time in weeks, if not months. It was only now that she was away, she'd admit that she'd been feeling burnt out and pressured these past few months. The phenomenal success of Sisters' Jewels had put a strain on all the sisters to create something bigger and better.

The farm had inspired her. As was her habit, she'd sketched her designs on paper first. Since she didn't have a scanner with her, she'd recreated her drawings on her computer using her art program. Along with the illustration, she'd added notes — colors, design possibilities and more. She was just getting started.

The new designs were floral, all treasures discovered while walking around the yard and just beyond. There was the clump of buttercups that bloomed at the corner of the old barn. The violets she'd discovered in a forgotten corner of the front yard. Daisies that grew in clumps alongside the fence. She'd drawn in enough of the background for each to give her a sense of place and perspective, to remind her of the farm when she was back in New York. There were dozens of varieties of other wildflowers, each color matching the birthstone of a month. The designs weren't anywhere near finished yet, but the basis for the collection was there.

Jackson shut down the computer and carefully laid it aside. Reaching out, he tugged her down into his lap. She went easily, really wanting to know his opinion. He had a great artistic eye and she knew instinctively that he wouldn't lie to her. He wouldn't be cruel, but neither would he sugarcoat his reaction. He would be honest.

She ignored the expanse of warm muscle and forced herself to sit up straight with her hands clasped primly in her lap when all she wanted to do was lean into his chest and nibble on his neck. She squirmed as her panties dampened. "Well?"

Jackson wrapped one arm around her waist, pulling her closer. She could feel the play of muscles in his thighs beneath the fabric of his jeans. He dropped his free hand onto her bare legs and began to trace a path from her knees to the top of her thighs. Her eyes almost crossed as he grazed the strip of skin just beneath the ragged edges of her jean shorts. They'd ridden up slightly when he'd pulled her into his lap and his fingers were incredibly close to her crotch.

She sucked in a breath and tried to shift her legs open without being blatant about it. Jackson just grinned and then let his fingers glide back to her knee. Just when she'd taken a deep breath, he trailed his hand upward again. The man was teasing her.

She frowned at him and he leaned down and kissed her. It was a quick kiss, over before it really got started. Yet it sent a blast of heat to her core.

"Your work is amazing, Emerald." He shook his head. "What you do and the fact that you have to come up with new ideas so often is incredible."

She felt her cheeks heating and knew she was blushing. Why this man's opinion meant so much to her she wasn't sure, but it did. "Thank you. I haven't done anything new in a while and I was starting to worry."

His hand dipped between her thighs, tracing the edge of her shorts. Close, but not close enough to where she really wanted him touching her. A low moan escaped her as she parted her legs, not even trying to be discreet about it. She wanted his hands on her. Everywhere.

"No need to worry." The low, gruff tone of his voice sent goose bumps racing down her arms and legs in spite of the heat. "You just needed a rest and a change of pace is all."

She licked her lips and his gaze followed her tongue. She did it again.

"Tease," he accused as his fingers brushed over the crotch of her shorts.

She sucked in a breath. "You're the tease, not me," she gasped as his knuckles grazed her sex. Even through the layers of her shorts and panties, she could feel the heat of his hand and the firmness of his strokes.

He chuckled, a low and sexy rumble deep in his chest. Emerald smiled and cupped his face in her hands. His fingers dipped beneath the hem of her shorts, seeking her heat. She lowered her face toward him. His breath was warm on her mouth. She parted her lips, almost able to taste him already. His fingers were close now. Just another half-inch. Emerald gave a breathy groan.

And was dumped back in her chair.

Sprawling against the seat, she struggled to sit up. Jackson's gaze was on the road and not her. She followed his stare and, sure enough, she could see the cloud of dirt coming toward the house. Struggling to her feet, she yanked down the legs of her shorts and made sure her top was tucked in. Her hair, which she'd bundled into a ponytail, was drooping slightly.

Swearing, she grabbed up her computer and sprinted for the back door. Jackson's hand shot out, catching her wrist as she passed him. She came to such an abrupt halt she almost tumbled back into his lap. Only his quick reflexes kept her from falling.

"Let go. I have to fix my hair and splash some water on my face or something."

"You look fine. Better than fine." She glared at him. That was fine for him to say. He looked as cool as a cucumber, if you ignored the large bulge pressing against the zipper of his jeans.

She glanced down the road and saw, not one, but two trucks headed their way. "That's your family," she hissed. The last thing she wanted was to look as if she'd just been tumbled in Jackson's lap. And, damn it, she'd never even got to finish getting tumbled. She groaned. The man was turning her into a sex fiend and making her crazy. "Let go."

He turned her loose, but not before his fingers trailed down the inside of her wrist, sending a rivulet of desire snaking through her. She stared at him. She'd never known that her wrist was an erogenous zone before. But everywhere on her body seemed to be where this man was concerned.

"Go," he encouraged as he gave her a light push toward the door. "I'll hold them off as long as I can."

Nodding, she scurried inside.

Jackson watched the screen door close behind Emerald and sighed, raking his fingers through his hair. He loved his family, but they had rotten timing. He stood as both trucks pulled into the yard. His muscles tightened and his hands fisted. Maybe they had news about Emerald's stalker. It was easy to forget about that problem when she was safe and warm, snuggled in his lap.

He swore and discreetly adjusted himself before walking forward to greet them. Taking a deep breath, he willed his erection to go down. His sister and brother-in-law climbed out of one vehicle while Nathan and Carly got out of the other one. Both women smiled as they strolled toward the porch. He gave them what he hoped was a smile. It seemed to work for the women, but both men gave him quizzical looks. He shook his head.

"What brings you all out here? Any news?" He wanted to send them all back to their trucks so he could go find Emerald and pick up where they left off. But that wasn't going to happen anytime soon. Rubbing the back of his neck, he tried to get a grip.

Because he was distracted, Erin had the back door open and was stepping into the kitchen before he realized it. So much for his promise to Emerald to divert them. He heard her greeting Erin and Carly, so he figured that everything was okay. He bent down to grab his glass of iced tea and saw the folder of his photos lying on Emerald's chair. Casually, he picked it up and tucked it beneath his arm.

"You okay?" Nathan eyed him cautiously.

"Yeah. Why wouldn't I be?" Oh great. Now both men were giving him strange looks. "Let's go inside with the women."

He herded them inside and was grateful to see his sister and sister-in-law comfortably ensconced at the table with tall glasses of iced tea before them. Emerald was at the counter, looking calm and gorgeous as ever. She smiled at the men as they entered and continued to bustle around. Within a minute, everyone had something to drink and a huge plate of fresh-baked oatmeal cookies had been passed around.

"These are delicious," Erin all but moaned as she took a bite. "I can cook, but I'm not much for baking."

"They're easy. It's my mother's recipe. I can write it out for you if you want." Emerald sounded so normal and unaffected by what had happened between them that Jackson wanted to growl. His body was still primed and ready.

"Not that I'm not glad to see you," his tone belied his words, "but is there some reason you're all here?"

Emerald leaned forward suddenly and he could see the worry in her beautiful brown eyes. "Have you found out anything?"

Abel shook his head. "Nothing. It seems as if your stalker is laying low now that you're away. He must have lost your trail after the last call he made to you and is waiting for you to make a mistake of some kind. It looks as if your investigator is in the clear."

"Either that or he's just playing it smart," Nathan added.

Emerald chewed on her bottom lip. Jackson wanted to soothe her abused mouth with his tongue. And he would. Just as soon as he got rid of his family.

"How are my sisters?" It had been agreed that Emerald wouldn't contact her family anymore just to be on the safe side. Abel had been in contact with the private investigator, who was in turn in touch with her sisters. It might have been excessive, but they preferred to err on the side of caution.

"They're good. Although Topaz seems to be a bit put out by her bodyguard." Abel chuckled. "Dane said that she's really giving this guy a run for his money."

Emerald smiled. "Topaz wouldn't like feeling restricted. We had a lot of that when we were growing up even though Mom and Dad were good about giving us as much freedom as they could. As long as she's safe, she can put up with it."

Nathan stirred in his chair. "From all I've been able to find out, everyone around you seems to be clean. No police records, unless you count your friend Derek Locke. He's had a few arrests for being drunk and disorderly."

Emerald nodded. "Derek's always been a bit volatile. His father casts a large shadow and has great expectations for his only son. In truth, I've always felt a bit sorry for him. But Derek is a great guy and has built quite a successful business."

Nathan continued. "Your ex-boyfriend has been sniffing around your sisters trying to find out your whereabouts."

Jackson could tell that surprised her. Her mouth dropped open and for a second she was speechless. She frowned and leaned closer to Nathan. "Beau? Why in the heck would he bother?"

Nathan sat back in his chair and settled his hands on his stomach. "You tell me."

Emerald looked bewildered. "We broke up months ago."

"Who broke up with whom?" Nathan queried. His wife elbowed him in the ribs and he sat up quickly. "What the heck was that for?"

"You could try being a bit more tactful, Nathan." Carly tossed Emerald an apologetic smile, still shaking her head at her husband.

"It doesn't matter." Emerald got up and began to pace the room. Jackson wanted to pull her into his lap and cuddle her. "I broke up with him when I caught him in bed with another woman."

Both women winced and then glared at the men. Nathan held up his hands to his wife. "Hey, it's not my fault." He turned back to Emerald. "Maybe he doesn't want it to be over."

She shook her head. "I made sure he knew it was over. Yes, he came around at first, apologizing and trying to get me to forgive him and take him back. But that didn't last more than a few weeks. Besides, I've only seen him a few times in the past couple of months. I'm sure it's not Beau. I don't know what to do, but I can't hide out here forever."

Jackson's hands fisted at his sides. She could damn well stay here until things were safe. "You can't go anywhere until the stalker is caught." His family all stared at him, but he ignored them. "Emerald," he all but growled her name. "It could be your ex-boyfriend, the delivery guy, your investigator or a complete stranger. Heck, it could even be

Derek Locke, even though you say he's nothing more than a childhood friend. People change. It's too dangerous for you to go home yet."

She waved her hand absently as she continued to pace. "I can't stay here indefinitely. Besides, my job here only lasts for a few more weeks."

Jackson pushed away from the table, coming to his feet. "The hell with the job." Reaching out, he snagged her arm and waited until she faced him. "Your safety is all that matters."

She glanced nervously at his family and then back at him. Why he felt the need to claim her in such a public fashion, he wasn't sure, but it was there inside him, goading him onward.

"It's not your decision, Jackson."

And that was the problem. Emerald had no real ties to him or this community. She could pick up and leave at any moment. The thought made his heart stutter and his stomach cramp. He pushed the fear aside and drew on his anger instead. "No, it's not. But it's not smart to do anything to get this guy going again, maybe even send him after your sisters."

He could have kicked himself the moment the words left his mouth. The fear in her eyes almost undid him. She wrapped her arms tightly around herself and he could see the fine trembling in her limbs. Unable to stand it any longer, he tugged her into his arms. "I'm sorry, babe." He rocked her in his embrace. "I don't think he'll bother your sisters, especially since they have bodyguards. He seems focused on you." He leaned back and stared down into her precious face. "Give it a while longer. Maybe your investigator can come up with something."

She sighed and nodded. "A few more weeks won't hurt, I guess. But I'd like to talk to my sisters. It shouldn't hurt if I call from here. I did it once already."

Jackson glanced over at Abel, who shrugged. Nathan shook his head. "It's risky." Jackson knew his brother was right, but he weighed the risk against Emerald's need.

"You can call them later tonight."

She nodded again and then pulled herself together. Taking a deep breath, she faced the audience seated at the table. "Sorry about that."

"Don't worry about it," his sister said.

"Totally understandable," echoed Carly.

They all turned to him and he knew he had to distract them from asking questions about his and Emerald's relationship. Since they both knew that she was eventually leaving, there was no point in getting into things with any of them. Their relationship was private between him and Emerald.

"There's something I've been meaning to talk to all of you about and now is as good a time as any." He pulled out Emerald's chair and seated her before yanking out his own, turning it around and straddling it.

"What is it?" He could see the curiosity in Erin's face.

He took a deep breath and took the plunge. "I want to buy your and Nathan's share of the farm."

Erin protested even as Nathan began to object. "There's no need for you to buy out our share of the farm. The damn place is yours and we all know it. It's your blood and sweat that's gone into it. If it hadn't been for you, we'd have lost it years ago."

"I agree with Nathan," his sister added, a mutinous glare on her face.

"But the two of you worked hard all these years and helped to pay it off."

"It was our home, Jackson." Nathan surged to his feet and planted his hands on the wood tabletop. "I might be younger than you, but I remember how things were. My God, you practically raised Erin and me. If it weren't for you, we wouldn't have had a roof over our heads, clothes on our backs or food on the table. If it had been left up to the old man, we'd have all starved." Anger was evident in every line of Nathan's body. "He hightailed it out of here so quick as soon as you offered to buy the place, he left a tornado in his wake. I don't know many other eighteen-year-olds who would have taken on the work of the farm and the burden of two younger siblings."

"It wasn't a burden, Nathan," Jackson said quietly. "You're my family. There's nothing I wouldn't do for either of you." He held up his hand before Nathan could protest again. "Look, you both have new families now and you," he turned to Erin, "you have a child on the way. You could use the extra money to make a fresh start."

"But where would that leave you?" Erin asked worriedly. "You'd have to take out a mortgage on the place to pay us, and besides which, I don't want your money."

"I can take care of my wife," Abel added softly but firmly.

"I know you can. I wouldn't have let you marry her if I hadn't thought that." Erin bristled, but Abel just grinned. "Look," he continued. "I have the money set aside for this. It's no hardship." Jackson glanced over at Emerald, needing to reassure himself that she was okay. Her eyes were luminous and she looked on the verge of tears. He wanted this done and his family gone so he could comfort her.

"Where the hell did you get that kind of money?" Jackson thought about ignoring his brother's question, but knew Nathan wouldn't give it a rest until he knew.

Pushing away from his chair, he stalked to the counter where he'd laid the folder. Grabbing it up, he returned to the table and dumped it in the middle. Photos scattered. "I have a hobby."

Erin reached out and picked one up. Nathan was more vocal. "So you took a few cute pictures as a hobby. So what?"

"A hobby." Jackson could hear the anger vibrating in Emerald's voice as she slowly stood and glared at Nathan, her hands fisted at her sides. Several curls had escaped from her ponytail and brushed against her chest, which was heaving with the force of her breathing. "The man is a bloody artist and his 'cute pictures' as you so quaintly put it are hanging in a gallery in New York, fetching a fine price." Jackson stood straighter, his shoulders going back as he watched Emerald in action. He'd never had someone stand up for him like this before. It made him feel strange inside, but it was kinda nice too.

"It's okay, Emerald." She was completely agitated and he wanted to soothe her. She was adorable when she was all riled up, and incredibly sexy. The fact that it was on his behalf made him want to grin from ear to ear.

"It's not okay. They need to understand just how important this is to you."

Abel and Carly were quietly examining the photos, but Nathan and Erin were watching the byplay between him and Emerald. "Look," he began. "I'm giving you the money and you can do with it what you want. End of conversation."

Of course, it wasn't the end, nowhere near it. As Nathan and Erin argued with him, Emerald and Carly began to make supper. By the time they sat down to a quick meal of fried chicken, salad and coleslaw, it was getting dark.

His brother and sister finally agreed to take a small portion of what he'd proposed. It wasn't what he'd wanted, but it was a compromise he could live with. He'd have the papers drawn up and then the farm would officially belong to him. A burden he hadn't realized he'd carried seemed to slip from his shoulders. He'd needed to own this place. To have something that was his.

Now he wanted them gone so he could celebrate with Emerald.

# Chapter Fourteen

**ဆ**

Emerald stood in the center of the kitchen and gave it one final inspection. Everything was as it should be. All the dishes were washed and put away, the leftovers were in the refrigerator and the floor had been swept. The crowd had left about ten minutes ago and Jackson had disappeared upstairs almost immediately.

She chewed on her bottom lip and then made herself stop. She'd thought she'd broken herself of that nervous habit years ago, but she'd been doing it a lot again lately. But it was no wonder she'd fallen back into her bad habit. With a stalker on her trail, she had a lot to be concerned about. And then there was Jackson.

She was rapidly falling for him, knew that she already had very deep feelings for him. Groaning, she scrubbed her hands over her face. Who was she trying to kid? She was in love with the man. It had happened so quickly, she hadn't had time to put up any barriers to protect herself. He had her heart whether he wanted it or not, and she had no idea how he felt about her. Oh, she knew that he liked her a lot and he was certainly sexually attracted to her, but she didn't know if it went any deeper than that.

Jackson was a private man. That much was abundantly evident. She couldn't believe that his family hadn't even known about his photography. Emerald raised her head, dropping her hands by her sides. She'd stood here and lectured Nathan on how important this was to Jackson. She'd had no right to interfere. This was a matter to be hashed out among family members. But she hadn't been able to sit there and let Nathan make light of Jackson's accomplishments.

Then there was the matter of the farm. Emerald shook her head in disbelief as she wandered over to stare out the window. Maybe it was because she was an outsider it was easier for her to see things as they were. Jackson loved this place, needed it in the same way that the rest of the world required air to breathe. It was in his blood. But even more, it was who he was. She understood the force driving him to create something that belonged just to him. After all, she and her sisters had done the same thing when they'd started their company.

Night had fallen over the farm. She stared up at the inky black sky and admired the yellow crest of the moon, surrounded by a scattering of stars. The natural spectacle gave her an idea for another design. She filed it in her mind for now, promising herself that she'd make some notes before she went to bed.

It was so dark here at night. Unlike the city, where artificial lights were everywhere, here there were only the lights from the house and the rest was darkness. Crossing her arms across her chest, she rubbed them, suddenly cold.

Strong arms wrapped around her from behind, chasing away the chills. Emerald leaned back against him and let his heat warm her. "Hey," he murmured as he nibbled the side of her neck.

"Hey," she breathed, tilting her neck to the side. He rewarded her by nipping at her earlobe and tugging on the silver and amethyst hoops that she wore.

"You looked deep in thought." Although she could feel his erection digging into the small of her back, she felt no impatience in him. He seemed as content as she did to just stand there and savor the closeness between them. "Emerald?"

What had she been thinking? The man always seemed to be able to scatter her thoughts. "I was just thinking about this afternoon and everything that happened with your family."

Jackson rested his chin on the top of her head and gently rubbed it back and forth. "I'm glad that everything is out in the open. It's something I've been wanting to do for a while now, but the time never seemed right until today." He hesitated before continuing. "Abel told me that Fred Kirby, the delivery guy, has been asking about you. Apparently he's been getting a bit adamant with your sisters, demanding to know where you are."

"Why didn't he tell me this?"

Jackson continued to move his chin back and forth across the crown of her head. "With everything else that went on here tonight, he forgot until he was getting aboard the truck to head home."

She nodded, trying to relax her suddenly tense muscles. Surely soft-spoken, slightly geeky Fred was no threat to her family. "He's been wanting me to talk to Beau about a computer game he's created. You know that." She'd told him everything when she'd made out her list of suspects.

"Yeah. Your investigator doesn't seem overly worried and neither, apparently, do your sisters."

She hated this. Hated being away from her family. Hated not knowing who was out there who wanted to hurt her and ruin her life. A lead weight rested in the pit of her stomach as she wondered if her life would ever be normal again. She'd never take normal, everyday living for granted for as long as she lived. Each day was a gift. Today had been an especially wonderful one.

Glancing out the window, she could see the reflection that she and Jackson made in the glass. He was so much larger than her, yet somehow they fit together in a way that looked and felt right. His big body hovered protectively behind her, his arms holding her close. She was surrounded by him, and for tonight, she wanted to bask in the closeness.

"Come upstairs with me." Jackson met her gaze in the glass and she could feel the sudden tension in his body. Did he think she'd refuse? She didn't speak, but nodded instead. He turned her, tucking her under his arm and guided her toward the stairs. He turned off the kitchen light as they left the room behind them. Emerald had a feeling she wouldn't be sleeping in her own bed tonight and that suited her just fine.

Neither of them spoke, but she didn't feel the need for words. She was content to just be in Jackson's company. They'd both talked a lot today, sharing deep, personal things. The time for talking was over. Now it was time to just feel.

He surprised her when he bypassed the bedroom and continued on to the bathroom. "Just a sec." He released her and grabbed a pack of matches off the counter, quickly lightly the four white pillar candles that were placed there. When they were all lit, he flicked off the light, leaving the room bathed in the gentle light.

She allowed him to tug her into the room. The large bathtub was already filled with water and several thick towels and washcloths had been laid out. Jackson reached for the hem of her top and began to pull it upward.

"The bathroom is much nicer than it was even a year ago. I did a lot of work on the place last winter. I tore down a wall and took part of the guestroom to make the bathroom larger. That allowed me to put in a separate shower stall and this bigger tub." Emerald tried to nod, but the tank top covered her head as Jackson tugged it off her and let it drop to the floor. Because her top had a built-in bra, she was naked from the waist up.

"God almighty," he muttered as he dropped to his knees in front of her and buried his face against her stomach. She automatically wrapped her arms around his thick shoulders, holding him to her. She sensed he was in an odd mood but wasn't quite sure what to do about it.

His lips grazed over her tummy as he nuzzled her. His tongue circled her bellybutton before snaking inside. She sucked in a breath, curling her toes into the mat beneath her feet. "Jackson?"

He muttered a curse and gave her belly one last open-mouthed kiss before surging to his feet. "Bath first." His fingers went to the button of her shorts, then the zipper. He wasted no time, tugging her shorts and panties down at the same time.

She was now totally naked, but he was still dressed. Yes, it was only his jeans, but it was still clothing. "What about you?" She reached for him, but he sucked in his stomach and took a step back.

"You do that and we won't make it into the bathtub." His jaw clenched and she could see the muscles working. The bulge in his pants was rather impressive.

"All right," she agreed as she stepped toward the bath. He was beside her in an instant, steadying her as she stepped over the side. Once she was settled back against the edge of the tub, he ripped open the front of his pants and skinned them down his legs. He hadn't bothered with underwear when he'd redressed earlier, so there was nothing holding in his erection. His cock sprang free, hard and ready, and she could see that the tip was already moist.

He took a deep breath, raking his fingers through his hair before stepping into the tub. "Sit up." She did and he slid in behind her, leaning back against the edge. He pulled her back against him until she was resting against his chest.

"This is nice." It was better than nice actually. She could feel his erection pressing against the cleft of her behind and it was heating her from the inside out.

He reached out and snagged a bar of soap and lathered his hands. When he was satisfied, he dumped the soap back into the holder. Starting at her shoulders, he began to massage his way down. She groaned as his fingers dug into her tight muscles, loosening then dissolving the tension. "That feels good," she gasped as he squeezed and released.

"I want you to feel better than good," he whispered wickedly in her ear. His hands traced the fragile line of her collarbone as his tongue traced the whorls of her ear.

Her legs moved restlessly and he hooked his own beneath hers and then spread his legs as wide as the tub would allow. It opened her completely and kept her from clamping her thighs together to find some relief from the need building inside her.

When his large, soapy hands covered the mounds of her breasts, she arched her hips. And when he traced her swollen nipples with his thumbs, she whimpered. Her pussy ached to have him inside her. Her inner muscles were clenching and relaxing in a rhythmic pattern.

"That's it," he all but purred as he rolled her nipples between his thumbs and forefingers. "You respond so quickly to me. It's such an incredible turn-on." He plucked at her nipples again, pinching them a bit harder this time.

"Jackson!" Emerald cried his name as her hips moved ineffectively. Her chest was heaving as she gasped for breath. The air around them was thick with steam and the passion flaring between them. Her body was alive, all the nerve endings tingling as desire pulsed through her. He'd only touched her breasts and she was close to coming.

"Tell me what you want." He gently bit at her earlobe before soothing the small sting away with his tongue. Water sloshed dangerously close to the edge of the tub as her hips pumped. She couldn't get much force behind her thrusts because his ankles were holding hers locked to the sides of the tub.

"I want—" She broke off on a moan as he carefully tugged on her nipples again.

"What do you want?" He continued to ply his fingers, teasing her, tormenting her. "Do you want me to touch you anywhere else? Maybe you'd like me to fuck your pussy with my fingers?" He nibbled at the base of her neck. "Would you like that?"

"Yes," she gasped. Reaching up, she grabbed one of his hands and thrust it between her thighs.

"That's it," he crooned. "Show me what you want."

She clamped her hand around his wrist and tried to get his fingers to touch the places she needed, but it was impossible. "Do it, Jackson," she demanded, thrusting her hips upward. Her back pressed hard against his cock and it was his turn to groan.

His fingers slid easily inside her. One. Two. Then finally, three. "Yes," she panted as he began to ease his fingers in and out of her hot, moist sheath. His thumb grazed her clitoris with every thrust of his fingers. It was too much. It wasn't enough.

She throbbed from head to toe. Even the roots of her hair ached as Jackson pushed her body higher and higher. The hand at her breast continued to pluck and tug at her nipples, first one and then the other. His face was buried in the curve of her neck, his breathing harsh as his fingers moved quicker and quicker in and out of her pussy.

Tension thrummed through her, getting tighter and tighter until she knew it had to snap. One final tug at her breast and a deep thrust of his fingers drove her over. Convulsing, she cried out his name. Mindlessly, she pumped her hips, wanting to milk every last sensation from the orgasm rocketing through her.

Jackson didn't stop, but kept up a steady rhythm until she was laughing and crying and begging him to stop. He slid his fingers from her core and wrapped his arms tight around her, hugging her to him.

Knowing he'd take care of her, she closed her eyes and lolled against him.

Jackson took one deep breath and then another. He was a hairsbreadth away from coming, and the last thing he wanted to do was spill his seed in the bathtub. But it wasn't easy. Emerald was so damn sexy. She gave everything to him whenever they came together. He'd never known another woman like her. The way she responded to him, it was if she'd been created especially for him. He touched her and her body immediately reacted.

Her cries and breathy moans had almost driven him over the edge. He grunted as she shifted slightly, pressing more firmly against his straining erection. She tilted back her head and when he looked down, she was smiling at him. It wasn't a big smile, but a sleepy, satisfied one.

His heart thudded heavily even as his cock throbbed. He didn't have any more time to waste. He shifted her from his lap and gripped the sides of the tub, hauling himself out. She gave a small shriek and a laugh as water sloshed everywhere, including over her. So much for being romantic. "Sorry about that," he muttered as he grabbed a towel and gave his body a few quick swipes.

"That's okay." Her dark brown eyes were soft and her lashes were spiky from where she'd grabbed the washcloth and given her face a quick wash.

What little makeup she'd been wearing had long disappeared. Not that she wore much. He was no expert, but he'd never noticed more than some lipstick and maybe some mascara, but he couldn't even be sure about that. She had such thick lashes naturally that she probably didn't need any. The fact that he was even thinking about women's makeup told him he was quickly losing his mind.

"Time to get you out of the tub." If she didn't get out soon, he'd climb back in and fuck her in the tub and he didn't want to do that. This time he wanted to take things slow and easy. That is, if he could manage to maintain enough control.

Reaching down, he helped her stand and then step out of the tub onto the thick bathmat. He flipped the plug open so that water would drain before grabbing a fresh towel and stroking it over her body. He wanted to linger, but he knew that he couldn't. His balls were so tight against his body they ached.

Tossing both towels aside, he blew out all the candles, grabbed Emerald's hand and tugged her behind him, leaving the bathroom behind. He could sense her confusion, but she went easily, not asking him any questions, for which he was very grateful. He wasn't sure he could actually explain the sense of urgency driving him. Ever since this afternoon at the pond, he'd had a need to join his body with hers and claim her.

Deep inside him there was a place that still held out a tiny hope that if he bound her to him physically with sex, then she might want to stay. Even as he thought it, he dismissed it. She had a life. He had a life. All they had was now. And by God, he planned to enjoy every moment of the now.

Entering his room, he led her over to the bed. She sat on the edge, never taking her eyes off him as he lit several candles he'd placed on the dresser and nightstand. He'd never tried his hand at being romantic before, but something about Emerald made him want to try. And he knew that women found candles romantic. Luckily for him, Erin had liked candles but hadn't taken them when she'd left home a year ago. He'd been able to find some tucked away in the storage closet.

He strode back to the bed, determination in every step. A condom was already on the bedside table. He ripped the packet open so he wouldn't have to waste time doing it later. This way, when he was ready to claim her, the condom would be ready and there would be no waiting.

"Lie back on the bed." He stood with legs braced apart, wanting to reach for her but knowing he wouldn't have much time once he touched her.

Emerald scooted up on the bed, reclining against the pillows. Something inside him relaxed slightly as she reclined. She looked incredibly right in his bed. Then she opened her arms to him and he was lost.

Kneeling up onto the bed, he braced himself over her and kissed her. Her lips always tasted sweet and he loved to lick and nibble them. They parted immediately and he stroked his tongue inside. Her hands clasped his shoulders, her nails digging into him. Just that slight touch made his cock jerk and he pulled back.

"What is it?" He could see the worry in her eyes. "Is there something wrong?"

He nodded. "Yeah." He took a breath and tried to ignore the pulsing of his cock. "If you touch me, it's gonna be all over before it really gets going."

"Oh." Her eyes widened, but he could see the pleasure in them as well. It was obvious that she liked knowing he wanted her that much.

"Yes, oh." An idea came to him as she stretched her arms over her head. "Leave them there." He sat back on his heels and watched her.

"Leave what where?"

Her breasts were firm, her nipples red from his earlier attention. He couldn't wait to taste them. "Leave your hands over your head and wrap your fingers around the slats in the headboard." He stroked a finger up the inside of her thigh, pleased when she gasped and opened her legs wider. "You can't touch me or I'll come too quickly. But I want to touch you." He paused for emphasis. "Everywhere."

Her fingers closed around the slats, but they were so thick she couldn't get a good grip on them.

"Can you hold them or do you need help?"

She licked her lips and he swallowed a groan as he followed the path of her clever tongue. "What kind of help?"

Jackson surged off the bed and hauled open a dresser drawer and pulled out a silk tie. It was one of two ties he owned. He stood at the head of the bed and stared down at Emerald, the gray silk in his hand. "It's up to you."

She stared at him for the longest time before giving a small nod. Quickly, he looped the tie around her wrists and then anchored them to the headboard. "Not too tight?"

She gave an experimental tug and shook her head. "No." Her voice was low and he detected a note of fear as well as arousal.

He climbed back on the bed, sitting between her spread thighs. "Remember, this is all about pleasure. If I do anything you don't like, just tell me. All right?" He wanted her excited but not afraid, never afraid of him.

"I trust you."

Jackson felt like yelling in triumph. His chest swelled. His cock twitched. She might not stay with him forever, but while she was here, she was his. Totally and without reservation. A man couldn't ask for more than that.

He scooted down slightly and picked up her right foot. "Even your feet are feminine and sexy." He firmly stroked the bottom with his thumb and watched her toes curl. "The arch is graceful." Raising it to his lips, he kissed the delicate curve.

"Jackson!" she shrieked, tugging at the bindings.

"Ah, you're ticklish." He moved upward to nibble on her toes, before sucking one into his mouth. Her cries turned to moans as his teeth lightly scraped over her toe.

He slowly kissed and nipped his way up her calves, first one and then the other, taking care to pay special attention to the dimples of her knees. Her breathing was getting faster. He glanced up and she was watching him with rapt attention. Her breasts were swaying with every gasp of air she pulled into her lungs. He'd taste them, and soon.

Her thighs were next. His fingers grazed the creases at the top as he licked the soft skin on the insides. He could feel her heat. Smell her arousal. Cream had already seeped from her slit and he sipped it from her thigh. She dug her heels into the mattress and arched her hips toward his mouth. He pulled back and blew gently on her heated core.

Her head thrashed on the pillow as she pulled on the bindings holding her captive. "Jackson," she breathed his name. His cock jerked in response.

Leaving her pussy behind, he rubbed his face across her softly mounded belly. He loved the feel of her skin against his face. He hadn't shaved and there was stubble on his jaw so he was careful not to press too hard against her flesh. Instead, he used it to tease her.

He nipped at the flare of her hips and the dip in her waist, moving ever upward. "I've been wanting to taste your nipples all night long. They're like juicy little strawberries just waiting to be eaten."

Emerald whimpered as he lowered his face, brushing his jaw over the soft mounds. "I love your breasts. They're large and firm and absolutely perfect." He straddled her torso as he plumped her breasts in his hands. Leaning forward, he nestled his cock between them and then squeezed them together.

He thought his head might explode, it felt so good. He moved forward, letting his cock slide between her breasts. "Open your mouth." Her eyes widened as she realized what he wanted, but she parted her lips, licking at them in anticipation. "I love your hot mouth and your sweet lips. Let me fuck your mouth." He released her long enough to pile several pillows behind her head to prop her up comfortably.

He positioned himself again, cupping her breasts in his hands and pressing them around his cock as he thrust. Her mouth opened, her tongue licking at the head as it passed. Jackson gritted his teeth as he jerked his hips back and forth, driving his cock deeper with each plunge. He thumbed her nipples as he continued and she moaned. The vibration almost sent him over the edge. If he wanted to finish this inside her tight pussy, he had to stop now.

He pulled back, but Emerald sat forward, trying to reach him. He gave a half-groan, half-laugh as he shifted out of her reach. He grabbed the open packet off the nightstand, pulled out the condom and rolled it on. "I want to be inside your hot pussy when I come this time. Your sweet mouth will have to wait for another time."

He positioned himself between her thighs, slid his hands under her ass and lifted her to his mouth. "First I'm going to eat you until you come. Then I'm going to fuck you until you scream."

Her eyes glazed over. "Yes," she hissed as he licked up one side of her slick folds and down the other. He flicked his tongue over her swollen clit before sucking it into his mouth and tugging. He could feel the cream seeping from her body, but it wasn't enough. He needed her to come again.

Holding her with one hand, he stroked the other one over her labia before sliding two fingers inside. He widened them inside her as he circled her clit with his tongue. Emerald cried out, her hips jerking as she came. Shocked by how quick she'd reached orgasm, he released her and stared down at her flushed face. Her hair was mostly out of her ponytail. Some of it was spread across his pillows while the rest of it was plastered to her face, neck and shoulders. Her hands were clenched into fists around the fabric of his tie and he wondered if it would hold, she was pulling it so tight.

When she sighed and relaxed, he positioned the head of his cock at her opening and pressed inside. Her inner muscles were swollen from her two orgasms, but he kept up a steady pressure until he was seated to the hilt. Reaching up, he tugged at the tie binding her to the headboard. He wanted his hands on her. Wanted to feel the bite of her nails in his skin as he fucked her.

Emerald helped and soon the silk tie was forgotten against the pillows. She groaned as he helped her lower her arms and he leaned down, planting kisses on her forehead, her cheeks, her nose and her chin.

Reaching up, she grabbed his head in her hands and kissed him. Hard. Jackson slid his tongue into her mouth and stroked it against hers. Now that he was inside her the sense of urgency that had been driving him was strangely missing. He was still balanced on a razor's edge and that was why he hadn't thrust yet, but he was content to just be inside her.

Gradually, the kiss gentled. Jackson raised his head to stare down at Emerald. "You're a very special lady." He brushed a damp curl off her forehead. Both their chests were slick with perspiration so they slid easily as he pulled back and then pressed forward again. "I know I said I wanted to fuck you until you screamed, but I've changed my mind." Pulling back, he pressed forward again. "I want to take it slow and easy and make it last."

"Slow can be good," she murmured as she clutched at his shoulders.

He continued the leisurely rocking motion, his eyes never leaving hers. Every now and then, he'd have to kiss her lips or her forehead or some other part of her face. There was no part of her that didn't fascinate him.

Her body clasped his cock in a tight blanket of warmth, the muscles contracting and relaxing around him. His release, when it came, was long and slow and he felt it in every cell of his body. His cock spasmed, filling the condom instead of her sheath. Emerald wrapped her arms around him and arched up. He felt her reach her own release, her pussy milking his cock until every drop of him was drained.

Totally spent, he collapsed. He managed, at the last second, to avoid completely squashing her into the mattress. He was still nestled inside her, but the bulk of his body was angled off her. It wasn't comfortable, so he dug his hands into the bed and pushed back. They both groaned when her body reluctantly released him. He rolled off the bed and staggered to the bathroom to clean up. When he returned, he blew out the candles and tugged the covers out from under Emerald before climbing into bed next to her.

She rolled into his arms, throwing one leg over his thighs and wrapping her arm around his chest. Her nose nuzzled against his chest hair before she finally settled down with a huge sigh. Her soft, even breathing told him that she'd fallen asleep that quickly.

Tucking her tighter against him, he ignored the heat and listened to the sounds of the night filter in through the open window. Totally relaxed, he drifted off to sleep.

# Chapter Fifteen

**ഇ**

Three days later, Emerald was still walking around in a daze. She'd spent each successive night in Jackson's bed. The man was insatiable, which was just fine by her. Shaking her head, she stared at the blank screen of her laptop. She was supposed to be working, but all she could think about was how yummy Jackson had looked when he'd left this morning.

She'd already been up and in the shower when he'd joined her. Jackson had made sure he'd washed every inch of her skin before he'd backed her against the tiled wall and taken her. Showering had never been so much fun.

Pushing out of her chair, she went to the refrigerator and grabbed the large container of iced tea. She'd consumed gallons of the stuff since she'd come here. The heat was still stifling and she knew that Jackson was beginning to get very worried about his trees and the crop.

She took a glass from the cupboard, as comfortable in this kitchen as she was in her own back in New York. As she poured herself some of the iced tea, she glanced out the window. New York didn't have a view like this. It wasn't just the scenery that drew her to this place, but the man who lived here. She wondered if, when this was all over, she might come back here for an occasional weekend or holiday. Maybe Jackson would enjoy that, maybe he wouldn't. Perhaps this was a time out of time for both of them and when it was over, it would be over for good. Only time would tell.

Deciding that she wasn't going to get any work done at the moment, she strolled out onto the back porch and sat in one of the chairs. It was a bit cooler here in the shade, but not by much. It was one of those summer days where it was so hot you could see and hear it.

Waves of heat shimmered in the air, which was thick and heavy. Even the insects seemed weighed down, moving slower as they buzzed around the flowers in the garden. A butterfly flitted by, landing on the porch railing not three feet from her. It slowly opened and closed its beautiful black-and-orange patterned wings. An idea for another line of products flitted through her mind as she watched a yellow butterfly glide past.

Sitting back, she rested her hands on her stomach and tilted her head back. She was wearing her usual uniform of jean shorts and a tank top. Her feet were bare and her hair was piled in a knot on the top of her head. It was the only way to survive the heat. Truth be known, she was actually enjoying it. Summer in New York was not pleasant when the temperature rose, but here it was different. There was no smog, no exhaust fumes from cars and no people with short tempers screaming. If she looked at the situation in a positive light, this was really a nice working vacation.

Thankfully, her sisters were both doing fine. Emerald still couldn't believe she'd forgotten all about calling them that first night. Okay, so she couldn't really blame herself, not with Jackson loving her so long and so…she didn't really have the words. He was wild and earthy one moment, sweet and sexy the next. Whatever he did, whichever way he made love to her, she was powerless to resist.

She squirmed in her chair as her panties dampened. Raising her glass, she had a long swallow before placing it down beside her chair. She ignored her pebbled tight nipples. What had she been thinking about? Oh yes, her sisters.

It had been the following night before she'd gotten the opportunity to call them. Jackson hadn't been pleased about her contacting them. Although the risk was minimal, he still felt that it was too much. He'd hovered around her while she'd been talking, glancing at the clock every two minutes. She'd ignored him and chatted with both Topaz and Sapphire.

"Are you sure you're all right?"

For the third time, Emerald reassured her older sister, "I'm fine. I'm perfectly safe. There's absolutely nothing to worry about."

"If you're sure."

She didn't lose patience with Topaz because she could hear the underlying worry in her sister's voice. "How about you two? Are you being careful?"

Topaz gave a most unladylike snort. Emerald laughed because it was so unlike her sophisticated older sibling. "I can barely go to the bathroom without *him* following me."

Emerald chewed on her bottom lip. She knew that Topaz was finding it very restrictive to have a bodyguard, but the Knight brothers were two of the best and Emerald was happy to have them guarding her sisters. "Any word from Dane yet?" She'd been praying that their investigator would turn up something. Anything.

Topaz sighed. "Nothing yet. But he's still looking. Oh, and Derek's been making a nuisance of himself."

"What does he want?" Emerald barely stifled a groan. She'd grown up with Derek and thought of him as a slightly obnoxious older brother. Because his father had been her parents' manager, he'd spent a large portion of his childhood in their home. They'd all hoped he'd grow out of his competitiveness, but with his father always pushing him harder and harder to succeed, he'd only gotten worse as he'd grown older.

Still, he was practically family so they all put up with him. Besides, like anyone, he had his moments where he could be incredibly sweet and kind. Like when he'd helped them produce the CD they'd given to their parents as a present. They wouldn't have been able to pull that off without Derek.

"He's just worried about you. He calls for an update almost daily, wanting to know if we've learned anything yet or if we know where you are."

"You didn't tell him, did you?" Emerald's stomach clenched. It would be just like Derek to rush out here to *protect* her.

Topaz gave a small chuckle. "No, we didn't tell him. We both know what he's like. He'd try to take over your life to protect you." She paused.

"What?" Emerald could tell there was something her sister wasn't telling her.

"Beau's been calling too. He's been adamant about getting in touch with you. Of course, Derek is convinced that Beau is your stalker."

Emerald sighed and began to pace. "That's just silly. It's been over between me and Beau for months." She felt Jackson stiffening beside her, but she ignored him. "Derek has an overactive imagination."

Topaz laughed. "Yes, he does. He's also convinced that Fred might be your stalker because he wanted you to take his computer game idea to Beau. Fred asks about you every day too."

They were no farther along in discovering who the stalker was than they were when she had left New York. "Maybe I should just come home." Tension was rolling off Jackson in waves. She didn't want to leave, not yet. But she couldn't leave her own life and her sisters in limbo indefinitely.

"No. You stay right where you are." Her words were decisive. Clipped. Topaz had gone into full big sister mode. "Derek is also worried about some country boy taking advantage of you in your vulnerable state. I told him he had nothing to worry about." There was a significant pause. "There is nothing to worry about. Right?"

Emerald avoided the question altogether, very aware of Jackson listening to every word she was saying. "I'll stay here for a while longer. But you're left handling everything at the store. That's not fair." She stopped pacing and leaned against the wall.

There was a prolonged silence on the other end of the line and Emerald breathed a sigh of relief when her older sister chose not to push the subject. "Sapphire still helps out and I hired a wonderful young art student to help out several days a week." She hesitated before plunging forward. "I'd been meaning to talk to you about this anyway. I think that you should be concentrating on developing product lines for Sisters' Jewels and not working in the store. I think that's part of why you burnt yourself out these past few years."

Emerald was struck dumb. She pulled the receiver away from her face and just stared at it. She heard her sister calling her name and reluctantly answered. "You don't want me there?" It had always been the three of them working together.

"Of course I want you here," Topaz insisted. "But only when you want to drop by, not because you have to work. I've already discussed it with Sapphire. She's agreed to let me hire someone else full-time so that she can work on her jewelry designs. There's also some talk of her doing a line that would be mass-produced and marketed at some of the better department stores."

"When did this happen?" Emerald felt like her world was changing around her while she was hidden away.

"We'd been approached before, you know that. Sapphire's come up with a line that she thinks would work. They've agreed to let her have final say over quality control, so she's happy." She could hear the concern in Topaz's voice. "This would allow Sapphire to really get on her feet financially and make a name for herself away from Sisters' Jewels. I think she needs that."

Emerald nodded. Her sister, although incredibly talented, had always been the most insecure of the three of them. "Then she should do it. As long as it makes her happy." It was hard to be making these decisions so far away from her family.

Usually, when there were major life or business decisions to be made, the three of them would order in and make a night of it sprawled out in their living room. Tears burned in her eyes. She really missed her sisters.

A large hand rested on the small on her back. She could sense Jackson's concern when she glanced back at him. His gaze narrowed when he noticed the tears in her eyes, but he said nothing. Instead, he wrapped his arms around her shoulders and tugged her back until she was leaning against his chest.

"Don't worry, Em." Her sister's soft voice washed over her. "We'll get it all worked out."

"I know." Her sister rarely called her by the shortened version of her name anymore. They all used their full names for professional reasons. Tears filled her eyes and she blinked them back as she cleared her throat. "I've been working again."

"Really?" She could hear the pleasure and surprise in Topaz's voice.

"Yeah."

"When can I see it?" The businesswoman was back in full force.

Emerald laughed, as she knew her sister had intended her to. "When it's done."

"Well then, why are we still talking?" Topaz softened her voice again. "I love you. Everything will be okay."

Tears threatened again. She wanted to hug both her sisters so badly at the moment. To feel their familiar embrace. "Mom and Dad still don't know anything?"

"No, and I think that's a mistake. Dad is not going to be very happy about this and I don't even want to think about what Mom is going to say."

Emerald didn't want to think about how this was going to hurt her parents. "There's nothing they could do except worry.

They've planned that extended trip to Europe for months. Let them enjoy it."

"For now, I'll let it go. But if we don't find any answers in the next few weeks or if something happens, I'm calling them."

"Okay. I can live with that."

"I have to go. My bodyguard is getting antsy. He says we've been on the phone for too long." Emerald could hear impatience, annoyance and something else that she couldn't quite place in her sister's voice.

"You sure you're okay with him?"

"Don't worry," Topaz replied dryly. "I can handle John Knight."

They said their goodbyes and Emerald hung up the phone. She'd barely had the receiver back in the cradle when Jackson scooped her into his arms and carried her straight upstairs to bed. She hadn't had time to think, let alone worry about anything.


The sound of a vehicle approaching broke into her reverie. Jumping from her chair, she hurried into the house, swearing under her breath when she realized that she'd left her glass outside. There was nothing to be done about it now. She closed the back door and locked it. It was probably only Erin or Nathan. She saw quite a bit of both of them these days. They were always checking on her to make sure she was okay. But she couldn't take any chances. As far as the rest of the town was concerned, she was long gone.

She went into her room off the kitchen and carefully tugged back a corner of the curtain. She tensed when she didn't recognize the vehicle, but relaxed when she saw the familiar logo on the side. It was the mail truck. Sweat trickled down her back, partly due to the heat, but partly due to fear. It was so easy to relax and feel safe, but there was still someone out there who meant her harm.

Watching from the window, Emerald waited as the mailman climbed out of his truck clutching a box. He ambled over to the door and knocked. He tried the handle, jiggling it several times before just leaving the package on the porch. Turning, he strolled back to the truck and hauled himself back inside. Seconds later, the truck was barreling down the road. She was alone again.

Unease filled her as she went straight to the door and unlocked it. It was just nerves, she assured herself as she tugged the door open. The package was indeed addressed to Jackson and the tension seeped from her body.

Shaking her head at herself, she leaned down and picked up the box, carrying it in and laying it on the kitchen table. She'd barely laid it down when the phone rang. She always let the answering machine pick up. Always. She wasn't supposed to be here. But she was so rattled by what had just happened, she didn't think. It was an automatic response that had her lifting the receiver and saying hello.

Dead air met her. She chewed on her bottom lip, not knowing if she should just hang up or continue talking. She could always pretend it was a wrong number. "Hello."

"Whore," the distorted voice spit at her. She froze, the receiver glued to her hand. "Did you think I wouldn't find you?"

"Who is this?" Anger surged through her blood, driving out all thoughts of caution.

Laughter filled her ear. Something was being used to distort the voice, but she could tell it was male. She pressed down the record button on the answering machine and prayed that it would work.

"I bought you that beautiful dress and you ran from me. That," he paused and it seemed even more menacing than his words, "displeased me."

Shivers raced down her spine. This guy was crazy. "Why would you send me a wedding gown? I don't even know you."

"Don't you?" His words were eerily calm. "Come home and all will be forgiven. Stay there and face the consequences."

"What consequences?" Fear for her sisters shot through her. Her hands shook as she clutched the phone.

"You'll see," he continued in that placid, almost pedantic tone. "Oh, did you get the package I sent you?" He was laughing when he hung up on her.

She turned to face the brown-wrapped package sitting in the middle of the table. It was addressed to Jackson. Terror unlike any she'd ever known filled her. Her stalker had found her. He knew where she was and he was threatening Jackson. She had to warn him first. Then she had to leave, and quickly. It was the only way to protect him.

But first, there was something else she had to do. Her fingers dialed the number posted by the phone. She felt detached, somehow removed from the situation. Logically, she knew it was from shock and fear, but she couldn't seem to care. When a man picked up on the other side, she didn't speak at first but could hear his deep voice on the other end.

"Who is this?" he repeated.

"Nathan?" she managed to push the word past her frozen lips.

"Emerald? What's wrong?"

She was trembling so hard that she had to lean against the wall for support. "He called here."

Nathan was quickly putting things together. "The stalker?"

She nodded until she remembered he couldn't see her. "Yes." The ice that had been encasing her began to thaw as anger began to flow hotly through her veins. "He sent a package too. And Nathan," she didn't quite know how to tell him this.

192

"I'm on my way there now, Emerald. Lock the doors and stay inside. Keep away from the windows."

"Nathan," she yelled. "The package was addressed to Jackson."

There was silence for a second on the other end and then Nathan continued as if she hadn't said anything that was particularly upsetting. "Where is the package?"

"On the kitchen table. Did you hear what I said?"

"Yes." His voice was clipped. "Go upstairs. Get as far away from the package as you can without leaving the house."

"Ohmigod. You don't think it's dangerous, do you?" Stupid question. Of course he thought it was dangerous. He wouldn't have told her to get away from it if he didn't.

"We're not going to take any chances. I'm going to have to call in the bomb squad. We don't have one here in Meadows, so it's gonna take a while to get them here." She could hear the sound of traffic and knew Nathan was moving as he talked to her. "I'll be there as quick as I can. When you see me, come downstairs and wait by the back door."

"Okay." From the noises she was hearing, she could tell that Nathan was in his vehicle and already on his way.

"Hang up this phone and go upstairs. I'll call back and you can answer on the cordless phone in Jackson's room."

Emerald licked her dry lips, wishing she had her iced tea. Was it only a few minutes ago she'd been sitting on the porch enjoying a perfect summer's day? It seemed a lifetime ago. "I'm hanging up now. Oh, and I taped the conversation with him. Or at least I think I did."

"Good. That's good." Nathan's calm, deep voice was reassuring. She knew she should hang up but didn't want to severe the connection between them. "Honey, hang up the phone and I'll call you right back."

She took a deep breath. She could do this. There was no reason to be this jumpy. It was just a phone call and a package. Nothing to hurt her. "Okay, I'm hanging up now." She turned to glance at the package one final time as she hung up the phone.

Shoes, she needed shoes in case she needed to run. Racing to her room, she grabbed her sneakers and a pair of socks. She'd put them on upstairs. As she entered the kitchen, the phone rang. Nathan was quick. She passed the table and was almost to the stairs when the explosion hit.

Something knocked her in the back and sent her flying through the air. She landed facedown at the base of the stairs, her face hitting the floor hard. Her head spun. Her entire body felt as if it were on fire. She coughed and realized that smoke was filling the air. Was the house on fire?

Digging her fingers into the floor, she dragged her body toward the front door. There was no going back through the kitchen. She thought about her laptop and moaned. It was certainly destroyed along with all of her new work. Which wouldn't matter at all if she didn't get out of here. It was getting harder to breathe and she coughed again.

The door seemed to be getting farther away rather than closer. Still, Emerald persevered. One inch at a time, she pulled herself closer to safety. When her hand hit the door, she almost cried in relief. The handle seemed a long ways away, but she pulled herself up, ignoring the agony in her back. Wrapping her hand around the knob, she turned and tugged. It didn't open. She tugged again, harder. Frantic now, she pulled again and again until a little voice in her head reminded her that the front door was locked. Jackson made her keep it locked at all times when she was home alone.

It was hard, but she forced her hand away from the knob and found the locks and turned them. Her head was spinning and something was in her eyes. She swiped at them and stared at her hand when it came back bloody. A siren rang out in the distance and she knew that Nathan was coming for her.

Determined now, she grabbed the doorknob, turned it and pulled. The door came back with such force it hit her.

Moaning, she dropped back to the floor. Fresh air hit her, reminding her of what she needed to do.

Shoving her shoulder against the screen door, she pushed it open, all but toppling onto the porch. She lay there totally spent, half in and half out of the house. Just as the world closed in around her, she thought she heard someone calling her name.

# Chapter Sixteen

Terror unlike anything Jackson had ever known flooded his veins as he raced toward the house. He'd been on his way home for an early lunch when he'd heard the explosion. He'd started to run when he saw the smoke and knew it was coming from the direction of the house.

Yanking his cell phone from his back pocket, he dialed the house. It rang and rang, but no one answered. Swearing, he disconnected and dialed Nathan's number.

"Emerald!" his brother's voice barked into his ear.

His gut clenched. "No, it's me. There's been an explosion at the house. Call the fire department and get out here."

"I'm almost there and the fire trucks are just behind me. Emerald heard from the stalker. He'd sent a package to the house addressed to you."

Bomb! Neither of them said it even though both of them were thinking it. "Just get here," Jackson snapped as he cut off the call.

He ran faster than he'd ever run in his life, his long legs eating up the distance. He practically flew through the orchards, past row upon row of apple trees, his feet thudding heavily against the parched ground. If Emerald were dead… He couldn't even finish the thought. His chest felt hollow, his legs like rubber, but he ran.

He broke from the fields and sped across the yard, taking the stairs in one leap. Smoke billowed out the back door, thick and oily. Ignoring it, he yanked aside what was left of the back door and plunged into the kitchen. Coughing, he tried to see, but the smoke obscured his vision. "Emerald!" He called her name again and again as he felt his way around the room.

He ducked into her room, but it was empty. Stepping into her small bathroom, he grabbed a towel and plunged it in the sink as he turned the cold water tap on full. When the towel was soaking wet, he held it over his head and mouth and hurried back into the kitchen.

Jackson dropped to the floor and began to search. He heard the crackle of fire but ignored it. Nothing mattered but finding Emerald. His hand hit the doorway leading to the stairs. Maybe she'd made it upstairs. "Emerald!" he yelled and then went into a spasm of coughing.

He continued to move forward, sweeping his hand out around him as he went. He paused when he thought he heard something. "Emerald!" he called again and then listened. There it was again, a soft moan off to his right.

Scrambling as fast as he could, he made his way to the front door. Lying halfway in and out of the house was Emerald. Blood covered her back, making him sick to his stomach.

"Emerald? Sweetheart?" He tossed away the almost dry towel as he rolled her over, wincing as he saw the smeared blood on her face and forehead. He knew it was dangerous to move her, but he didn't really have any choice. He had no idea how bad the fire was, but the smoke itself was a hazard.

Picking her up, he stumbled into the grass as Nathan swerved into the yard and came to a screeching halt. His brother jumped out and hurried toward him. "Is she all right?"

Jackson shook his head and coughed. "I'm not sure, but I couldn't leave her in there." He sank down into the dirt with Emerald still clutched tight in his arms.

A multitude of sirens filled the air and within minutes the entire yard was filled with fire trucks, police cars, an ambulance and the vehicles from every volunteer firefighter in the area.

Jackson didn't care about the fire. The only thing he cared about was the woman being gently loaded onto a stretcher. He held her hand tight, refusing to let it go. Harry Flynn, the paramedic on board, didn't even try to stop him from going with them, but just told him to stay out of his way. Jackson hunched down on the bench across from her as Harry worked on her back. It seemed that the cuts on her face were superficial and most of the blood was from her nose. Jackson winced as he imagined the force with which she must have hit the floor.

Emerald moaned and he squeezed her hand tighter. "It's okay, Emerald. I'm here."

She moved her lips and he leaned closer to hear her. She licked her dry, chapped lips and tried again. His name was more of a breath than a spoken word, but he heard it, felt it, right in the center of his chest.

"I'm here," he told her again. Reaching out, he brushed her hair out of her face. She was lying on her stomach so he could only see part of her face. What he could see was battered and smoky, but to him she was still beautiful. All that mattered was that she was alive and that she would recover.

Two hours later he was sitting in a corner of the waiting room with his head bowed and his arms resting on his legs. His hands were clasped and he was doing something he hadn't done much of in years—he was praying.

He'd had way too much time to think in the last two hours and he'd faced some pretty hard truths. He loved Emerald. There was no two ways about it. He didn't care if the house burned to the ground as long as she was okay. He'd have rather died in there today with her than to live without her. He released the death grip he had on his hands and rubbed one of them over the back of his neck. Man, he had it bad.

He also loved her enough to protect her and then set her free. Whatever it took to make her happy was what he wanted.

It was enough. It had to be because it was the only choice he had.

He looked up when footsteps approached, but it wasn't the doctor. It was his family. He wasn't surprised to see them all here and stood as they approached. Nathan and Abel looked grim and concern was written all over Erin's expressive face.

"How is she?" Erin threw herself into his arms and he automatically closed them around her, drawing strength from her nearness.

"I don't know. No one has told me anything yet. I guess they're still working on her."

Nathan glanced his way and then headed for the nurses' station. As a police officer and part of the official investigation, he might be able to find out something. Jackson sure hoped so, because he was quietly going crazy waiting for news.

Erin drew back and stared up at him, her blue eyes cloudy with distress. "How are you?"

He shook his head. "I'm fine."

Erin looked as if she might argue the point, but thankfully let it drop. "The house is surprisingly okay. There wasn't as much fire damage as we thought. Mostly smoke. The kitchen table and floor are a write-off and the room will need to be painted from top to bottom. Some of the kitchen cabinets may have to be replaced. I'm not sure about that. Other than that, a good cleaning will go a long way to setting the place back to rights."

He gave her a quick squeeze before releasing her. "Thanks for sticking around until the fire was out."

She patted him on the arm. "The police and the fire marshal are out there investigating, but there's little doubt that the package contained some kind of bomb."

They all paused when Nathan came striding back. "The nurse said that the doctor would be out in a minute."

Jackson nodded as he raked his fingers through his hair. He hated not being able to do anything. Emerald was somewhere behind the large swinging doors at the end of the hallway, and she was alone. He needed to be with her.

"Why don't you sit down?"

His sister's voice penetrated his thoughts and he gave her a soft smile. "Don't worry about me, honey. Other than smelling a bit smoky, I'm fine."

"Did the doctor check you for smoke inhalation?" Abel stepped up beside his wife, wrapping his thick arm around her shoulders.

"Yeah." Jackson realized that his voice was slightly hoarse. That, coupled with the fact that he was covered in soot, was making him appear much worse than he was. "I'll be back to normal in a day or two."

Erin looked relieved and even the tight set of Nathan's shoulders eased slightly. Jackson felt anything but relaxed or relieved. That wouldn't happen until he knew what was going on with Emerald. As if his thoughts had finally summoned him, the doctor pushed through the door and headed toward the waiting room. Jackson met him halfway.

"How are you holding up, Jackson?" He'd known Dr. Williams his entire life, but right now he wanted to shake the man to get him to hurry.

"I'm fine. How's Emerald?"

"She's a lucky lady. Whatever device set off the explosion, it wasn't all that powerful, but she's still fortunate that she wasn't standing right next to it when it went off. The fact that her back was turned means that it took the brunt. We removed some flying pieces of debris, mostly shards of wood from the kitchen table. She hit her face when she fell forward, but her nose isn't broken. Mostly, she's bruised and shaken. There are some minor burns on her back as well, but they'll heal with little problem." He clapped his hand on Jackson's shoulder.

"She'll be hoarse for a few days because of the smoke, but physically she'll be as good as new in a week or two."

Jackson cleared his throat, almost overwhelmed by the news. "Can I see her?"

"Sure. She's been asking for you. After you see her, we'll get her cleaned up and moved to a room."

Nathan stepped forward. "Is someone with her now?"

Dr. Williams nodded. "The officer you sent showed up about the same time I started working on her. He's posted right outside her door."

Jackson stared at his brother, thankful for the precaution. It hadn't even occurred to him that Emerald might be in danger here at the hospital, but it should have. "Have you contacted Hatcher?" It was important that Emerald's investigator in New York know about this latest development.

"Yeah. I talked to him and the detective in charge of the case back in New York. We'll be sending them all the information on the bombing as soon as we get a report together. In the meantime, he knows what's going on." Nathan hesitated. "I talked to her sister's bodyguard as well. He answered the phone when I called, so I explained the situation to him. You should probably call them later."

"I will." He rubbed his hands over his soot-covered jeans and glanced at the doctor.

"Follow me." The doctor gave them all a nod and headed back toward the heavy closed door of the emergency room.

"Don't worry about a thing with the house," Erin said. "We'll take care of everything." He turned and gave Erin a grateful smile as he stepped inside the doors. They swung shut behind him, shutting his family on the other side. He followed the doctor to a room at the end of the hall. A uniformed officer nodded as they passed. That was one of the benefits of living in a small town—a stranger would stand out like a sore thumb.

"She's a bit groggy, but don't worry. She truly will be fine."

"Thanks, Doc." Jackson pushed through the door, pausing just inside.

Emerald was lying facedown on the pristine white mattress. He could smell the smoke from here. Or maybe it was himself he smelled. He took a deep breath and went to her side. Her face was pale and he could see the smattering of small cuts on her cheek. Her nose looked slightly swollen, but not too bad considering the blood she'd had on her face.

His hand was trembling ever so slightly when he reached out to stroke her hair. The ends were a bit singed, but nothing a trim wouldn't take care of. He swallowed back the lump forming in his throat. He was so damn grateful she was alive.

She stirred and her eyes fluttered open. "Jackson," she croaked.

He winced at the sound of her voice. Her throat sounded incredibly sore. "I'm here." Stroking the side of her face, he leaned closer to her. "Everything is okay. You're going to be fine."

"The house?"

"To hell with the house. I've got insurance." He wasn't sure it would cover a mad bomber, but he didn't care. She flinched at his harsh words and he gentled his voice as much as he could. "The house isn't important. The only thing that matters is that you're going to be all right."

She nodded, her fingers plucking at the sheet beside her. "I'm sorry." Her red-rimmed eyes filled with tears.

Jackson eased down onto the mattress next to her, careful not to jar her. "What are you sorry for?"

"I brought all this trouble to you." A lone tear spilled out of the corner of her eye, nearly breaking his heart.

"I'm not sorry." He brushed her hair over her shoulder and gently wiped the tear from her cheek. His thumb caressed the side of her face. "I'm glad you came into my life." Leaning down, he brushed his lips lightly against hers.

Emerald gave a soft sigh and parted her lips. It was a brief kiss, but they both needed the connection, the intimacy of it. Jackson sat back, lightly stroking his hand over her shoulder. "Me too," she breathed and then started to cough.

"You need to rest." He started to stand, but her hand shot out, catching his. She winced as the movement shifted her battered body. "Don't worry," he promised. "I'm not going farther than that chair."

Her fingers slowly released his and she sighed. "You should go and get cleaned up. Maybe check on your house. It's selfish of me to keep you here."

"If it's selfish, then I'm selfish too," he assured her. "I don't want to leave you." The memory of hearing the explosion and the realization that Emerald was inside the burning house was still too fresh. He wanted to haul her into his arms and keep her there for at least a month, if not longer.

Her eyes were beginning to droop. Staying awake was becoming more difficult for her by the second. "My sisters?"

He knew what she wanted. "I'll call them."

"Don't let them come here." He could hear the frantic worry in her voice and sought to calm her.

"I'll make sure that they stay where they are and that their bodyguards are aware of the situation." Bending forward, he brushed a kiss over each of her eyes. "You just rest and concentrate on getting better. I'll take care of things until that happens."

"All I need is a nap."

He almost smiled at the fierceness in her voice. He had no doubt she'd be back to her usual independent self in no time at all. In the meantime, he'd watch out for her. "I know," he soothed.

She snuggled her face into her pillow and sighed. "My work burned," she mumbled as she drifted off to sleep.

Jackson winced, knowing that was another blow to her that could be laid at the stalker's feet. There was nothing more to say, so he stood and watched her until he was sure she was asleep. He was just moving away from the bed when the door opened. A nurse walked in. She was an older lady and had been a friend of his mother years ago. "Mrs. Patterson," he nodded.

"How are you holding up, Jackson?" By now he had no doubt that everyone in town knew about his and Emerald's relationship. He'd worry about the implications of that later. Right now, he was more worried about Emerald's rest being disturbed.

"I'm okay," he stated briskly. "She just went to sleep." He could hear the challenge in his own voice and saw the twitch of the nurse's lips as she tried not to smile. "I'm being an ass, aren't I?"

Mimi Patterson shook her head. "No, you're being concerned." She kept her voice low, which Jackson appreciated. "We'll clean her up when she wakes. Why don't you go home and get cleaned up." She shook her head as she reached out to pat his arm. "Or at least go to your sister's place if yours is too bad. I'm sorry about the fire."

"Thanks." Jackson's head was spinning with the sudden realization that he might not even have any clean clothing. Even if the upstairs was okay, it was going to smell of smoke. "I'm not leaving her."

She nodded as if she'd figured that would be his reply. "Then why don't you at least get someone in your family to get you a change of clothing? You can shower here." Her eyes were kind and understanding as she gave him a soft smile of encouragement.

"Yeah. I can do that." He glanced over at Emerald's still form, huddled under the sheet.

"I'll stay with her until you get back. All of them are still in the waiting room." She squeezed his forearm and then strode briskly around to the far side of the bed.

Jackson's hands clenched at his sides. It was hard for him to leave her now that he was finally by her side, but he knew the nurse was right. He'd feel better if he showered and changed. He'd get Nathan to loan him some clothes until Erin could get back out to the house and assess the situation better. If his clothing wasn't too bad, she could launder some for him and pack him a bag. He wasn't leaving this hospital until Emerald went with him.

Determined, he strode out of the room and back toward the waiting area.

Emerald slowly became aware of her surroundings. Her head was pounding, her throat was parched and her entire body was one big ache. A moan escaped her lips as she shifted.

A hand brushed the side of her face and she frowned. That touch was very familiar. Forcing her eyelids to open, she blinked when she saw only darkness. It took a few seconds for the eyes to adjust and for her to realize that it was night. The drapes in the room were open and the light of a lone streetlight illuminated the room. She was in the hospital. Memory came flooding back and she moaned again.

"Emerald." Of course it was Jackson touching her. He'd saved her life.

She licked her lips and tried to speak but all that came out was a croak. The tip of a straw brushed her lips and she latched on to it and began to suck. Cool, refreshing water flowed into her mouth and down her dry throat, the abused tissues sucking in the life-giving fluid.

"Take it easy," he admonished softly when she began to cough. He eased the straw away until she'd stopped and then pressed it back against her mouth. This time she was more cautious. He patiently waited until she'd had almost two cups of water and was satisfied.

Feeling much better, she stared at him, trying to see his features in the dark. "Why are you still here?" It was obviously the middle of the night. Not that she wasn't happy he was here. She was, but he had a multitude of problems of his own to deal with.

"I told you I wouldn't leave you." His voice was low and deep and filled with determination. Of course he was here. He wouldn't be Jackson, the man she loved, if he wasn't here.

"What about the farm?" It was hard to talk, but there were things she needed to know.

"The farm is fine. Erin and Abel will handle things for a day or two. Nothing for you to worry about." He stroked her hair and her face as if to reassure himself that she was truly okay.

"Of course I'm worried. The apple crop will be ready to start harvesting any day now and your house was just torched by a maniac stalker." Her voice rose with each word until it was a hoarse shout.

"Erin says that the house isn't that bad. The main damage is in the kitchen, but the rest of the place just needs a good cleaning."

Emerald thanked God for small miracles. "I'll pay for any damages, of course." She'd have to contact the bank and draw on some of her savings.

"You'll do no such thing." Anger, tight and controlled, vibrated in his voice. Uh-oh. Jackson was well and truly pissed with her.

"It's only right," she began, but was cut off when he lifted her into his arms. She was so shocked that it took a second to realize that he had avoided the bandages on her back. Even angry, he was incredibly careful with her, concerned about her well-being. He settled back into his chair with the sheet tucked firmly around her, not even disturbing the IV that was pumping fluids and medication in her abused body. She hadn't even noticed the needle in her hand until he'd moved her. "I'll take care of the farm, Emerald." It was said with such finality that she knew the subject was closed. For now. She'd bring it up again when she was released from the hospital.

"When am I getting out of here?" The darkness surrounded them as his arms wrapped around her. She felt safe and cared for. The heavy thud of his heart was a comfort as she leaned her face against his chest. He'd showered and changed. She inhaled clean scent of soap instead of smoke, but beneath it was the unique smell of Jackson — warm, musky and all male.

"Tomorrow afternoon, the doctor said."

She nodded. "I don't smell like smoke anymore." That wasn't exactly true. There was still a light tinge of it, but it was mostly gone.

"Yeah, the nurse gave you a sponge bath earlier. You were mostly out of it at the time." Emerald nodded as a vague memory flitted through her brain. "I brushed your hair, but we didn't wash it. That's why you still smell some of the smoke. The nurse gave me some dry shampoo, she called it, to brush through your hair. It helped some."

Conversation lagged as they both enjoyed the pleasure of simply touching one another. Emerald rubbed her hand over his chest, wishing it were his bare skin instead of a soft cotton T-shirt. Jackson ran his hand up and down her arm. The only sound in the room was the gentle inhalation and exhalation of their breaths, punctuated by the background noises of the hospital.

"You should sleep." The low rumble of his voice made her smile.

"So should you," she countered.

He gave a short bark of laughter and she felt his lips brush the top of her head. Maybe it was the dark of the night. Maybe it was the intimacy of the situation, but she found herself wanting to talk about Jackson, to find out as much as she could about the man she loved. Finally, she asked a question that had been troubling her since her arrival at the farm. "Why don't you have any animals on your farm?"

Jackson gave a huge sigh. "If I answer, will you promise to sleep?"

"As long as I'm satisfied with your answer," she retorted.

He snorted and then rested his head back against the chair. "When I was a kid, my grandfather had a couple of horses. When he died, my father sold all but the oldest one. Nobody wanted him. I loved old Elvis."

"Elvis?" she laughed. She could sense more than see Jackson's smile as she tilted up her head to look at him. The light from the window outlined his features, making them appear blunter and more rugged than usual.

"Yeah, Granddad was a big Elvis Presley fan. Anyway, Elvis the horse died the next winter and that was the end of all the horses. We had a couple of dogs when we were kids, a few cats. But that was mostly Mom's doing and not my father's."

"He didn't like animals?"

Jackson lowered his head until he was looking straight at her. "My father didn't like anyone or anything. At least not back then. I have no idea what he's like with his new wife."

"You don't know?" It was appalling to her that he and his siblings seemed to have no relationship with their father. Her family was so close.

"Never met her. The old man moved away just after I turned eighteen and bought the farm from him. He landed in Florida, met a woman and remarried. I'm not even sure where he lives now. We lost contact several years ago."

"That's sad." Her heart ached for Jackson. He'd been so young to be abandoned by the only parent he'd had.

"That's life," he countered. "Now go to sleep."

"But what about now? Why don't you have a dog or a cat?"

His arms tightened slightly around her before they relaxed. "Habit, I suppose. The old barn cat died a couple years back and then when Erin and Nathan moved out, there didn't seem to be much point."

That struck Emerald like a punch to the gut. Jackson had learned the hard way that animals die and people don't stay. He kept to himself so that no one or nothing could hurt him. Emerald swallowed hard. She wasn't sure that she was any different to him.

Would he send her on her way when this was over or would he ask her to stay? Was Jackson even capable of loving her or had he closed himself off to that deep emotion? Oh, she knew he cared about her. She was his lover and he was a decent and responsible man. She cringed at the thought. She didn't want to be just another responsibility to him.

Too much to think about right now. Her temples were throbbing and her lungs ached. As if he knew she was hurting, Jackson began to stroke her hair, occasionally rubbing her temple. "Sleep. Everything will seem better in the morning."

She wasn't sure of that, but she closed her eyes and snuggled closer to him, absorbing his caring and his heat. The air-conditioning in the hospital made her shiver. Jackson pulled her closer and the steady beat of his heart lulled her to sleep.

# Chapter Seventeen

ഔ

"I need to leave today." She said the words for at least the tenth time since she was released from hospital. Jackson ignored her this time as he had the other nine times. "You know I'm right," she continued.

He turned and pinned her to the seat with a hot blue gaze. She swallowed hard and tried to ignore the fluttering in her heart and in her womb. "You're not going anywhere. Not until this stalker is caught. If you leave now," he continued reasonably, "you might draw the threat back to your sisters in New York."

That was a deep concern. She'd called her sisters this morning and had spent a half-hour on the phone convincing them that she was fine. Topaz had taken it upon herself to call their parents in London and now they were on their way back to New York. Emerald didn't have it in her heart to be angry at her sister, although at this point, she'd have preferred to have her parents as far away from her as possible. At least that way she'd know they were safe.

"No arguments?" Jackson was staring at her with concern now as they drove down the highway toward the farm. Abel or Nathan, she wasn't sure who, had driven his truck to town this morning and delivered it and a change of clothing for both of them to the hospital. Emerald appreciated the loose cotton shorts and oversized T-shirt that Erin had packed for her. She wouldn't be wearing a bra for a while, although her back was much better today.

"No. I know I can't go back to New York, but I can't stay here either." She was a danger to whomever she was around.

"You can't run forever, Emerald. Now that we know that he knows you're here, we can take steps to protect you."

She swallowed hard as she stared out the window. Jackson would protect her, but at what cost to himself and his property? "It's not just you who might be at risk. Have you thought about that?" She turned as far as the seat belt would allow and faced him. "Your family might be at risk as well."

"Abel and Nathan will take care of themselves and the women." He sounded so confident and so chauvinistic she wanted to smack him.

"They can't stop a bomb, Jackson." She'd done everything to get him to understand, but he was being stubborn. Well, she was stubborn too and as soon as she felt up to it, she was packing her bags and leaving. She ignored the pain deep in her chest and the churning in her gut. She *had* to leave to protect him.

He didn't answer her, but she hadn't expected him to. There was nothing more to be said as far as she was concerned. Jackson kept his eyes on the road, but his fingers tightened perceptibly around the steering wheel. Sighing, Emerald turned to peer out the side window. She was going to miss the unspoiled countryside around her. For a city girl, she'd gotten used to the peace and quiet real quick.

Jackson turned up the road to the driveway. They were here to pick up some clothing before heading over to Erin's place. Trucks and a few cars lined the road, with more parked around the back of the house.

"What the heck…" Jackson pulled to a stop, turned off the ignition and sat back and stared. The house was a beehive of activity. A slow smile turned up the edges of his mouth, softening the harsh planes of his face.

"What's going on?" Men were talking as they sawed and painted. Women were trooping to and fro, carrying buckets of dirty water outside and dumping them before turning around and marching back inside.

"Looks like the neighbors have come to call." Jackson opened his door and climbed out as Abel strode toward him. Not wanting to miss anything, Emerald pushed open her door and slid out of her seat, ignoring her aches and pains.

"Glad you're here." Abel slapped Jackson on the back. The blow would have felled a lesser man. Abel's hands were the largest she'd ever seen. Jackson never even flinched.

"What's all this?" Jackson sounded more bemused than concerned.

"Everyone heard what happened." Abel turned to her with regret on his face. "The entire town knows about you, the stalker and the bomb."

"How?"

Abel gave a chuckle. "Nothing works quite like the country grapevine. Folks monitoring the police band heard about the bombing. The firefighters and paramedics knew about you. The hospital staff knew you were brought in because of your injuries in the blast."

Abel arched his eyebrow, making her laugh. "Okay. I get the picture." She watched the beehive of activity with growing interest.

"Nathan decided the best thing to do was to set things straight. So he went to the diner yesterday afternoon and laid things out for folks. Carly's been doing the same all day today. We figured a stranger would be easier to spot if everyone in town and the surrounding area was looking for him."

Emerald was uncomfortable with the idea that everyone knew her business, but it did make sense. "But what does that have to do with all these people?"

"Heck, darlin'. Folks started arriving as soon as the police gave the okay. The actual fire damage was minimal. Most of it came from smoke and water. People have been cleaning and scrubbing throughout the night. This is the second shift."

"Wow." Emerald didn't quite know what else to say. The community of Meadows was unlike any she'd ever experienced. It also said a lot about Jackson that all these people would leave their busy lives to come and help.

"We had to put in a couple new windows in the kitchen, but everything in the room has been cleaned and floor has been hauled up. We also decided it was better to just haul out the walls and redo the drywall. The bottom cabinets were a write-off, so we tore them out and replaced them. Paul Werner at the hardware store sent out some that will match the existing ones."

Jackson nodded as he watched the activity. A few folks had looked their way, but for the most part, they just kept on working. Emerald wondered if he was as overwhelmed as she was. Sidling up beside him, she tucked her hand into his. His fingers closed around hers as he tugged her closer.

"We should get you inside." Voice gruff with emotion, Jackson led her toward the porch.

People stopped as they approached. Some nodded while others stopped to offer their sympathy about her injuries and the damage to the house. Names flew at her so quickly she couldn't keep track of them all. There was what had to be the entire Applebee family, the Martins, the Werners, Dirk Marshall and his brother Peter, the Essex sisters and the list went on and on.

A few of them mentioned that they were fans of her parents' music. Emerald felt their genuine concern as she made her way into the chaos of the kitchen. She blinked at the transformation. New walls had been installed, taped, plastered and were now in the process of being primed. Pristine cabinets were going in and a new sink was being installed. The floor was nothing but plywood, but Emerald had a feeling that would be changed by the end of the day. Two new windows replaced the ones that had been damaged in the blast.

Erin walked toward her with a huge grin on her face. "What do you think?"

Emerald's answer came straight from the heart. She didn't even have to pause to think about it. "I think you people are amazing."

A large man of about fifty with a wild, gray beard gave a hoot of laughter, but she could see the pleased gleam in his eyes. "This is nothing, little lady. We'd have rebuilt the whole house if we'd had to."

She could see the sincerity in his eyes and again marveled at this place and the people who lived here. "Since this was my fault, I want to help."

The man was already shaking his head. "From what I heard, it ain't your fault. You just got out of the hospital, so the only thing you're allowed to do is sit and watch." His eyes twinkled with mischief. "I'd have thought it was every woman's dream to sit and boss a bunch of men around."

She laughed, unable to resist his humor. "Emerald Jewel." She held out her hand and he reached out and engulfed it with his huge paw of a hand. "Francis Parker. My missus is here somewhere. You'll meet Frannie later. She's a big fan of your parents, but don't be letting her wear you out with questions about them."

"Now, Francis, don't you be frightening that young woman before she even meets me." Emerald had to blink twice when she saw who she assumed was Frannie Parker. The woman was about half the size of her large husband. Her hair was an ash blonde and sleekly styled. Delicate was the only word for her. She walked up to her husband and gave him a playful swat before introducing herself. Before she knew what was happening, Frannie was leading her upstairs. Emerald glanced behind her to find Jackson surrounded by the men working in the kitchen.

"Don't you fret none," Frannie continued as they made their way up the stairs. "We'll have the worst of it taken care of by dark." Emerald just nodded as the older woman led her to the clean spare room and made her lie down. Suddenly exhausted by it all, she snuggled on her side beneath the covers and fell asleep.

It was quiet when she awoke. She had no idea how much time had passed, but it was dark outside. Seems she'd slept most of the afternoon and evening away. She sensed Jackson's presence even though she couldn't hear him. Sitting up, she pushed her hair out of her eyes and saw him leaning against the wall by the window, looking out over the land. When he heard her, he glanced her way.

"How are you feeling?"

She stifled a yawn and took stock of her body before answering. "I actually feel pretty good." Even her voice sounded better. It was still husky, but not quite as raw. "How about you? I didn't mean to sleep the entire day away." And she was rambling, nervous without knowing why.

Jackson levered himself away from the wall and strode toward her. It was then she noticed the rifle in his hands. She swallowed hard. It brought home once again just how much danger surrounded her.

"You needed the rest." His voice was low and warm as he sat down beside her. The mattress dipped and she slid closer to him. He cupped her face with his hand, leaned down and kissed her. It was a soft, gentle kiss, but it made her toes curl beneath the covers.

There was so much caring in that tender caress that it brought tears to her eyes. She blinked them back, but it wasn't easy. She'd found herself on the verge of tears several times since the explosion. A nurse at the hospital had told her to expect to be more emotional, that it was a normal thing after going through such a traumatic event. Emerald thought it had more to do with her depth of feelings for the man seated next to her than the explosion.

She could have sat there and kissed Jackson all night long. He used his lips and his tongue, plying them lightly against her mouth before slipping inside. Warmth filled her, adding to the sleepy, dreamlike quality of the night. She whimpered as he pulled back.

"Are you hungry?"

"I guess." She knew she should be hungry, as she'd barely picked at her breakfast and lunch.

"Come on then." Jackson held out his hand as he stood. She slid out of bed, stopping long enough to shove her feet into her sneakers before she took his hand.

But he didn't lead her downstairs as she'd expected, but down the hallway to his bedroom. A small table had been set up in front of the window. A grouping of tea lights sat in ceramic holders in the center, illuminating the bounty set out on it. There was fresh bread and biscuits, sliced deli meats, several kinds of cheese and cold iced tea. And sitting there in the center was the perfect cherry cheesecake.

"Ohmigod," she moaned, her stomach suddenly grumbling.

Jackson shook his head but chuckled as he propped the rifle against the windowsill and sank down into the large leather chair that was pulled up next to the table. He gave her hand a tug and she went willingly into his lap. "I guess you're hungry after all."

"I guess I am," she agreed as she wiggled around trying to get comfortable. "When did everyone leave?"

"About a half-hour ago." Leaning forward, Jackson quickly began to assemble a sandwich.

"I want some of that chicken." Under her guidance, Jackson made her a chicken sandwich with Swiss cheese and mayonnaise. She held the plate in her lap and moaned in pleasure as she took the first bite. She chewed and swallowed. "This sure beats hospital food."

They didn't talk much while they ate, but it wasn't an uncomfortable silence. Jackson passed the occasional comment about the work being done, filling her in on a few details, but other than that, both of them were at ease in the quiet. There was an intimacy in the moment that filled her with contentment.

When she finished her sandwich, Jackson took her plate and laid it back on the table. Then he dished up a huge slab of the cheesecake. Emerald licked her lips in anticipation as he broke off a piece with his fork and lifted it toward her. "Open up."

She parted her lips and he slid the cheesecake into her mouth. Flavor exploded onto her taste buds and she moaned as she chewed. "This is incredible."

"Frannie Parker made it."

"The woman is a culinary genius," she managed to get out as Jackson sent another piece sliding into her mouth. It was even better than the first taste had been.

Being a smart man, Jackson fed her two bites for every one he took. It wasn't long before she felt full enough to burst, but she managed to eat the last piece as she looked longingly at the rest of the cheesecake.

Jackson pushed the plate aside and sat back, studying her. "Don't worry. You can have more later."

Slightly embarrassed to be caught lusting over the rich treat, she sat back and sighed, totally replete. Jackson reached down and pulled her sneakers off her feet, letting them fall to the floor with a thud. Her socks followed. The evening was warm, but there was a hint of coolness on the air.

"Do you think we'll finally get rain?" That had been a topic of concern among the women working upstairs. Emerald had lain in bed half listening to their conversation as she'd drifted off to sleep. Many of the families raised animals or crops of some kind and it had become a concern for them all. The heat wave had held them in its grip these last few days of August.

"Probably by tomorrow at the latest." The flickering candlelight accentuated the harsh planes of Jackson's face. His jaw was darkened with stubble and his blue eyes were hooded as he stared at her. It was obvious to her that the weather was the last thing on his mind.

She shivered as his gaze raked over her body from her face, down the curve of her neck to her breasts. Unconfined by a bra, her nipples were pressed tight against the fabric of the T-shirt she wore. Jackson's eyes went lower, over her belly before coming to rest on the mound of her sex.

Unconsciously, she arched her hips toward him, drawn by the intensity of his gaze. She wanted him to touch her. Needed to share herself with him at least one more time. She was determined to leave him to protect him. Tomorrow, she promised herself. Tonight was for them.

His fingers were dark against the light color of her shorts. Deftly, he pulled at the ties cinching the soft fabric around her waist. Inserting his hand into the opening, he pushed downward, his fingers slipping beneath her panties and moving unerringly toward her slick folds. She bit her lip to keep from crying out as his fingers stroked over her mound, sliding through the neat thatch of curls that covered it. She parted her legs and he teased her clit with his fingers before finally touching her aching flesh.

Cursing, he jerked his hand away and began to tug her shorts and panties off. She lifted her bottom, helping him any way she could. When she was naked from the waist down, he turned her so that she was facing away from him. A second later his shirt was tossed to the floor and his hands gripped the hem of hers. She raised her arms over her head, marveling at how careful he was as he drew the fabric over her head.

His lips, warm and firm, caressed her back as he moved from one cut to the next. "I'm so sorry you were hurt." Emotion threatened to overwhelm her as he continued to kiss every hurt he could reach. She shivered and his arms came around her immediately. "Are you cold?"

Was he kidding? If she were any hotter, she'd self-combust. Heat flooded her core and cream flowed from it. Her nipples puckered tighter as his hands slid up her torso, coming to rest just beneath the heavy mounds. He draped her legs over his and then slowly spread them. The move left her wide open to his touch. The cool air flooded over her hot flesh, the contrast making her moan.

His large hands covered her breasts and kneaded them. Her nipples dug into his palms, demanding attention. His thumbs stroked the edges of her areolas, never quite touching them. Moaning, she undulated her body, pushing her chest forward, wanting him to touch her the way she needed.

"I've never been as scared in my life as I was when I realized that you were in trouble." His voice was low, his tone serious. Lips, warm and firm, grazed the back of her neck. His teeth scraped sensually across her nape, sending goose bumps down her back and arms.

"I'm fine." At this moment, she was better than fine. Jackson's large body was surrounding hers, encompassing her in his protection and heat.

She gasped when his thumbs finally flicked over her distended nipples. "You're more than fine." As he continued to play with her breasts, she could feel the heat and shape of his erection pressing into her lower back. He was still wearing his jeans, but there was no mistaking the large, thick feel of his cock. She wiggled, wringing a groan from him.

"Minx."

"Tease," she retorted.

Jackson chuckled, one of his hands dropping from her breasts and smoothing down her stomach. His fingers sifted through her pubic hair and went straight to the damp folds hidden below. Now it was her turn to groan as two large fingers slipped past the entrance to her sheath and pressed deep.

She moved her legs restlessly, trying to get his fingers farther inside her. One slow inch at a time, he pulled them out, curling them upward as he went. One of them scraped across a sensitive spot, making her cry out. Blood pumped thickly through her veins as every nerve ending in her body was sensitized. This wasn't going to take long. She was primed and ready for release.

With everything that had happened, she needed this. Needed the reconnection with life, with Jackson. He thrust his long, thick fingers inward, pushing past the resistance of her inner muscles. They contracted and relaxed, gradually pulling him inward. His thumb caressed the taut bud of nerves at the apex of her sex. Her hips moved of their own accord.

"That's it," he crooned. "Come for me, Emerald. Let me feel your hot cream on my hands." He bit the curve of her neck where it met her shoulders, making her entire body jerk. She could feel everything inside her tensing. Gathering. Waiting.

The hand at her breast continued to ply one puckered nipple and then the other, drawing both to a tight point. Looking down, she watched his darker-hued hand caress the pale mounds before tugging on the stiff, red peaks. It was an incredible turn-on to see him touching her, arousing her.

Her lungs were working harder. The air was almost too thick and heavy to breathe. "Jackson," she gasped as she undulated her hips. His fingers were working faster, thrusting and retreating from her core.

"Come for me." His hips jerked, pressing more firmly against her back. His hand tightened around her breast. His heavy breathing was hot against her throat. "I want to feel you come apart in my hands. I've got you. Let go, Emerald." The last was a hoarse plea and she responded.

Her entire body tightened and then exploded. Heat flooded her. She cried out, tipping her head back against his shoulder. He swooped down and captured her mouth with his, swallowing her scream of ecstasy. She felt as if she were suspended in air. Jackson surrounded her, holding her. All she had to do was feel the release sweeping through her, embrace it. And she did.

When the final aftershocks shimmered throughout her entire body, she sank back against him. His tongue sank deeper into her mouth, devouring her. When he dragged his fingers from her core, she cried out. Releasing her lips, he buried his face in the curve of her neck, dragging air into his lungs. She could feel the heavy rise and fall of his chest and the frantic pounding of his heart.

Exhausted and drained, yet totally content, she relaxed. His arms tightened around her. "That was just the beginning." She shivered at the sensual promise in his voice.

Her toes curled as he stood with her still clasped tight in his arms. Carrying her to the bed, he laid her in the center. She almost cried out in protest when he pulled away, but he didn't go anywhere. Instead, he stood there watching her.

She was totally naked, but she wasn't embarrassed or uncomfortable. She felt absolutely wonderful. His eyes narrowed as she stretched sensually, letting her arms and legs slide over the dark green comforter. "Mmm, I feel good."

"You're going to feel even better," he promised. His hands went to the front of his jeans and slid the button open. The rasp of the zipper was loud above the sound of their breathing.

"Come here." She held her hand out to him and he reached for it. Their fingers almost touching.

An explosion rattled the glass in the window.

"What the hell?" Jackson raced to the window and swore. His hands were fastening his pants as he snatched up the rifle and hurried back to the bed.

She'd grasped the comforter, draping it around her. Fear wrapped around her heart. "What is it?"

"The old barn."

He grabbed his phone and hit the speed dial. "Nathan. He's hit the barn. Send the fire department. Hurry." He hung up and placed the phone in her hands, wrapping her fingers around it. "If anything else happens, call Nathan. He's got a man watching the road to the farm. They should both be here in a few minutes." He strode to the door.

"Wait." She jumped off the bed and ran to him. "Don't go out there."

He cupped the back of her head in his big hand. "I have to. He's out there just waiting for a chance to get to you. Stay in here with the doors locked."

"It's a ploy to get you out of the house."

"I know." Leaning down, he dropped a hard kiss on her lips. "But I have to keep him from getting close to the house." He turned and hurried down the stairs. She was hard on his heels.

The smell of fresh paint filled her nostrils, reminding her just how dangerous this stalker was. She should have left this afternoon. But it was too late for that now. "Don't go," she pleaded.

"I have to." His face was grim as he unlocked the back door. "Lock this behind me and then go back upstairs and wait for Nathan."

Opening the door a crack, he slid out and disappeared into the shadows. Emerald locked the door and raced back upstairs. If there was a chance she could do anything to help him, the last thing she wanted to be was naked. Ignoring the twinge in her back, she ran into the bedroom, dropped the comforter, grabbed her shorts and began to dress.

# Chapter Eighteen

ॐ

Jackson kept to the shadows as he moved stealthily toward the barn. He didn't see much in the way of flames yet. Thankfully, he'd sent off the last load of alfalfa and hay a few days ago. There wasn't much left in that barn, but the wood was old and dry and would go up like tinder. He didn't even want to think about the orchards beyond. With the dry weather, the entire place could go up quickly.

He didn't care.

If the place burned to the ground, he'd rebuild and replant. It was all replaceable. The only thing that mattered was keeping Emerald safe. The deputy would be at the house within seconds and he would keep her safe. As long as he was between her and the barn, her stalker would have to go through him to get her.

He stood in the shadow of an old oak tree just beyond the yard and watched. Nothing moved. He inched forward, drawing in a deep breath and letting it out slowly. The rifle was solid in his hands. He'd never shot a man before, but he knew he'd do it without a moment's hesitation to protect Emerald.

Sweat rolled down his back as he eased up to the open door of the shed. He could hear the crackle of fire as it began to eat at the structure. He needed to close the door. That would help cut off the supply of oxygen and slow the flames. At least he hoped it would.

Jackson slipped in the door, trying to see through the thick, black smoke and the dark of the night. He grabbed the edge of the door and began to pull. Something. A sound, a movement or just plain instinct told him he was no longer alone. He jerked at the last second, but he wasn't fast enough. Something hard glanced off his head and hit his shoulder. He dropped to the dirt. The sound of a door closing seemed impossibly loud above the crackle and roar of the growing blaze.

The stalker was heading toward the house. Toward Emerald.

Cursing himself for falling prey to the stalker's tricks, he shook off the pain in his head and pushed to his knees. The rifle was still in his hand and he slung it over his shoulder. It was incredibly hard to push himself to his feet, but he did it. Something slick ran into his eye and he brushed it away. His fingers came away sticky and he knew it was blood. Ignoring it, he staggered to the door and pulled. Jammed!

Turning, he faced the growing inferno behind him. There was no getting out through the back way. Lurching forward, he plunged through the blaze and dove into the tool room. The smoke made seeing impossible. Going totally by feel, he ran his hands over the wall until he found what he was searching for.

The handle was smooth and familiar and he gripped it tight with both hands. Three steps were all it took until he was facing an outside wall. Drawing it back over his shoulder, he threw every bit of his strength behind it as he struck forward. The axe bit into the dry wood, sending chips flying everywhere.

Emerald hauled on the rest of her clothing and then pulled on her shoes. Grabbing the cell phone, she shoved it in her back pocket as she pounded down the stairs. She needed a weapon.

Stumbling into the kitchen, she swore under her breath. With everything torn up, she didn't know where to find anything. She didn't dare turn on a light and give away her position to her stalker.

Worry for Jackson was eating at her. She loved him. There was no denying it any longer. And if they both lived through this, she was going to tell him. She was also angry with him for going out there alone to face her stalker. He should have stayed with her where she could keep an eye on him.

God, she was losing her mind. Making her way over to the kitchen drawer, she yanked the top one open and reached in. Sure enough, her fingers folded over the handle of a small paring knife. It wasn't much, but she had no idea where to find the knife block that usually sat on the counter.

Closing the drawer, she went to the kitchen window and peered out. Where was Jackson? For that matter, where was the deputy? Biting her bottom lip, she debated going outside. The problem was that Jackson thought she was inside. There was always the possibility that he might shoot her by accident if she went out. She was well and truly stuck inside. Something else she was going to yell at him about when this was over.

Calm. She took a deep breath. She needed to stay calm. The sound of glass tinkling caught her ear. Her room downstairs. There was no time to run. He'd surely hear her. She eased back into the corner of the dark room and stayed very still. Footsteps grew louder. The roaring inside her head intensified until it deafened her. Where was Jackson? Had he been hurt? Her fingers tightened around the handle of the knife, which was down by her right thigh.

"Emerald! Where are you?"

She bit her lip to keep from gasping and tasted blood. The voice sounded vaguely familiar, but with her heart pounding so loud in her ears she couldn't quite place it. She didn't move. Didn't dare to breathe.

"Your lover is dead," the voice intoned calmly. Her stomach roiled, but she refused to believe him. She couldn't believe him. Jackson had to be okay.

"You can't hide from me," the voice continued, moving ever closer. Her fingers tightened on the blade. "This is all your fault. If you'd only listened to me, none of this would have happened. It's all your fault."

Disbelief filled her, followed by acute betrayal as recognition hit her.

"You need me. If you'd done what I asked of you, I wouldn't have had to do this." He sounded perturbed more than anything.

Anger pushed out the disbelief and betrayal, filling her until nothing else existed. This man had ruined her life and threatened the people she loved. This was no nameless, faceless fan. This was a man she'd known all her life, a man who'd sat at her parents' table for dinner many, many times.

The light came on so suddenly it blinded her. He was on her before she had a chance to react. The back of his hand hit her face, driving her head back into the wall with a sickening snap.

But she was beyond pain, beyond fear. If Jackson was hurt, he needed her and this man was standing between them. He was dressed as suavely as usual, his expensive suit immaculate, his imported shirt and tie crisp. But his hair was disheveled, his face darkened with soot and his eyes flat and cruel. How had she not seen this before?

Without a thought, she attacked. Bringing the knife up as she went. But he was quick and jerked to the side. Instead of hitting his heart, the blade sank into his shoulder. He howled with fury and hit her again. Emerald tumbled to the floor and he was on her in a second. His hands wrapped around her throat, his fingers squeezing the life out of her as he thumped her head against the floor.

"All you had to do was marry me and make a record. If you wanted to do it, your sisters would have fallen in line. What person doesn't want fame and fortune? I would have made millions and the old man would have gotten off my back for once. Was it too much to ask for you to just do this one thing for me?"

Emerald clawed at his hands, trying to fight, but it was becoming impossible. He was literally choking her to death. The handle of the blade still stuck out from his shoulder and she used her last bit of strength to reach out and twist it. Yelling, he fell away from her.

Rolling to her side, she coughed and gasped for breath. Her lungs desperately pulled in air. He grabbed her by the hair and began pulling her toward the door. "You're coming with me. It's not too late. We can still make this work." His voice was calm, almost conversational, as if he were asking her to join him for an afternoon tea.

She was dealing with a madman. There was no sanity left in his dark blue eyes.

"Let me go," she managed to choke out.

He turned and looked down at her and shook his head. Blood seeped from the wound in his shoulder, but he didn't even seem to notice. He straightened his tie with one hand, keeping the other securely tangled in her hair. "I can't. We belong together. You'll see."

"What will your father say?" The words were barely a whisper, but his reaction was anything but.

He yanked on her hair, pulling her to her feet. "He will be pleased." He dragged her head back so hard she thought her neck might snap.

She was running out of time. Clenching her hand into a fist, she drove it into his groin as hard as she could, just as Jackson had taught her. He dropped to the floor like a stone, dragging her with him. While he curled into a ball, groaning and crying, she grabbed his hand and pulled. She knew she'd left quite a bit of hair with him, but she didn't care. She had to escape.

Crawling, she headed for the door. His hand gripped her ankle, yanking her back. Her head bounced off the floor and light exploded behind her eyes. The world seemed to dim and she struggled to remain conscious.

The click of a gun's hammer being pulled back was as loud as an explosion. Emerald froze. "I'm sorry," he said as he sat up and aimed the weapon at her. "But you're not cooperating. This won't work if you don't cooperate." He spoke to her as if she were a child who had been slightly naughty. Where were the police?

As if on cue, she could hear the sirens in the background.

"Bitch." He struck her again. She felt her lip split. "You called the cops."

"Of course I did." She spat the blood away. "I didn't know it was you." If she could make him believe she might want to go with him, maybe she'd get a chance to overpower him.

He slowly stood and stared at her, his eyes suddenly sad. That frightened her more than his anger. "No. You won't go with me." Disappointment filled him. "Maybe you're not the one. You were my first choice, but Sapphire would do just as well. They could sing as a duo instead of a group. Or maybe she could have a solo career. She's young and beautiful enough."

"Derek." His name came out as a hoarse whisper, but he heard her. His head snapped down to meet her gaze. "It's not going to happen." Terror filled her as she thought about him going after one of her sisters.

"Of course it will," he continued calmly. "No one will know who did this." He tilted his head to one side as if considering something. "Maybe I'll frame your old boyfriend, Beau. Or perhaps that interfering investigator you hired. I'll console Sapphire over your death. It will be so sad, but the publicity it will bring to your family will push your parents' records sales up. We can reissue their greatest hits album and add the new song that you and your sisters recorded for them. It was too good." His finger tightened slowly on the trigger.

"You owed it to me and to the world to share your talent. You thought yourself too good to sing, to let me represent you. I bet you're sorry now."

Emerald gathered her strength. Her only chance was to roll quickly and tackle him. "Derek." She added a pleading note to her voice. The sirens were getting louder.

"Goodbye, Emerald."

A shot rang out as she rolled to one side. She expected to feel the bite of the bullet somewhere in her body. Had he missed?

A roar filled the air as a huge body flew into the room, tackling Derek where he stood swaying and sending them both to the floor. Emerald dragged herself up onto her hands and knees just as Jackson sent Derek's gun flying. Drawing back his fist, Jackson struck the other man in the face, over and over again. Blood flew as Jackson pummeled him.

Emerald forced herself to move. If he kept this up, he'd kill Derek and that would lead to another set of problems. Crawling toward him, she threw her arms around his shoulders. "Stop." It was almost impossible for her to speak, but she managed. "Stop, Jackson, please."

Jackson's large body shuddered, but he stopped. Turning his back on Derek, he pulled her into his arms. "Are you hurt? Did he hurt you?"

Unable to speak, she buried her face in his chest and shook her head. Jackson was safe. Her sisters were safe. She was safe. Nothing else mattered. The rest would heal in time.

Sirens blared, car doors slammed and footsteps pounded up the porch steps. "Holy shit," someone said as they entered the kitchen. Emerald knew that the newly painted walls and floors were covered in blood.

Nathan was suddenly crouching in front of them. "Ambulance is on the way." He turned to watch as several other deputies dealt with the unconscious man on the floor. "That him?"

Emerald nodded and lifted her head from Jackson to stare at her former friend. "Derek Locke."

Nathan swore. "The son of your parents' former manager?"

"Yes." She looked away from him, not wanting to see his face again.

"The barn is gone, but they should be able to keep it from spreading." Nathan glanced around. "Why don't you both come on outside? We'll sort this all out after you've both been to the hospital." Nathan tried to help, but Jackson wouldn't release his hold on her.

Staggering to the porch, he dropped into one of the chairs. One of the deputies brought them a blanket and Jackson wrapped it around her. She hadn't even realized she'd been shivering. "Your poor face." He feathered his fingers over her cheeks.

"It doesn't matter." She burrowed closer to him, desperate for his heat. "I thought he'd killed you." Her teeth were chattering now. "I couldn't have borne that."

"He tried, but I don't kill easy." Holding her close in his arms, they both watched the barn burn as the volunteer firefighters worked to keep it from spreading. Not two minutes later, the first drop of rain hit the ground and then another. The skies suddenly opened up and began to send a steady shower to the ground. The summer heat wave was over as suddenly as it had begun. The parched dirt began to soak up the moisture. Emerald shivered. Summer was over.

When the ambulance arrived, Jackson carried her to the back and climbed inside with her still tight in his embrace.

# Chapter Nineteen

## ℘

It was a very different scene a few days later when Emerald got out of her car and stared at the blackened remains of the barn. Her life had changed irrevocably, but the world still moved on.

Jackson had stayed with her the first night, but then she'd felt him pulling away from her. He'd only had to stay overnight for observation and the next morning he was gone, citing his need to be back on the farm. She understood it, truly she did. It was September and the harvest was now in full swing. Jackson was working day and night trying to pick up the pieces of his life.

The authorities had interviewed them both separately and the police back in New York had found all kinds of evidence of Derek's obsession with her in his apartment. She'd demanded all the details, needing to know in order to cope with her ordeal.

Her parents and sisters had descended on the hospital the next day, creating quite a stir in Meadows. They were all staying at the B&B in town until she was well enough to leave.

Her mother had cried and hugged her; her father had stared at her with a sad look in his eyes that had her bursting into tears. He'd gathered her into his strong arms, telling her everything was all right even as he admonished her for not telling them about the stalker. Her sisters hovered, showering her with love and attention.

Her family had met Nathan, Carly, Erin and Abel, but Jackson was conspicuous by his absence. She made excuses, but she could see the questions in her parents' and sisters' eyes. Thankfully, none of them asked any. She wasn't sure she'd have any answers.

Emerald was grateful that her car had been parked in the newer barn or it would have gone up in flames, and that Erin had been kind enough to collect it and drive it into town. Her new friend had figured that she might want her own transportation and Erin had been right.

This was one trip that Emerald insisted on making alone. She was hoping to see Jackson for herself and talk to him. She loved him and wanted to stay. But after what happened, she wasn't sure how he felt. He'd been injured and almost killed, his home damaged, lost his barn, had his livelihood threatened and had been forced to almost kill a man. All for a woman he'd met only a few weeks before. She wouldn't blame him if he couldn't wait to see the last of her.

That's why she was here.

She straightened her sundress, smoothing out nonexistent wrinkles, and started toward the house. The screen door pushed open and Jackson stepped out. She stopped, just drinking in the sight of him. From the tip of his scuffed boots to the tips of his reddish-brown hair, he appeared even more ruggedly handsome than she remembered. He was wearing faded blue jeans and a T-shirt, which was his normal work wear, but he made it look incredible.

His sky-blue eyes narrowed as he examined her from head to toe. Her body tingled, her nipples tightened. If she'd been wearing panties, they would have been damp, but she was naked beneath the dress. It had a built-in bra and that was good enough. She had plans. She only hoped Jackson would cooperate.

Her heart was pounding, her palms sweating as she took a few steps closer to the house. It was ridiculous to feel nervous all of a sudden, but she was. These next few moments were crucial to the rest of her life.

"How are you feeling?" She shivered as his voice washed over her like a gentle caress.

She licked her dry lips. "I'm good. How about you?"

He stood there as still as a statue, his wide shoulders straining the seams of his shirt and the soft fabric of his jeans molded to the thick muscles in his thighs. "I'm fine." His face showed no emotion as he continued to watch her.

"Do you have a minute to talk?" How polite they were. Watching them, you'd never know that they'd had hot, sweaty sex many times before. They were acting like strangers who'd just met.

"Sure." He motioned her toward the porch swing.

Emerald wiped her hands on her skirt as she strode forward. Ever the gentleman, Jackson seated her first. He towered over her for a moment before lowering himself to the bench seat beside her.

She slid off her low-heeled sandals and pushed gently. The swing began to sway. With his eyes, Jackson tracked her bare feet and up her calves until they disappeared beneath the hem of her dress.

"What will happen with the barn?" There was a large blank space where the structure had stood.

"I'll rebuild something smaller and more efficient. The old barn was too big and not very economical anyway." He shrugged as if it were no big deal.

"Will your insurance cover it and all the equipment inside?" She knew he'd lost a tractor in the blaze and that kind of thing cost big money. She clenched her hands in her lap. The monetary aspect of things had worried her while she'd been laid up in hospital.

His lips thinned, and she could see the muscles in his jaw twitching as he clenched it tight. "Money is not a problem." He glanced at his watch. "Is there anything else? I have to get back to work."

Emerald's stomach jerked. This was not going as she'd planned and now he was angry with her. Sighing, she took a deep breath and plunged forward. "What about us?"

His booted foot came down heavy on the porch as he stopped the swing from moving. He stared off into the distance, not looking at her. "What about us?"

A light breeze brushed her skin and teased the ends of her hair. A crow cried out as it pitched low in the air before swooping upward again. A bee buzzed as it went from flower to flower in the planter on the edge of the porch. Emerald wasn't quite sure what to say to that. She swallowed the lump in her throat. "You're going to pretend that nothing happened between us."

Jackson swore and dragged his hands through his hair before swiveling on the swing to face her. "Damn it, Emerald. What do you want me to say? It was great. It was fun. But we both know that you have a life back in New York and the only reason you're here is because of your stalker. That threat is gone now, so I guess it's time for you to go home."

Anger bubbled and boiled inside her. How dare he try to reduce what they'd shared together. "So it was fun, was it?"

"Yes, it was. Did you think it was more?" For the first time ever, she couldn't get a read on Jackson. It was as if he'd closed himself off from her. She wasn't having it.

"Silly of me if I did, isn't it? If it was *fun*." She put all the emphasis on the last word. "Then we should finish what we started in the bedroom the night of the barn fire." With righteous fury guiding her, her fingers went to the buttons at the front of her dress and began sliding them from their holes. If it was a good time he wanted, she'd give him one he'd never forget.

"What the hell are you doing?"

"What does it look like?" The dress was open to her waist, exposing her naked breasts. Turning suddenly, she threw her leg over his thighs, straddling him. His hands gripped her waist, holding her steady as she grabbed the sides of his head and yanked him closer. "I'm having fun." She slammed her mouth down on his.

For a moment he didn't move. The heat of embarrassment began to fill her. Oh God, she was making an absolute fool of herself. Then he groaned, his fingers tightening around her waist as he hauled her closer.

His lips ground against hers as he devoured her mouth. His tongue plunged past her teeth, tasting and stroking. Her hands slid from his head down to his broad shoulders. She wanted his shirt gone. Needed to feel his warm skin beneath her fingers.

Jerking the material up, they broke the kiss long enough for her to drag his shirt over his head and toss it aside. Jackson tangled his fingers in her hair, dragging her back down so he could nibble and lick at her mouth. She felt as if he were eating her alive. All her doubts disappeared beneath the growing heat. There was no denying the explosive connection that existed between them.

"Jackson," she gasped his name when he trailed hot, open-mouthed kisses down her throat. He licked at her collarbone. Her thighs clenched around his. Her pussy was hot and wet, aching for him to fill it.

"You are so damn beautiful." His voice was gruff and ragged as he tore at the remaining buttons on her dress. One of them clattered to the porch floor as he gave one final tug. The dress parted, exposing her totally to his view. Her breasts were heavy with desire, her nipples puckered into tight, rosy nubs. She took a deep breath and they swayed. Jackson cupped them in his hands and buried his face between them.

Emerald clutched at his shoulders, feeling the tenseness of his muscles. She arched forward, pressing her mound against the bulge in his jeans. They both moaned at the pressure. She did it again, undulating her hips in a pleasing rhythm.

"Emerald, you have to stop or I'm going to come in my pants." Jackson was panting hard now, his chest rising and falling with each harsh breath.

"I don't care," she muttered. She was past caring. It had been days since she'd even laid eyes on him and she needed to touch him, to reconnect with him, to feel him beneath her hands. Part of her loved the fact that he seemed to be as vulnerable to her touch as she was to his.

He growled low in his throat as his lips latched on to one of her nipples, drawing it into his mouth as he began to suckle. Emerald cried out, dragging her hands down his chest, gently scraping his flat brown nipples with her nails. His entire body jerked and he tore his mouth from her body.

Reaching between them, he ripped open his jeans and shoved his underwear aside. His cock sprang forward, hot and ready. She grasped his shaft in her hands, pumping them up and down. The plum-shaped head was dark and engorged with blood. The veins that ran down the thick length pulsed against her palm, and as she pumped, a bead of whitish liquid seeped from the slit. She wanted to taste it but settled for spreading it over the tip with her thumb.

Jackson dipped his fingers between her thighs, a deep rumble of pleasure coming from him when he touched her damp heat. She tilted back her head and cried out as he stroked two of his fingers into her core and then dragged them back out again.

"More," she demanded as she squeezed his cock.

Jackson grabbed her hips and lifted her until she was up on her knees. Using her grip on him, she guided him to her. The thick head of his erection squeezed past her opening. She loved the way he stretched her each time he entered her. It was tight, but he fit as if they'd been made especially for each other.

Cupping his face in her hands, she watched his expression as she slowly lowered herself onto his cock. He hissed out a breath from between clenched teeth. His blue eyes flickered with the flames of lust, searing their expression onto her soul.

When she was seated as far as she could go, she wiggled her hips and managed to take him even deeper.

"Hold on to me." She had no idea what he planned to do, but she trusted him implicitly. Grabbing on to his shoulders, she held on tight.

She felt his right thigh flex and then the swing began to move. Emerald wrapped her hands around his neck, twining her fingers together as Jackson clasped her hips in his hands and began to guide her.

As the swing moved forward, he dragged her close. As the swing drew back, he held her away from him, his cock sliding out until only the head remained inside. This time when the swing came forward, he drove back in hard and deep. Emerald cried out as fire shot from her core to flood the rest of her body.

She began to work with Jackson, catching the rhythm, anticipating each swing. Using his right foot, he kept the swing moving at a slow and steady pace. Emerald writhed in his arms, panting and moaning as desire spiraled higher and higher within her.

A light sheen of perspiration covered her body and Jackson's shoulders were slick beneath her hands as she stroked them. She felt the familiar contractions begin deep in her womb. Her inner muscles flexing and relaxing. Getting tighter. Tighter.

Jackson slipped one of his hands between her legs and stroked her swollen clitoris. That was all it took to drive her over the edge. Her hips jerked, slamming forward, driving him deep and hard. Contractions rippled through her core, squeezing his cock tight.

She felt the flood of his seed as it filled her, the hot jets of semen pumping through his shaft and into her body. Her inner muscles tightened around him, wringing moans from both of them. Aftershocks were still pulsing through her when she collapsed forward.

Jackson's strong arms came around her. There was almost a desperate feel in the way he held her so tight that she could barely breathe. Wrapped in each other's arms, neither of them spoke. As the minutes ticked by, Emerald could feel the closeness slipping away and she didn't know what to do to hold it.

Knowing she couldn't stay like this forever, she slowly pushed herself upright. She bit her lip to keep from crying out as the move made his still semi-erect cock flex within her.

Jackson swore and eased himself from her. "We didn't use a condom." His voice was flat.

Flustered now that the heat of passion was past, Emerald grabbed the edges of her dress together and began to button them. "It's okay. I'm on the Pill and I've never had sex without a condom before so you don't have to worry about disease." She fastened several buttons, not looking at him. It was cowardly, but she didn't want to face him until she was covered again.

"I'm clean too. I've never had sex without a condom. I knew it felt too damn good."

She stopped what she was doing and scrambled out of his lap. His hands tightened briefly and for a split second she thought he might pull her back into his lap. But the moment passed and he let her go.

His eyes tracked down her body as she stood and she realized that the bottom of her dress was still askew, revealing her damp, glistening pubic hair. Twitching the dress closed, she fastened a few more of buttons, ignoring the one that was missing near the bottom. When she looked back at him, he'd just finished fastening his jeans. She felt hot, sticky and uncomfortable, but Jackson barely had a hair out of place.

Leaning back against the swing with his shirt off, he appeared cool and composed.

"There's nothing for you to worry about." The heat from his eyes had faded, replaced by the cool, closed expression he'd had when she'd first arrived. "So where does this leave us?" She locked her knees and fisted her hands in her skirt to hide their trembling.

His eyes narrowed as he pushed out of the swing. She took a step back. A muscle twitched beneath his eye as he stared at her. "Right where we started." He bent down and snagged his T-shirt, turning it right side out before pulling it back over his head. "It was fun, Emerald. It was great. But we both know that your life isn't here on this farm. Your work, your life is in New York."

Emerald felt curiously detached as she watched him, a peculiar numbness coming over her. Her heart felt as if it had shattered into little pieces. He wasn't going to ask her to stay. Didn't want her to stay. She'd gone into this knowing there were no promises or guarantees, but God how it hurt.

It wasn't his fault that she'd fallen in love with him, but he didn't love her. Like he'd said, they're both adults and they had a good time together. Now it was over. She wouldn't make a scene even if it killed her. He'd saved her life for heaven's sake. The least she could do was get out of his life and let him rebuild what her coming had shattered.

"I'll pack my things and go."

Jackson nodded. "That's probably for the best." He opened his mouth as if he might say more, but closed it again. The muscles in his jaw were tight and his hands were fisted as he stalked away from her. He stopped at the bottom of the steps and for a second she hoped and prayed that he might turn around and come back to her. One word from him and she was ready to admit that she loved him and wanted to stay.

Tension surrounded them. Emerald could almost feel an invisible thread between them, holding them together. Then it

239

snapped as Jackson thumped down the steps and hurried across the yard. He didn't look back.

She watched him until he disappeared from sight, swallowed up by the orchard. Tears filled her eyes, slowly overflowing and trailing down her cheeks. Swiping at them, she shuffled into the house. The room she'd stayed in had escaped most of the damage from the kitchen fire, but it had been cleaned and aired. Emerald yanked her bag out of the closet and began to stuff her clothing into it. It didn't take her long. Her laptop was gone, destroyed in the explosion, but she'd get another. She still had her sketchbook with all her original drawings and ideas. Not that she'd ever forget the farm or the man who lived here.

Dragging her bags out to her car, she threw them into the trunk and slammed it shut. She went into the house one last time and walked through it. Standing in the doorway to Jackson's room, she stared at the chair where he'd held her so tenderly while he'd fed her. Her eyes strayed to the bed and her feet moved forward as if some unseen force were propelling her.

She sat down on the bed and inhaled, dragging Jackson's unique outdoorsy scent into her lungs. A shirt was tossed onto the end of the bed and she picked it up, bringing it to her nose and sniffing. It smelled like him. Standing, she tucked the shirt beneath her arm and left. Her bare feet made no sound on the stairs as she padded down to the main floor. She ignored the fresh, new kitchen as she strode through it, didn't stop to admire the brand-new maple trestle table situated in the center of the room. Tears pricked her eyes, but she wiped them away.

She was alive and her stalker had been caught. That was all that mattered. She'd shared an incredible few weeks with an exceptional man and now it was over. It was time to move on with her life.

Tilting her chin up, she walked out of the farmhouse and closed the door behind her. Stopping long enough to snag her sandals, she hurried to her car without looking at the porch swing. Emerald slid into the front seat of her car, shut the door and turned on the ignition in one smooth motion. She backed the car away from the house and headed down the road, refusing to look in the rearview mirror as she drove away.

Jackson watched from the edge of the tree line as Emerald left the house for the last time and got into her car. His fingers dug into the trunk of the tree to keep from running to her and dragging her back inside. He didn't want her to go, but he had no right to keep her here.

Their relationship had been intense because of the circumstances that had brought them together. But he knew that her life was not here. She was a city girl, reared in a famous family. Her family and her career were in New York. He was a farm boy through and through and could never be happy anywhere else.

These past few weeks had been the best of his life. Emerald had filled a void he hadn't even known existed until she'd arrived. Smart, funny and beautiful, she'd brought joy and sunshine to his mundane existence. There was no doubt in his mind that he loved her. He could easily picture growing old with her, rearing a family together. But that wasn't in the cards.

He loved her enough to let her go.

He knew himself well and knew there would never be another woman for him. Emerald, with her curly black hair and her gypsy looks was the one for him. Any other woman would pale in comparison.

As the car pulled away, he took a step forward, reaching out his hand as if he could somehow stop her. He blinked as his eyes began to sting. It was only dirt on the breeze, he assured himself as he dragged his hand over his eyes. As the car disappeared from view, he turned and slowly trudged back to work.

# Chapter Twenty

**ဆ**

Emerald stared at her computer screen, her eyes burning from overwork. All she'd done since she'd returned home to New York was work. She'd not only managed to recreate all the work she'd lost when her computer was destroyed in the kitchen explosion, she'd outlined an entire new collection as well. *Seasons*, she was calling it.

So far she'd created summer, which consisted of wildflowers such as daisies, buttercups, violets and a multitude of others, along with butterflies and bees. It was colorful and dramatic and would look wonderful on cards, stationery and journal covers, not to mention a line of accessories that would be ready for next summer.

Now she was starting the work on the fall collection. She wanted rich burnt orange, red and gold as her palette. She'd done some research on the area surrounding Meadows, seen some pictures of the autumn season, but it wasn't the same.

Pushing her chair away from her desk, she rose and went to the window. Staring out, she took in the sights and sounds of the city. People and traffic bustled up and down the busy streets. Horns blared, people shouted. What had filled her with energy and excitement only months before now just annoyed her.

Slamming the window shut, she leaned her head against the glass and took a deep breath. She longed for the clean air of the countryside, the sound of the birds twittering in the morning, the silence. She wanted to be back on the farm with Jackson.

But she had to stop thinking about him. What was done was done.

"Are you okay?" Emerald almost groaned aloud. It was Topaz. Both she and Sapphire had been watching her like a pair of hawks since she'd returned home.

Summoning up a weak smile, she turned from the window. "I'm fine. I've finished the summer collection and started on autumn."

"That's good." Topaz strolled into the room, looking chic and sophisticated in a cool green linen suit. Chunks of amber circled her wrist, set in an intricate band of silver. It was one of Sapphire's pieces. Emerald, in her jeans and Jackson's shirt, felt like a wrung-out dishrag next to her sister.

As Emerald watched warily, her sister went to the desk and examined several finished designs for the summer line. Her stomach clenched and she realized she was slightly nervous. With everything that had gone on with the stalker and her design block before that, it had been quite a while since she'd created anything this special.

"This is wonderful." Topaz carefully laid the drawings back on the desk. "They have a vibrancy and realism that's amazing. Sapphire is already designing the jewelry to go with this line." Topaz turned and leaned back against the desk, crossing her arms across her chest. "She'd very excited about the wildflowers and she has an entire butterfly collection in mind."

"That's good." Emerald was pleased but she couldn't really work up any enthusiasm.

"Yes, it is." Her sister pushed away from the desk and sighed. "When are you going to tell us what's wrong?"

"There's nothing wrong. I'm fine." The words came automatically and Topaz frowned at her.

"No, you're not." Her sister's voice was flat as she strode forward, determination in every line of her body.

"Am I late?" Sapphire hurried into the office, slightly breathless as she balanced three large beverage containers and a bakery bag in her hands.

"We haven't started yet."

Emerald stared from one sister to the other. "What's going on?"

Sapphire plunked what Emerald suspected were café mochas and a selection of treats from Althea's Bakery, a favorite of all three sisters. The only time they brought out this much chocolate and calories was when there was a serious discussion on the table.

Topaz wrapped her arm around Emerald's shoulders and propelled her toward the comfortable couch and chairs that created a sitting area in the office. Sapphire had already curled up in one of the chairs and was busily opening the bag and setting cream puffs and éclairs onto paper napkins.

She found herself seated on the sofa with her café mocha in one hand and a cream puff in the other. Topaz pinned her with her golden-brown eyes and Emerald swallowed. She'd seen that look many times before and knew that time had run out.

"Tell us what happened." Topaz's voice was like velvet over steel. If Emerald didn't spill the story, her sister would end up on Jackson's doorstep demanding answers.

Emerald opened her mouth to once again say that nothing happened. Instead the entire story tumbled out from deep inside her. She told them about running and how she stumbled upon the job at the farm. She left out nothing as she spun the story of what had happened when she and Jackson met and what had followed. She poured her heart out, stopping occasionally to sniff back the tears that threatened.

"So you see, it's nobody's fault that I fell in love with him. We're both adults and there was no commitment on either side. It was an intense affair and now it's over." And if she said it enough times maybe she'd even start to believe it.

Sapphire handed her a tissue, which Emerald took gratefully. Topaz, on the other hand, was thinking, and that was always dangerous. Her older sister sipped her café mocha thoughtfully. "The man insists you stay with him, doesn't seem to care that his home is almost destroyed and risks his life for you?"

Emerald nodded. "Jackson's one of a kind. He felt responsible for me." Her heart clenched. "He's big on responsibility."

Topaz was shaking her head. "The man loves you." She said it so matter-of-factly that Emerald sat up straighter.

"How can you say that? He sent me away."

"No, he didn't." Topaz laid her drink on the table and reached out and took Emerald's hands in hers. "He set you free. Don't you get it? From everything you've told us, his actions show that he has deep feeling for you."

"The sex between us was explosive," she muttered, feeling her cheeks heat. She'd skipped over those parts of the story. They were too private, too special to share even with her sisters.

Topaz shook her head emphatically. "No. I'm not buying that. The guy thinks he's doing you a favor by letting you come back to the city and your life here."

A seed of hope began to bloom within her and she suddenly realized that she'd never really lost it. "He did keep saying that my life was in New York and his was on the farm."

Sapphire came over to sit beside her, offering her a quick hug. "I'd say he was too afraid to ask you to stay just as you were too afraid to tell him you love him. He would no more ask you to come live on the farm than you'd ask him to sell it and move to New York."

"You really think so?" She so wanted her sisters to be right. It was an idea that she'd mulled around in her own mind, but Jackson didn't seem to be afraid of anything. Except from what she'd learned about him, he'd isolated himself to keep from being hurt. His family had all left him, leaving him alone on the farm. He didn't even have a pet for heaven's sake.

"I do." There was a certainty to Topaz's words that had Emerald raising an eyebrow in question. "I saw him one night. I'd already left the hospital, but I'd forgotten my sweater and went back for it. The door was slightly opened and I peeked in just in case one of the doctors or nurses was with you. He was standing there watching you sleep."

"I never knew he was there." Emerald was shocked. As far as she'd known, Jackson had left the next morning and not returned to the hospital. He'd never told her any differently.

"I think that was the point," Topaz pointed out. "The way he looked at you…" Her sister's voice trailed off. She cleared her throat and continued. "I didn't say anything sooner because I didn't want to interfere. I kept hoping one or both of you would come to your senses." Topaz arched her brow and Emerald felt her cheeks heating at the implication. "Let's just say that if that man doesn't love you, he should be making movies because he's a damn fine actor." Topaz grinned at both of them. "And he's hot too, if you go for the rough and rugged type."

All of them laughed. It was well known that Topaz only dated Wall Street, three-piece Italian suit kind of men. Topaz glanced away as if embarrassed. Emerald squeezed her sister's hand tight. "Thank you for sharing that with me."

"You're welcome." When she faced them again, all signs of embarrassment and discomfort were gone and Topaz appeared to be back to normal. "The thing I want to know is, what are you going to do about it? You going to just give him up without a fight?"

That's what she'd done. It occurred to her that she was as bad as Jackson, hiding from her love for him to keep from being hurt. She should have sat him down and laid all her cards on the table. Her old life no longer suited her and it was time for a change one way or another.

Determination filled her as she grabbed an éclair and took a big bite. She hadn't eaten much the past few weeks, her appetite nonexistent. It was suddenly back with a vengeance and she was starving. As she chewed she realized she'd already been thinking about making a big change. If her relationship with Jackson didn't work out, she was still going to go ahead with her plans.

One way or another the time had come.

Wiping her sticky hands on a napkin, she took a sip of her drink and laid the cup on the table. "I've got a plan."

Jackson glared at his sister. "I'm fine."

"You certainly seem fine. You've been like a bear with a sore paw ever since Emerald left." Erin crossed her arms over her chest and tapped her right foot on the floor.

Jackson didn't know whether to be angry, amused or totally exasperated. His family had barely given him a moment's peace since Emerald had left. His chest tightened and he swallowed back the ache that always accompanied thoughts of her. Jackson took a deep breath and ran his hands over his face. "Look, I know I've been a bit tense, but the bulk of the harvest is in, the barn is being rebuilt and everything is going back to normal."

"Are you sure that's what you want?" His sister was too perceptive for comfort.

"That's the way it has to be." His voice was flat, leaving no room for further discussion.

She looked as if she might say more, but thankfully left it at that. Coming up to him, she wrapped her arms around his waist and hugged him tight. He could feel the slight bulge of her tummy against him, reminding him that at least part of his family was happy. "I'm making fried chicken for supper. There's plenty if you want to drop by." Pushing away, she smiled at him. "I promise we won't lecture or ask questions. I'm just worried about you."

He felt like an ungrateful wretch. "I know." Leaning down, he kissed her forehead. "But there is nothing to worry about and you need to be concerned about yourself and my niece or nephew." He patted her tummy, making her laugh.

"It's your job to worry about me and it's mine to worry about you." She headed for the door. "If you don't show up for supper, I'll bring you some leftovers tomorrow."

"Good deal." He walked out to the porch and leaned against the railing, watching as she climbed in her truck and left. It was closing in on the end of September and Emerald had been gone for more than three weeks. The harvest was in full swing, with the bulk of it done. He was on the homestretch and things looked good for the farm. He owned the land as far as his eye could see. This should be the best time of his life.

Instead, there was a never-ending ache deep inside him. It had taken him a while to figure out exactly what it was. It plagued him throughout the day as he tried to work himself into exhaustion and late at night when he tried to sleep. As he lay awake in bed night after night, it had finally occurred to him that he was lonely. And not in the way he'd been when Erin and Nathan had moved out. This went straight to the very marrow of his bones.

He missed Emerald.

He missed her smile, the way she nibbled on her bottom lip when she was thinking about something. He missed talking to her, sharing small moments of his day and listening as she shared hers. He missed walking into the house in the evening and smelling supper mingling with the soft scent of her perfume. His arms ached to hold her at night and many times he rolled over in his sleep, reaching for her only to awaken when she wasn't there.

He loved her.

There was an empty hole where his heart had been. He still worked and functioned, but the joy was gone from life. She'd taken it with her when she'd driven away. Or when he'd driven her away, a voice in the back of his head reminded him. He'd wondered a million times if she would have stayed if he'd asked. But then, he'd remind himself that she needed to go back to her old life. The time they'd had together had all but been forced upon her by circumstance. Jackson needed to be sure that what she felt was real.

He'd already decided that once the harvest was done, he needed to make a trip to New York to visit the gallery that handled his photographs. He planned to call on Emerald while he was there. Maybe take her to dinner and talk.

Groaning, he buried his face in his hands. Truthfully, he wanted to swoop into New York, kidnap her and drag her back out here with him. "You'll be lucky if she even wants to see you," he muttered as he raised his head. Now that she was back to her old life it would be very easy for her to forget all about him.

He'd been thinking about the trip to New York since Emerald had left, but what had sealed his fate had been the arrival of his photos from the developer. He'd sent several rolls, including the ones he'd taken of Emerald that day at the pond.

When he'd first seen them it had been like being hit in the head with a two-by-four. Sexy, mischievous and all woman, she'd stared back at him. The light and shadows had played over her creamy skin, making him want to touch it. He'd spent hours looking at her heart-shaped face, dark brown eyes and curly black hair. Wet and sleek, she was like some mystical creature come to touch the mortal realm and share some of her magic.

That's what she'd done to him. She'd touched something deep within him and he knew he'd never be the same. So no matter what happened, he knew he had to take the chance and go to New York. If he didn't try, he'd never be able to live with himself.

Pushing away from the railing, he raised his arms over his head, his muscles bunching and straining against the seams of his T-shirt. It was time to get back to work. The quicker the harvest was completely finished, the faster he'd get to New York. He only hoped that Mother Nature cooperated.

As he stepped off the porch, he heard a vehicle approaching. He swore under his breath, praying it wasn't another well-meaning member of his family. All of them had taken to dropping by at odd hours to check on him. As much as he appreciated their concern, it was starting to drive him insane.

He squinted as a car came into view, not recognizing it at first. His heart stopped and then began to pound the closer it got. Cold sweat rolled down his back. It couldn't be, but it was. The vehicle pulled to a stop and the door opened. As if he'd conjured her with his thoughts alone, Emerald stepped out and closed the door.

"Hello, Jackson."

Emerald couldn't stop staring at him. After not seeing him for over three weeks, she wanted to soak up everything about him. He looked just as she remembered — good enough to eat.

He was tanned and fit and strong. He hadn't changed at all. Or so she thought until she took several steps closer. Then she saw the truth. There were new lines around the corners of his eyes and dark circles beneath them. He hadn't been sleeping any better than she had. That gave her hope that maybe he'd missed her as much as she'd missed him.

His mouth thinned into a firm line and his fists clenched at his sides. Not exactly the reception she'd been hoping for, but she wasn't giving up. She was here and she was committed to her course of action. He would listen to her. She'd make him.

"Emerald." Like a man in a trance, he took a step toward her and then jerked himself to a halt. "Why are you here?"

This was it. This was the moment she'd come all this way for. "We have some unfinished business between us."

Now he appeared perplexed. His eyebrows furrowed and he frowned. "What business?"

"Do you mind if we sit?"

He stepped back and motioned her forward. She didn't bother going to the door. Instead she went to the swing and lowered herself onto the bench seat. Jackson didn't sit next to her, but perched on the railing instead. Crossing his arms over his chest, he stared at her, looking cool and aloof. But she could see beyond the façade. The loneliness in his eyes mirrored what she saw in her own daily.

"What was so important you came all this way instead of just calling or e-mailing?"

Her back stiffened and she glared at him. If she didn't love him so much, she'd be tempted to smack him for acting so obtuse. "You know darn well why I'm here."

His eyes widened and he straightened. "Why don't you tell me?"

The low cadence of his voice made her shiver. It reminded her of all the times they'd made love and he'd whispered in her ear, praising her, telling her how much he enjoyed touching her. She shivered and ignored the fact that her nipples were hard nubs and her panties were already wet.

"I love you." She'd meant to talk a bit more and maybe bring the subject around to them, but the words had just come out of her.

He appeared shocked. All the color seemed to drain from his face, leaving him pale, which was amazing considering the golden hue of his tanned skin. The blue of his eyes seemed to darken to the color of a summer storm the longer he stared at her. "What did you say?"

"I said that I love you." Rising, she went to him, standing so close that she could feel the heat from his body even though they weren't quite touching. "I didn't want to go. I want to stay here with you."

251

"But your life, your career, your family is in New York." He held his body so stiffly she could see the outline of all the muscles in his arms. His jaw was tight, the vein in his temple throbbing.

"My family lives in New York, but we can all visit. My career is portable. I'm no longer involved in the daily running of the store. Topaz is hiring more help and both Sapphire and I are branching out even though we'll both still be designing mostly for Sisters' Jewels."

She took a deep breath, inhaling the outdoorsy scent that reminded her so much of Jackson. It had finally faded from the shirt that she'd taken and she'd missed it. "As for my life, well, New York no longer suits me."

Jackson's eyes narrowed, his eyes like lasers studying her. "You say that now, but what about in six months or a year?"

She shrugged, trying to still the racing of her heart, trying to pretend that the rest of her life wasn't on the line. "Whether I stay here or not, I'm not going back to New York. If you don't want me here, I'll drive around the country until I find a new place for myself." It wasn't what she wanted, but she was a strong woman and realistic. It might hurt like hell, but she'd eventually get over Jackson. Maybe in ten or twenty years.

"You're sure."

"Absolutely." Reaching out, she touched him for the first time, her hand grazing the edge of his jaw. Beard stubble rubbed against her skin, sending tingles shooting to all the nerve endings in her body. "I love you, Jackson."

"Thank God." He dragged her into his arms, all but smothering her, he held her so tight. She could feel the heavy thump of his heart against hers. His muscles rippled in his shoulders as he scooped her into his arms, his face still buried in the crook of her neck. She could feel him trembling as he carried her across the porch and into the house. "I can't let you go again."

"You don't have to."

His boots thudded on the floor and then up the stairs. Emerald felt as if she'd come home. She was where she belonged. They were meant to be together. They'd work out the details later. For now, she needed to touch him and have him touch her. To come together, two bodies joining as one. Everything else could wait.

# Chapter Twenty-One

## ❧

Jackson was afraid to blink, almost afraid to breathe. It seemed too much of a miracle that Emerald was once again in his arms where she belonged. Carrying her into his bedroom, he reluctantly let go of her legs, letting her feet fall to the ground. He stroked his hands over her hair, loving the way it curled wildly around her face. He didn't say anything, almost too overwhelmed to speak.

She'd come back to him.

For the first time in his life, someone he loved had come back to him. He realized his hands were shaking when he reached for the buttons on her blouse. One at a time, he slipped them from their holes, unwrapping her like a present. He wasn't in a hurry. Instead, he wanted to savor every inch of skin he exposed.

Peeling back the fabric, he slid it down her arms and dropped it. She was wearing a bra that was the color of ripe peaches. Bending down, he nuzzled her neck. She smelled like summer—warm and lush, with a hint of something floral. He'd missed her scent and had only changed the covering of his pillows when it had finally faded.

He ran his finger along the lace that edged her bra. It looked incredible against her lightly tanned skin. She sucked in a breath when he stroked his thumb over her nipple. It was already puckered tight, pressing against the thin fabric. A low rumble started in his chest as he went down on one knee in front of her.

"Jackson?" She steadied herself, clutching at his shoulders.

"Let me," he murmured as he pressed hot, open-mouthed kisses on her tummy. "Let me undress you. Let me have you."

"Yes," she sighed as his hands slipped around her sides to her back. His fingers made quick work of the closure on her bra and he slid the straps over her arms. She released her grip on him long enough to let the garment fall to the floor.

Clad only in faded blue jeans and sneakers, she was a sight to behold. Her full breasts rose and fell with every deep breath she took. Her rosy nipples were tight, begging to be touched and tasted.

"God, you're beautiful." He breathed in her scent as he buried his face between her breasts. His hands molded to her ass, squeezing and caressing.

Emerald tugged at his T-shirt, pulling it over his head so that he had no choice but to release her long enough for her to drag it off. Her eyes were dark pools of chocolate brown, her lips wet and pink. He wanted to devour her, to eat her up from head to toe.

He needed her naked. Now. It only took him a second to undo her jeans and push them over her hips and thighs. When they bunched at her calves, he had her lift one foot at a time as he yanked off her socks and shoes before pulling off her jeans.

She was wearing a skimpy pair of panties that matched her bra. The thin scrap of fabric barely covered her mound. He knew a lot of women shaved themselves these days, but he liked the fact that she didn't. He skimmed his fingers up the inside of her thighs, tracing the crease at the top. Emerald sucked in her breath and widened her stance. Her fingers tangled in his hair, drawing him closer.

His cock was so hard that it was almost painful as it pressed against the zipper of his jeans. His body was screaming at him to fuck her, but his mind wanted him to go slow, to arouse her to such a fevered pitch that she'd beg him to take her.

Growling as he tried to balance both sides of himself, he hooked his fingers in the edges of her panties and gave them a tug. They slid downward, exposing her pubic hair.

Jackson slid his arms around her waist as he kissed her stomach. He couldn't get enough of touching her, needing to reassure himself that she was indeed real and not some figment of his overworked imagination.

Sitting back on his heels, he parted her sex with his thumbs, exposing the damp, pink flesh. Leaning forward, he licked up one side and down the other. Emerald gasped and then groaned, pushing her hips forward.

"You like that, do you?" He traced the slick folds with his fingers before licking them again.

"Yes," she cried as her hips jerked.

Jackson pressed one finger inside her core. She was hot and wet and it was all for him. He thought he might come on the spot. His balls were heavy and tight, his shaft pulsing with hunger. He withdrew his finger, ignoring her cries of dismay and pushed two fingers past her tight opening.

She moaned, her nails digging into his scalp. "I need you. Jackson!"

Surging to his feet, he tumbled her back onto the bed. As she lay there wide-eyed and panting, he unlaced his boots and yanked them off. Quickly, he divested himself of his socks, jeans and underwear.

He couldn't wait any longer. He'd spent too many long nights dreaming and fantasizing about her being here. "Spread your legs." Kneeling up on the mattress, he watched her, unable to take his eyes from her.

Her legs parted, welcoming him. She held her arms out to him and he crawled forward, covering her with his body. He gripped his cock in his hand, guiding it to her opening. As he squeezed the bulbous head of his cock, he closed his eyes and groaned. If he weren't careful, he'd come before he had a chance to get all the way inside her.

Emerald's hair was spread across his pillows. Her mouth was open on a cry of need, her eyes wide and wild with desire. He took a deep breath and pushed a little further. Her hands fisted in his sheets as her legs came up to wrap around his waist, dragging him closer.

Planting his hands flat on the mattress by her head, he flexed his hips, thrusting forward until he was buried to the hilt. They were both gasping for breath now. Their lungs pumping in and out.

"I can't last long," he gritted out.

"Neither can I," she panted as she tilted her hips upward.

Jackson pulled his hips back and slammed them forward. The headboard hit the wall with each thrust, the springs on the bed squealing in protest. They were both slick with sweat and their wet skin made a slapping sound as they came together. Emerald's pussy sucked his cock deep with every thrust.

It wasn't enough. He needed to touch her so deep that they were melded together as one. Sitting back, he lifted her legs over his shoulders. As he drove forward, her inner muscles clenched hard around his shaft, milking it, massaging it.

The vein in his temple was pounding, matching the throbbing in his cock. His balls were drawn tight. As he thrust into Emerald's welcoming flesh, he watched her face. Her lips parted on a groan. She writhed on the bed beneath him, unable to control the depth or timing of his thrusts. Her breasts swayed with his movements in an erotic dance, her nipples hard nubs that he longed to taste.

"Jackson!" she screamed his name as her hips thrust upward. He felt her heels digging into his shoulders with surprising force.

He slammed his hips forward. "Come for me." Pulling back, he thrust again and again. Harder and faster. His skin felt as if it were stretched too tight over his frame. Every cell in his body was crying out for release. He could feel it building. His balls clenched and he felt the surge through his cock.

Her pussy spasmed around his shaft. Her sweet cries of release filled his ears. He roared her name as he came, hot cum flooding her. His head was spinning, but he kept pumping his hips, drawing out both of their releases until they were both spent.

Reaching up, he carefully lowered her legs back to the bed and withdrew his semi-erect cock. Emerald whimpered, her limbs sprawled on the bed, her eyes shut tight. He collapsed facedown on the bed next to her, reaching out one arm to drag her close.

Jackson could hear the sounds of the day seeping into the bedroom now that the passionate explosion had passed. The wind floated into the room, bringing its cool breeze to help ease their heated flesh. The drapes swished against the glass. The wind-up clock ticked on the bedside table. Satisfaction deeper than anything he'd ever imagined filled him.

He rolled onto his back and dragged Emerald on top of him. She muttered as she rooted around to get comfortable. Finally she sighed and relaxed, her head tucked beneath his chin, her legs sprawled on either side of his.

He yanked a corner of the comforter over her and kissed the top of her head. "I love you," he whispered as he kissed her again.

He wasn't even sure that she'd heard him until she muttered, "Love you too."

Closing his eyes, he relaxed for the first time in weeks.


Emerald felt something tickling her nose and sniffed, batting at it with her hands. She hit hard, male flesh and froze. It all came flooding back to her—the passionate lovemaking between the two of them.

Had he told her he loved her?

A heavy hand stroked over her bottom and she arched into it. A male chuckle followed. Slowly, she raised her head to look at him. A lock of hair was plastered to his forehead, his jaw was covered with dark stubble and there was a gleam in his blue eyes. This was *her* Jackson, the man she loved. She'd missed him so much the past few weeks.

Her nipples brushed against the hard planes of his chest, making them tingle. She felt the hardness of his cock growing and pressing against her softer belly. Jackson stroked his fingers down the cleft of her ass, rimming the tight opening with one finger before reaching lower to stroke her pussy.

She was sweaty, sticky and tired, but she felt...she wasn't quite sure how to put it. Complete. Satisfied. As if she'd finally come home.

Jackson surprised her by lifting her off him and then sitting up in bed. Grabbing the pillows, he propped himself up. "We need to talk."

She started to reach for the sheet, but then stopped. It wasn't as if there were any secrets left between the two of them, at least not in the physical part of their relationship.

Sitting up, she wrapped her arms around her legs and waited.

"What happened with Derek?" That wasn't exactly what she'd expected him to say, but she supposed they needed to settle what had happened.

"He hired some sixteen-year-old kid to hack into my e-mail account, credit card account and eventually into my sister's phone records." That was how he'd eventually found her. "He promised the kid that he'd help him get a recording contract. Derek knows all kinds of people in the music business and introduced the kid to some of them. He spun some story about trying to find his girlfriend because they had a fight and the boy bought it.

"Right now, Derek's in a psychiatric hospital being assessed. If he's deemed competent enough to stand trial, it will happen somewhere down the road." She wasn't sure how she felt about Derek. He'd tried to kill her and Jackson, but she remembered him as a young boy as well, laughing and playing with her and her sisters.

"How do you feel about that?" Jackson was watching her, his blue eyes hooded.

"I'm not sure," she replied honestly. "Part of me wants him put away for good so that he can't cause any more harm, but the other part of me remembers that he was a good friend for years."

"That's understandable." His voice was gentle and she wanted to be in his arms. These past weeks had been unbearably hard. Her life as she'd known it had been ripped apart, and it wasn't just her own life that had changed.

Her entire family had been rocked by this. Derek had been like a part of the family and the betrayal went deep. And all because he'd believed that if Emerald and her sisters cut a record and it was successful, his father would finally respect him. With her at his side, he'd finally have the kind of success he always felt he deserved. It was all so sad.

Derek's father had cut all ties with the family, which hurt her parents as well. They were torn between wanting to help their longtime manager and friend and supporting their daughter if the matter came to trial. Not that there was any doubt. There wasn't even a choice, but that didn't mean it was easy for any of them. In fact, it was a mess for everyone.

She stared down at Jackson's chest and let it all pour out, telling him everything that had transpired in the weeks that she'd been away. In return, he told her about his visits from the police and about the harvest.

Emerald had no idea how long they talked, but finally there seemed to be nothing left to say. She still hadn't looked at Jackson. Nothing had been settled between them. She'd told him that she loved him and they'd had wild, passionate sex.

While it felt wonderful, it didn't give her any indication as to where they went from here.

She opened her mouth to ask, but closed it as he began to speak. "I was coming to New York." Her head snapped up and she stared at him in disbelief. He gave a self-deprecating chuckle. "Hard to believe after I practically kicked you off the farm, isn't it?" He sighed and scrubbed one hand over his face before continuing. "Thing is, I wanted you to stay from the beginning, but I needed to be sure. Needed you to be sure that this wasn't an aberration brought on by the situation you were in."

"I understand." And truly, she did. Didn't mean she liked it though. Narrowing her eyes at him, she continued. "But if you ever try to do anything like that again, I won't be responsible for what I do."

A slow grin split his face. "Fair enough." He reached for her then and she all but threw herself into his arms. Cupping her face in his large hands, he leaned so close that their noses were touching. "I love you, more than you can even begin to imagine. The light was gone from my life when you left. I want you to stay here with me forever."

Emerald held her breath. Was he asking what she thought he was asking?

"Marry me." He kissed her lips softly, gently. "Marry me and share my life. If you want to live in New York, I can sell the farm."

Shock vibrated through her. That he'd even offer to do such a thing meant everything to her. "You'd do that for me?"

"Whatever it takes." There was no doubting the sincerity and determination in his eyes.

"Yes." All the weight that she'd been carrying the past few months slid away. "But I want to live here." This felt right. There would be challenges as they melded their lives together, but they would face them together.

"You won't be sorry." He peppered her face with kisses.

"I know." She reached for his lips, the passion that always seemed to be simmering between them rising again.

The rumble of a large truck drifted in through the window. "Ignore that. Whoever it is, they'll go away," Jackson murmured as he nibbled on her earlobe.

She groaned, wanting to sink against him. "No, they won't." As if to prove her point, a loud horn blew.

Jackson dropped his head back to the pillow and sighed as she scrambled off the bed and grabbed her jeans. She didn't bother with underwear as she shimmied into her pants. "Come on."

He rolled off the bed, yanked on his jeans and shirt and grabbed his boots as he followed her down the stairs. She finished buttoning her blouse as they walked through the kitchen.

Two burly men were waiting outside when they stepped out onto the porch. "Can I help you?" Jackson asked.

One of the men strode over. "Where do you want the stuff put?"

"What stuff?"

"Jackson." She tugged on his arm until he faced her. "That's my furniture. I'm moving in."

His face went blank and she began to get worried. Then he threw back his head and roared with laughter. Snatching her into his arms, he twirled her around until she got dizzy. He finally stopped and let her feet touch the ground again, but he didn't let her go.

"Pretty sure of yourself, weren't you?" The creases at the corners of his eyes deepened as he smiled.

"Not sure, no. But I had lots of hope."

He kissed her then. A short, hard kiss filled with promise.

"Don't mean to interrupt." She could see the laughter in the man's face as he rubbed his jaw in an attempt to hide his smile. "But we got a schedule to keep."

Jackson slung his arm around her shoulders and they walked to the back of the truck. "Let's see what we've got."

It didn't take them long to get it all sorted out. She didn't have too much stuff, but enough. Most of it was put in her old room off the kitchen until they could figure out what to do with it. Within an hour, the boxes and furniture had been stored and the men had been given a cool drink and were on their way.

Jackson stared at the mound of belongings stuffed into the room and grinned. "That saves us the trouble of having to go to New York to get your things."

She smacked him on the arm, but he only laughed. She'd never seen him this happy before and it made her heart sing.

"Are you sure about this?" All humor was gone and he was his serious self again. "You're the one leaving your home."

"Yes, I'm sure."

"What about your career?" He tucked a lock of her hair over her ear and then dropped his hand by his side.

"I can work from here. In fact, this room would make a great office for me. That is, once I get all the other stuff out of it."

"Whatever you want to do or change is fine with me. This is your home now. We can get rid of any furniture we don't need any longer. If Erin or Nathan don't want it, we can donate it to the church for their yearly fundraising sale."

"We'll work it all out," she assured him.

He grabbed her hand and tugged her close. "I know we will." Bending down, he kissed her neck as his hands roamed over her ass. "Where were we when we were so rudely interrupted?"

Emerald laughed and wrapped her arms around his neck. "I'm not sure. Maybe you could remind me."

She was scooped off her feet and Jackson was charging back up the stairs before she had a chance to blink. "I plan to remind you again and again and again." His voice was rough with desire as he captured her lips with his.

It was a good plan. A stupendous plan, she thought as he laid her on the bed and reached for the opening of her blouse.

# Epilogue

**&**

Jackson leaned against the trunk of an old oak tree in the corner of the yard and watched his wife chatting with her sisters. Not far beyond, Erin was talking to his new mother-in-law. He couldn't keep the grin off his face. The woman had insisted that he call her Moon and not Mrs. Jewel. It was strange, but then again, there was nothing normal about the family he'd married into.

Like her daughters, Moon had black hair and brown eyes. The outfit she was wearing was flowing and colorful, but it looked really good on her. It reminded him of Emerald. Moon looked much too young to have three grown daughters between the ages of twenty-eight and thirty-two. As if she sensed his gaze on her, she looked over and gave him a wave before going back to the conversation with his sister.

Aloysius, on the other hand, wasn't anyone's idea of an aging hippie. His steel-gray hair fell to his shoulders and was tied back at the nape with a leather thong. His tailored suit fit his wide shoulders to perfection and his black eyes missed nothing as he kept an eye on his wife and daughters.

Jackson hadn't been surprised to get a visit from Aloysius before the wedding took place. His wife and daughters might consider him laid-back, and he was, with them. The rest of the world had to contend with his shrewd mind and ruthless demeanor. Surprisingly enough, they'd gotten along from the moment they'd met. Aloysius knew that Jackson would do anything to protect Emerald and that was good enough for her father.

"How you doing?" Nathan handed him an ice-cold bottle of beer as he took a sip from his own.

Jackson took the cold brew and thought for a minute before replying. "I'm doing good." Actually, he was doing better than good. He looked ahead and all he could see was years of life with Emerald. Contentment swelled within him as he sought her out again.

She hadn't worn white, but he hadn't expected her to. Instead, she'd chosen a long flowing gown in a deep emerald green. The sleeves were long, but the bodice was cut low and cupped her breasts to perfection. The dress was fitted along her torso and hips before it flared out slightly and fell to the floor. She'd piled her hair on top of her head, fastening it with a jeweled comb that he recognized as one of Sapphire's designs. Other than that, the only jewelry she wore was the diamond solitaire that he'd given her as an engagement ring.

Her sisters wore identical dresses but in different colors. They were similar to Emerald's gown but the hem only came to their knees instead of falling all the way to the floor. Topaz's was a rich golden hue while Sapphire's was a deep blue. They indeed glowed like jewels as they flitted around the garden.

Patio lights had been strung and a buffet had been set up in the new barn. Since they'd only had a few weeks to pull together the wedding, they'd decided to keep it small and have it here at the farm. The new barn had been left unused and now guests milled around, chatting, laughing and occasionally dancing to the music of the small three-piece band they'd hired.

The wedding was elegant—much like the woman he married—but simple enough to suit his taste. The ceremony had passed in a blur, but he'd never forget the moment he'd slipped the golden band on her finger, making her his. They'd eaten good food, drank a few toasts, cut their cake and danced.

Jackson's body began to swell the longer he watched her. She was his now. They belonged together.

"Boy, you've got it bad." Abel slapped him on the back as he came alongside Jackson, almost knocking the wind out of him.

He turned and glared at his best friend as he snorted. "Like you can talk."

Abel's eyes heated as he found his wife in the midst of the small gathering. "I think it will soon be time for us to go home. Pregnant women need their rest, you know."

Jackson laughed and shook his head. "Go. The quicker the rest of you leave, the faster I can get Emerald inside."

Nathan chuckled and inclined his head. "Carly has to get up early for work tomorrow morning. We need to leave."

Both men sauntered across the lawn to collect their women, but they didn't leave right away. It took a while for everyone to say their goodbyes. Jackson strode over to stand at Emerald's side as she hugged his sister and Carly. The men stood back and watched them chatter. Finally, Jackson leaned down and whispered in Emerald's ear, "For God's sake, you can see them tomorrow."

Everyone around him burst out laughing. He'd meant to whisper, but obviously they'd all heard what he said. He shrugged, totally unrepentant. He wanted his wife and he wanted her now. Maybe in five or ten years he wouldn't want her every minute of the day, but he wouldn't bank on it.

Aloysius came up and shook his hand as he ushered his wife and daughters to the car. Thankfully, they were staying in a local B&B. He really liked his new in-laws. The few townspeople who'd been invited all said their goodbyes and a half an hour later, he and Emerald were standing on the back porch by themselves.

Stars were sprinkled across the dark night sky and the moon was a sliver of silver. The harvest was done for the year and now the long winter would give them both time to meld their lives together.

Jackson stood behind her, his arms wrapped around her. There was a nip in the air. Frost wasn't too many days away. "Cold?"

She shook her head and leaned back against him. "No." Her voice was low and with the darkness surrounding them, there was an intimacy to the moment that he didn't want to disrupt.

They stood there for the longest time, peering over the land that was in his blood. The fact that she was standing here with him, sharing it, made the moment perfect. "I love you."

She sighed deeply as if inhaling his words. "I love you too." She hesitated a moment and then pulled away from him. "I got you a present."

He smiled, thinking how much she was going to enjoy what he'd gotten for her. "I got you one too."

"Me first." She hurried in through the house and returned a moment later with a huge box that had holes in the top. His suspicions grew when the box moved. She peered coyly at him through her lashes. "I kept it over at Erin's place. Abel slipped the box inside the door a few hours ago."

A low whine emanated from inside the box as Emerald set it on the porch. She flipped open the lid and a furry brown head popped up. Jackson reached down and plucked the pup from his makeshift kennel. "How you doing, little guy?" The puppy licked his face, squirming to get closer.

"His name is Martin. You need a dog to keep you company while you're working in the fields. You've got all winter to train him, so he'll be ready to go with you next spring." Emerald stared at him almost defiantly.

Jackson knew she'd remembered their conversation about the farm not having any animals. He shook his head and chuckled as he lowered the little guy back into his box. "He's perfect. Now wait here while I get your present."

It only took him a minute to go to his office and collect his present. Her eyes widened when he stepped back out onto the porch. He laid the small kennel beside the box and opened the door. A tiny black kitten pranced out, her big green eyes blinking as she peered up at them and let out a plaintive meow.

"Oh, she's beautiful." Emerald scooped up the kitten and snuggled her. A loud purring sound filled the air around them.

"I thought you could use some company for when I'm gone in the days." He couldn't take his eyes off her as she and the kitten bonded. "Her name is Onyx."

"I love it." Emerald bit her lip. "Do you think they'll get along?"

"Only one way to find out." Taking the kitten from her, Jackson placed it in the box with the puppy. The kitten hissed, but the puppy licked playfully at her. Onyx made a show of ruffling her fur and hissing a few more times, but the puppy was woefully unconcerned. Within five minutes they'd both settled down, the two of them curled up side by side.

"Thank you." Emerald's eyes practically glowed as she opened the door so he could carry the box inside. He set it down in the laundry room, making sure the kitten's litter box was there, along with water for the two of them.

"You're welcome." He turned off the light and shut the door, praying the puppy wouldn't set to howling at least for an hour or two. He leaned against the door and pulled Emerald into his arms. "Thank you for making me the happiest man in the world today."

Her finger traced over the buttons on his crisp white shirt. His body tightened in anticipation of the night ahead. He hadn't let her out of his arms for a single night since she'd returned to him. Not even last night, even though she'd scolded that he wasn't supposed to see the bride the night before the wedding. He'd informed her that she could sleep wherever she wanted, but he was going with her.

He lifted her into his arms, savoring the weight and feel of her against him as he made his way through the kitchen and up the stairs. As he carried her across the threshold of their bedroom, he glanced down at her. He knew it was a cliché, but she glowed. Damn, but she was a beautiful bride.

His arms tightened as he carried her across the room and laid her on the bed. She opened her arms to him and he came down on the mattress beside her, pulling her into his arms. His mouth lowered to hers.

She belonged to him now, his very own jewel.

# Also by N.J. Walters

ട്ര

*eBooks:*

Amethyst Dreams

Amethyst Moon

Anastasia's Style

Awakening Desires: Capturing Carly

Awakening Desires: Craving Candy

Awakening Desires: Erin's Fancy

Awakening Desires: Jackson's Jewel

Awakening Desires: Katie's Art of Seduction

Beyond Shadows

Dalakis Passion 1: Harker's Journey

Dalakis Passion 2: Lucian's Delight

Dalakis Passion 3: Stefan's Salvation

Dalakis Passion 4: Eternal Brothers

Dalakis Passion 5: Endless Chase

Drakon's Treasure

Ellora's Cavemen: Dreams of the Oasis IV *(anthology)*

Ellora's Cavemen: Jewels of the Nile IV *(anthology)*

Ellora's Cavemen: Legendary Tails IV *(anthology)*

Ellora's Cavemen: Seasons of Seduction III *(anthology)*

Entwined Hearts *(anthology)*

Jessamyn's Christmas Gift

Lassoing Lara

Out of Shadows

Project Alpha 1: Embracing Silence
Project Alpha 2: Have Mercy
Project Alpha 3: Sweet Charity
Seeking Charlotte
Summersville Secrets 1: Annabelle Lee
Summersville Secrets 2: Heat Wave
Summersville Secrets 3: Lily Blossoms
Tapestries 1: Christina's Tapestry
Tapestries 2: Bakra Bride
Tapestries 3: Woven Dreams
Tapestries 4: Threads of Destiny
Tapestries 5: Embroidered Fantasies
Tempting Tori
Three Swords, One Heart
Tracking Talia
Unmasking Kelly

### *Print Books:*
Candy Caresses *(anthology)*
Dalakis Embrace *(anthology)*
Ellora's Cavemen: Dreams of the Oasis IV *(anthology)*
Ellora's Cavemen: Jewels of the Nile IV *(anthology)*
Ellora's Cavemen: Legendary Tails IV *(anthology)*
Ellora's Cavemen: Seasons of Seduction III *(anthology)*
Erin's Fancy
Enticemnets *(anthology)*
Feral Fixation *(anthology)*
Katie's Art of Seduction
Overtime, Under Him *(anthology)*
Summersville Heat *(anthology)*

Tapestry Dreams *(anthology)*
Three Swords, One Heart
White Hot Holiday Vol 3 *(anthology)*

# About the Author

&

N.J. Walters worked at a bookstore for several years and one day had the idea that she would like to quit her job, sell everything she owned, leave her hometown and write romance novels in a place where no one knew her. And she did. Two years later, she went back to the same bookstore and settled in for another seven years.

Although she was still fairly young, that was when the mid-life crisis set in. Happily married to the love of her life, with his encouragement (more like, "For God's sake, quit the job and just write!") she gave notice at her job on a Friday morning. On Sunday afternoon, she received a tentative acceptance for her first erotic romance novel, Annabelle Lee, and life would never be the same.

N.J. has always been a voracious reader of romance novels, and now she spends her days writing novels of her own. Vampires, dragons, time-travelers, seductive handymen and next-door neighbors with smoldering good looks all vie for her attention. And she doesn't mind a bit. It's a tough life, but someone's got to live it.

N.J. Walters welcomes comments from readers. You can find her website and email address on her author bio page at www.ellorascave.com.

## Tell Us What You Think

We appreciate hearing reader opinions about our books. You can email us at Comments@EllorasCave.com.

# Why an electronic book?

We live in the Information Age—an exciting time in the history of human civilization, in which technology rules supreme and continues to progress in leaps and bounds every minute of every day. For a multitude of reasons, more and more avid literary fans are opting to purchase e-books instead of paper books. The question from those not yet initiated into the world of electronic reading is simply: *Why?*

1. *Price.* An electronic title at Ellora's Cave Publishing and Cerridwen Press runs anywhere from 40% to 75% less than the cover price of the exact same title in paperback format. Why? Basic mathematics and cost. It is less expensive to publish an e-book (no paper and printing, no warehousing and shipping) than it is to publish a paperback, so the savings are passed along to the consumer.

2. *Space.* Running out of room in your house for your books? That is one worry you will never have with electronic books. For a low one-time cost, you can purchase a handheld device specifically designed for e-reading. Many e-readers have large, convenient screens for viewing. Better yet, hundreds of titles can be stored within your new library—on a single microchip. There are a variety of e-readers from different manufacturers. You can also read e-books on your PC or laptop computer. (Please note that Ellora's Cave does not endorse any specific brands.

You can check our websites at www.ellorascave.com or www.cerridwenpress.com for information we make available to new consumers.)

3. *Mobility.* Because your new e-library consists of only a microchip within a small, easily transportable e-reader, your entire cache of books can be taken with you wherever you go.

4. *Personal Viewing Preferences.* Are the words you are currently reading too small? Too large? Too... ANNOYING? Paperback books cannot be modified according to personal preferences, but e-books can.

5. *Instant Gratification.* Is it the middle of the night and all the bookstores near you are closed? Are you tired of waiting days, sometimes weeks, for bookstores to ship the novels you bought? Ellora's Cave Publishing sells instantaneous downloads twenty-four hours a day, seven days a week, every day of the year. Our webstore is never closed. Our e-book delivery system is 100% automated, meaning your order is filled as soon as you pay for it.

Those are a few of the top reasons why electronic books are replacing paperbacks for many avid readers.

As always, Ellora's Cave and Cerridwen Press welcome your questions and comments. We invite you to email us at Comments@ellorascave.com or write to us directly at Ellora's Cave Publishing Inc., 1056 Home Avenue, Akron, OH 44310-3502.

Make each day more *EXCITING* With our

# Ellora's Cavemen

CALENDAR

## www.EllorasCave.com

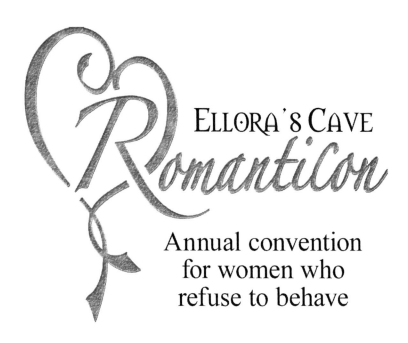

ELLORA'S CAVE

*Romanticon*

Annual convention
for women who
refuse to behave

Discover for yourself why readers can't get enough
of the multiple award-winning publisher
Ellora's Cave.

Whether you prefer e-books or paperbacks,

be sure to visit EC on the web at
www.ellorascave.com

for an erotic reading experience that will leave you
breathless.

LaVergne, TN USA
03 April 2011
222661LV00001B/159/P